Catherine Prentic[e ...] e.
"Don't worry, it's n[...] [th]e hospital. We
need you to be on [the show] *Professional Match*. All you
have to do is answer a few questions and get in a plug
for Western Memorial."

"No, thanks." Martin rose and walked round the desk,
signaling—he hoped—that the matter was closed. "I
don't watch TV. I'm really busy and—"

"And?"

"And to be honest..." He hesitated, then decided to let
her have it. "I think this sort of thing...this puffery...is
ridiculous. Empty-minded drivel. It has no place in
medicine."

"Other than that, though," she said with a straight face,
"you kind of like it?"

Martin resisted the urge to soften what he'd said with
a joke or a crack; even to his own ears he'd sounded
self-righteous. But he had more important concerns.
"I don't have time for this."

She turned to leave, then took a step back into the
office. "Since you don't watch TV, you probably read a
lot. I was just thinking there's a character in Dickens's
A *Christmas Carol* you'd probably recognize." A tight
little smile, a flutter of her fingers and she was gone.

Dear Reader,

Martin and Catherine and the other characters in this book have been a part of my life for so long, it's incredibly exciting to have the opportunity to introduce them to a wider audience.

If all fiction is a little bit autobiographical, it's certainly true in this case. Although I've lived in California for many years, I'm originally from Great Britain and, like Martin, have never quite got used to eighty-degree weather at Christmas—or fake frost on the windows. I also share some common bonds with Catherine, including the struggle to raise two children as a single parent. For many years I worked in the public relations department of a large medical center, and more recently have written extensively about neonatal intensive care units for a number of publications, including the *Los Angeles Times*.

The specialized world of the NICU and the dedication of those who work in it never fails to impress me. But while modern medicine is responsible for breathtaking advances, it can also raise difficult and complex questions for which there are no easy answers. This was the inspiration for my story. I hope you enjoy it.

Janice Macdonald

The Doctor Delivers
Janice Macdonald

TORONTO • NEW YORK • LONDON
AMSTERDAM • PARIS • SYDNEY • HAMBURG
STOCKHOLM • ATHENS • TOKYO • MILAN • MADRID
PRAGUE • WARSAW • BUDAPEST • AUCKLAND

ISBN 0-373-71060-7

THE DOCTOR DELIVERS

Copyright © 2002 by Janice Macdonald.

Visit us at www.eHarlequin.com

Printed in U.S.A.

To my Mum,
who is nothing at all like Catherine's mom and who never
stopped telling me she believed in me. And to Joe,
who had to endure me talking about Martin in my sleep.

Thanks for all your support.

CHAPTER ONE

PHONE CRADLED between her head and shoulder, Catherine Prentice padded around the kitchen in a ratty yellow robe and thick woolen socks listening to her mother ramble on about colon irrigation. Her mother, who had never met a disease she couldn't make her own, or self-medicate with the latest wonder cure.

Through the window, Catherine could see out into the small backyard. The grass needed cutting and Santa Ana winds had tossed purple bougainvillea blossoms over the rippling turquoise waters of the swimming pool, a picturesque effect marred by the floating aluminum chair and a double page of the *Los Angeles Times* sports section.

She dumped oatmeal into the saucepan for the children's breakfast. On the phone, her mother moved on to St. John's Wort and how it had really helped the woman downstairs and maybe she'd try it herself if Wal-Mart had it on sale. Sounds from the living room suggested that her ten-year-old son and his six-year-old sister were engaged in mortal combat. Catherine yelled for a cease-fire. *Who ordered this day? Make it go away. I had something different in mind. Something wild and exotic.* The yellow, happy face clock on the kitchen wall told her it wasn't even seven. She had an insane urge to go back to bed and stick her head under the blankets. She was trying to imagine actually doing this when, in a blur of sound and movement, the children burst into the kitchen.

"Listen, Mom..." Catherine cut short her mother's description of the heartburn that had plagued her since the previous evening's spaghetti dinner, promised to call later and hung up the phone. "Okay, you guys." She regarded her children. "What's going on?"

"Make Julie quit sticking her feet in my face, Mom." Peter, small for ten, his face dominated by large glasses, glared at his sister whose halo of blond curls and wide blue eyes gave her a deceptively angelic look. Peter's breathing had an asthmatic rattle and his chest heaved slightly with each intake. "She knows it makes me mad and she keeps doing it."

"I'm not sticking my feet in his face." Julie kicked her pajama-clad leg high and stuck a small pink foot in Peter's face. "I'm airing them out."

"You need to, they stink," Peter said.

"They do not." Julie stuck out her tongue. "Yours stink. Yours stink worse than anything else in the world. They stink like two hundred million skunks."

"Peter, you need to use your inhaler. And then go pick up your homework from the bedroom floor. Julie—" Catherine pointed the wooden spoon she'd been using to stir the oatmeal "—you go get dressed before breakfast. Go on. Move it, I have to be at work early today."

On the stove, she caught the oatmeal just as it was about to erupt over the edge of the pan. She turned down the burner, then reached into the cabinet for brown sugar. Absently, she watched it dissolve into the oatmeal, her thoughts already on the day ahead. In her office at Western Memorial, where she worked in the public relations department, there were news releases waiting to be proofed, a half-finished newsletter article and a reminder that she still needed to track down the elusive Dr. Connaughton.

She'd promised the producer of *Professional Match* that Connaughton would be happy to appear on tomorrow's show, but Connaughton hadn't answered any of her pages and when she'd gone up to the NICU to track him down, he'd been with a patient's family.

"Mommy." Julie tugged at the belt of her robe. "I have to tell you something. Peter keeps calling me a geek."

"Ignore him, sweetie. Please go get dressed, okay?" Maybe she'd goofed by promising Connaughton's participation. The show was fluff, a sort of career-oriented version of *Love Connection*, but her friend Darcy watched it every week and, according to marketing, it had exactly the demographics Western was targeting. Personnel had given her the names of three unmarried physicians. Two of them, thrilled to be chosen, had already taped segments. Now she had to find Connaughton.

The phone rang again. "Mom, I said *I'd* call *you*. I'm trying to get the kids off to school…what? Mom, listen to me, okay? Unless you have a prostate you didn't tell me about, Saw Palmetto isn't going to help you. I've got to go, okay? I'll call you tonight to see how you're feeling. Yeah, I love you, too. Bye." God. She rubbed at the knot of tension that seemed to have taken up permanent residence in the back of her neck. "Okay, kidaroonies," she called. "Who's ready for yummy oatmeal?"

"I'm not hungry," Peter said.

"I don't want oatmeal," Julie said. "I hate oatmeal. I want eggs."

"You had eggs yesterday. Today's oatmeal day."

"*Nah hah.* It's Wednesday." Julie cackled at her joke. "It's not oatmeal day Mommy, it's Wednesday."

Catherine turned from the stove to smile at her daughter. A little girl in a Big Bird nightie and a gap where just two days ago she'd lost the first of her baby teeth. *God, it had to get easier than this.* Thinking about work when she was home with the kids, thinking about the kids when she should be focused on work. Wanting to be there for everyone, but never quite being there for anyone. Peter, still in his pajamas, hadn't touched his oatmeal.

"Peter, eat your breakfast and get dressed. And please use your inhaler. I can hear you wheezing." She made a mental note to call his allergist when she got to work. Call the allergist then go find Connaughton. A niggling feeling told her he might be difficult. He was new on staff and Catherine had never met him, but a nurse on the unit had rolled her eyes at the mention of his name.

"How come we never have the kind of cereal I like?" Julie asked, scowling at her bowl of oatmeal. "I like the kind of cereal Nadia gets. Nadia gets good cereal. Nadia lets us have Little Debbies for breakfast."

Nadia. Catherine held her breath and counted to ten. Slowly. Nadia—her onetime best friend and, as of a month ago, her ex-husband's new wife. Just hearing Nadia's name was enough to ruin Catherine's day. Sometimes she entertained herself by picturing Nadia ballooned up to two hundred and twenty pounds with a bad case of cellulite. Nadia could eat a case of Little Debbies and never gain an ounce. *To hell with Nadia. She didn't want to think about Nadia.* "Okay, guys, let's get this show on the road." Arms folded, she looked at Julie. "If you're finished, go get dressed."

"I want some juice. Please." Julie grinned. "See, I said please."

"I noticed that," Catherine poured apple juice into a Big Bird glass. Her daughter was a *big* Big Bird fan. "That's very good." As she dropped a kiss on the top of Julie's head, she heard Peter's asthmatic rattle, louder now. She watched him for a moment. Never a robust child, his drawn face and laboring chest reflected the effort of each breath. "Not feeling so good, huh? Where's your puffer?"

He shrugged, and she pulled a pale blue inhaler from the cabinet drawer and waited while he used it. She had them stashed everywhere. Without intervention, mild wheezing had a frightening way of developing into a full-fledged attack. Like the last time he'd stayed at his father's. She'd blamed the rain and the dog Gary had bought—even though he knew Peter was allergic to dogs. Gary had blamed her for upsetting Peter by making a big deal about a missing homework assignment. *And* forgetting to pack an extra inhaler. Which she was absolutely certain she'd done. But Gary, a trial attorney, was a master at verbal self-defence...and attack. She glanced at the clock and wondered whether she should try and make an appointment for Peter this morning and risk going into work late again.

"Daddy said Peter wheezes because you don't dust enough." Julie had returned to the kitchen after dressing herself in the clothes Catherine had set out the night before. Yellow leggings and a bright red woolen sweater. "Daddy said Nadia likes to clean house because it's good for Peter's asthma."

Catherine opened her mouth to speak. Closed it. *Let it go.* She saw with relief that the inhaler was working. Peter's breathing looked less labored, the wheeze not so audible. She poured more juice for both kids, stuck a piece of bread in the toaster for her own breakfast. *Doesn't dust enough.* The words branded into her brain. Maybe Daddy should keep his lame-brained opinions to himself. Okay, she *had* to let it go. She spent far too much time obsessing over what an incredible jerk Gary could be. She spread a smear of peanut butter on the toast and resisted the urge to dip the spoon into the jar for a soothing mouthful.

"Daddy said he's the luckiest man in the world to have Nadia." Julie's legs dangled from the chair. "I like Nadia, she's pretty."

Catherine looked at the spoon in her hand, still poised over the open peanut butter jar. *She is only six,* she reminded herself. *She isn't trying to hurt you. You can kill*

Gary later. Nadia too, just on general principle. Angry, she dug the spoon into the peanut butter, brought it to her mouth. And didn't taste a damn thing. Which further incensed her.

"Daddy said when we come to live with him and Nadia, I can pick my own bedroom in the new house," Julie said. "And I'm going to get twin beds so if you get lonely you can come and sleep in my room."

Catherine slowly replaced the lid. "If I get lonely?"

"When we go to live with Daddy."

"Jeez, Julie, you're so lame." Peter reached across the table to push her shoulder. "Dad told you not to say anything."

"Owww," Julie squealed. "Peter pushed me, Mommy."

THE DAY CONTINUED on a steady downhill drift. In the office, Catherine discovered a stack of news releases that should have gone out yesterday, managed to spill a cup of coffee over the top one and splash it down the front of her cream wool skirt. And Martin Connaughton continued to play hard to get. At noon, on her way down to the lobby to meet her boss, she paid another visit to the unit.

As she pushed open the double doors to the NICU, a rush of green scrub-suited figures flew past her wheeling a Plexiglas case. She watched as they pushed it to an empty spot in the row of bassinets, watched as a nurse reached inside and lifted out a red, wizened baby, watched, transfixed, as the nurse applied sensors to the baby's skin then threaded a tube into its tiny mouth. And then she couldn't watch anymore. Heart racing, she turned away and stared hard at a bunch of pink Mylar balloons, but they dissolved in a blur of tears.

Peter had spent six weeks in an NICU. Even ten years later, she could vividly recall it all. The hot lights and machinery, the alarms that shrieked like police sirens when

JANICE MACDONALD   13

babies forgot to breathe, the nurses sitting vigil. Frantic
suddenly to be somewhere else, Catherine hurried to the
nurses' station and forced herself to smile at the clerk behind the desk.

"I'm looking for Dr. Connaughton," she said. "Is he
around?"

"He was a while ago." The clerk had white-blond hair
and burgundy lips. Half a dozen small gold earrings ran up
the side of her left ear. She peered out at the rows of bassinets, shrugged. " I don't see him now. Did you try paging
him?"

"Three times."

"And he didn't answer." She smiled knowingly. "Yeah,
well, he's kind of famous for ignoring pages. That and being late for everything. It drives Dr. Grossman up the wall.
They don't get along," she whispered. *"At all."*

The knowledge didn't do much for Catherine's mood,
nor did the fact that she was now five minutes late to meet
her boss. Breathless from running down five flights of
stairs, she pushed her way through the crowd of visitors
and employees in the lobby. She found Derek in front of a
makeshift stage watching Western's employee choir singing "Winter Wonderland" under a canopy of stylized
snowflakes. He wore a leather bomber jacket opened to
show a pale cream shirt, a lavender tie patterned with math-
ematical equations and an expression of barely concealed
impatience.

"You're late." He handed her a paper cup. "Libations.
Hot apple cider, I think. Courtesy of the auxiliary. Too bad
it's nonalcoholic."

Catherine smiled, not sure how to respond. Derek Petrelli
was a puzzle she hadn't quite solved. While administration
clearly respected his ability to court the media, he made a
virtual art form of flouting convention. Flamboyant and
openly gay, he either behaved as though things were too

tedious to endure or, for no apparent reason, turned almost childishly manic. She suspected that he saw her as a sub-urban hausfrau forced back into the workplace and easily shockable. Which was, in fact, pretty close to the truth.

"How are you doing with *Professional Match*?" he asked during a break in the choir's offerings. Have you found anyone yet?"

"I'm still trying to reach Connaughton. That's *why* I was late. I went up to the unit to see if I could find him. He hasn't answered any of my pages."

"Connaughton." Amusement played across Derek's face. "Uh-oh."

"What?"

"I didn't know that was who you'd lined up."

"Personnel gave me his name. You don't think he's right for the show?"

Derek shrugged. "He's telegenic enough and he has an accent of some sort, Irish, I think. A little detached and aloof at times, but he's got that brooding quality women go gaga for. Supposedly, he and Valerie Webb are an item."

"Valerie Webb? The pediatrician?" Catherine stared at Derek. "She's Julie's doctor."

He grinned. "News flash. Physicians have sex lives."

"I realize that, Derek…" She felt blood rush to her face. *God, who ordered this day anyway?* "Anyway, about Con-naughton," she said after a moment. "I told the producer he'd do the show. You think—"

"I think it might have been prudent to wait until you'd cleared it with Connaughton." Derek paused to sip his ci-der. "The man is not exactly easy to work with. Either he'll withdraw so you think you're talking to the wall, or fly into a rage. When I had to turn down his request for publicity for that drug addict program he runs…" He rolled his eyes. "It wasn't pretty. I didn't dare tell him the thing is deader than a dodo. Of course, you didn't hear that from me.''

Catherine sipped the cider. "Of course not."

"Let me try and explain Connaughton." Derek brought the rim of his paper cup to his lips, thought for a minute. "He's a cowboy. A thorn in administration's side. Never met a rule he couldn't break. A brilliant doctor, which is one of the reasons they haven't booted him out, but something of a law unto himself."

Catherine felt the day slip down another notch. This time a year ago, the most complicated thing she'd had on her mind had been Christmas shopping and what kind of cookies to bake for the PTA bake sale. Now she was dealing with outlaw doctors and contemplating custody battles. Her left temple throbbed.

"But don't let him intimidate you," Petrelli said. "*Professional Match* is the most popular morning show in this area and it reaches the audience we want. Getting Connaughton on would be worth God knows how much in advertising. Be firm with him. I'd do it myself, but I've got a meeting downtown."

"And if he does refuse?" She thought of the unanswered calls she'd made to the unit. "Should I try to line up someone else?"

"Connaughton's too tough for you to handle?"

"No, I didn't mean that." The paper cup had started to crumple, and she tossed it in the trash. "I just meant—"

"You've been with Western for how long? Two months?"

"Nearly three."

"Still on probation though."

"Well, yes." Her stomach did its familiar flip-flop thing. "I, uh…is there a problem?"

"Mmm." Derek examined the paper cup he held as if it were an object of great interest. "Well, that's the whole theory behind probation, isn't it?'' He turned the cup, peered inside, inspected the pattern of holly berries around the rim. ''Wait and see how things go. Ask me in a couple of weeks. Meanwhile, work on getting Connaughton for *Professional Match*.'' He drained the contents and smiled up at her. ''Imagine your job riding on it. That should get the adrenaline flowing.''

DR. MARTIN CONNAUGHTON leaned his head back against the seat of his battered black Fiat and closed his eyes. He'd had to get out of NICU before he lost it. An hour earlier, the Washington baby had died, and one of the residents had said it was probably a good thing.

''Some make it. Others don't,'' the resident had said. ''I never really believed that kid was salvageable though.''

Martin listened to the dry rustle of Santa Ana winds in the eucalyptus trees, smelled the heated air through the car's rolled-down windows. He hated the word *salvageable* and had yelled at the resident for using it, but he couldn't mourn Kenesha Washington's death. What haunted him was her short cruel life.

After a moment, he opened his eyes. Through the windshield, he watched the pink and white blossoms on the oleander bushes tremble in the wind. A strip of eucalyptus bark whipped across his line of vision. In the arid air, his eyes and mouth felt parched, the skin on his face dry and stretched taut across his skull.

One of the E.R. physicians claimed that the number of attempted suicides rose when the Santa Ana winds blew. Martin believed it. He was from Northern Ireland, more accustomed to enveloping mists and soft rain. California's hot, roaring winds with their banshee-like howls seemed sinister, full of dangerous energy. They made him tense and edgy, as if he'd offended a malevolent presence who would soon exact revenge.

He ran his finger under his collar—unsettled by the Santa Anas, by thoughts of Kenesha Washington and by the knowledge that today marked the fifth anniversary of his wife's death. Five years. Enough time that it was no longer Sharon he really mourned, but what had happened to his own life in the years since her death. Somehow it had drifted so far off course that he'd started to wonder about the direction in which it now seemed headed.

In the next week, he had to make a decision. A medical team, leaving to set up a pediatric hospital in Ethiopia, had invited him to join. It was a two-year commitment, similar to other expeditions in which he'd participated, with doctors he knew and respected, yet for some reason, he couldn't commit.

"But we were counting on you," the group's leader said when Martin had asked for more time to decide. "Most of us have family considerations, mortgages, all that stuff. We're not as footloose and free to wander as you are." He'd laughed. "Don't tell me, you've settled down."

Martin had laughed too, but the laughter was hollow. He could leave without creating a ripple. At thirty-eight, he had few possessions. The Fiat, the sloop he lived on in the Long Beach Marina, some books and an eclectic collection of music that leaned toward Celtic traditional. Back in Belfast, his family, or what remained of it—was far removed from his life.

After a week of sleepless nights searching for reasons not to go to Ethiopia, he'd finally come up with just one. The WISH program. He ran his hand across his jaw, seldom smooth even when he took the time to shave closely, and felt the coarse stubble of his beard.

WISH was about Kenesha Washington. Kenesha, the tiny junkie. Shaking, sweating, born in need of a fix. He stared down at the medical journals that littered the Fiat's floorboards. Kenesha, who had never seen the sun or the sky.

Never known anything but the brightly lit world of the NICU and people who did painful things to her.

With a sigh, he unfurled himself from the Fiat and started across the parking lot. Wind whipped at his hair, blew gritty dust into his eyes. At the edge of the lot, he stopped at a brightly painted mobile home covered with images of pregnant women, smiling under banners that read: WISH—Women, Infants, Staying Healthy.

He unlocked the back door, climbed inside. Dust motes swam in a beam of sunlight, settled on boxes of charts and folding chairs stacked against the walls. Until a week ago, the camper had rolled through the streets and housing projects of Long Beach providing free medical services to crack-addicted mothers. Now it sat idle in the lot, the prognosis grim.

His reaction to the news that Western's executive committee had essentially pulled the plug on WISH had prompted Edward Jordan, the hospital administrator, to suggest, once again, that Martin consider taking an anger-management course. Jordan apparently saw nothing amiss with the idea of packing the indigent off to other facilities, or with turning the vehicle into a mobile cappuccino bar.

Filled with a dull anger that demanded an outlet, Martin began sorting through manila folders in one of the packing boxes. Maybe it was him. Maybe he lacked the insight to see that two-dollar lattes were a better reflection of the upscale image Western's public relations department wanted to project. And maybe it really was time for him to move on.

Which he would. After he gave WISH one last chance. In a couple of hours he was scheduled to make a presentation to the executive committee. The prospect of going to them, hat in hand, galled him but if he could prevent one child from going through what Kenesha Washington had, the effect would be worthwhile.

A knock on the side of the van broke into his thoughts, and he turned to see Dora Matsushita, one of the social workers in the unit, peering through the open door.

"I thought that was you I saw loping across the parking lot." She held up a bag of oranges. "From my tree. It's a bribe." She winked. "I need a few minutes of your time."

"Ah, sure, I can always be bought with oranges." With a grin, he bent to take the bag and help her into the van. Dora had a bit of the rebel about her, a quality he admired. When they first told him to phase out WISH, he'd ignored the injunction, rounded up a small volunteer staff and taken the van out himself. Dora had been behind the wheel. A small, spare, fiftyish woman, she was a shrewd assessor of character, as quick to set straight a muddleheaded administrator as a young father.

"I want to talk to you about this little fifteen-year-old girl," she said.

He listened, frustration building. Twice that week he'd been warned about admitting new patients, told that one more infraction would result in his dismissal. That threat didn't trouble him as much as the knowledge that WISH would almost certainly die without his involvement.

"I'd like to, Dora. I'm not sure I can. We'll know later this afternoon." He told her about the upcoming presentation. "It's the last hope we have. I've got all the supporting data, all the clinical documentation—"

"Oh, Martin." She shook her head. "Facts and figures aren't going to do it. Show some emotion. There's a rumor up in the unit that you've got two temperatures, ice cold or—"

"Boiling over." He shrugged. "I know, I've heard it all. So what should I do then, break into a chorus of 'Danny Boy'?"

"WISH is *your* baby." She ignored his attempt at humor. "Your *passion*. No one who didn't care would put all the effort you've put into it. Let it out. Let yourself feel. Show the committee how important the program is to you."

He turned away and stared through the dusty window and out to the windswept parking lot. An image of Kenesha's face, contorted in a silent scream, filtered through his brain. Dora might be right, but emotional expression wasn't his specialty. He turned to look at her again, shifted uneasily under her steady gaze.

"I was just thinking," she said after a moment. "About these girls that come through WISH. By the time we see them, they're usually right on the edge. They can go one of two ways—completely destruct, or get their lives together and find some peace."

She paused and in the beat of silence, he heard the distant wail of an ambulance. He rolled the manila folder into a cylinder, unrolled it, tapped it against his chin. Without moving his head, he raised his eyes up at Dora. She sat with her hands folded in her lap, her expression impassive.

"Before they can find that peace and move on, they have to drop all the baggage they came in with," she said. "Let go of who they thought they were and what they thought they knew." She waited a moment. "I suppose, in a sense, you might say that something old has to die for something new to be born."

DORA'S WORDS still rang in his ears as he walked into Western's main lobby, but the sight of all the fake snow momentarily distracted him. Piles of it, flocking the branches of a massive Christmas tree, piled in drifts upon window ledges, heaped upon the roof of the Santa's cottage. Streamers of sunlight shone like a benediction, filling the lobby with tropical warmth. Underneath his lab coat, the scrub top stuck to his back.

Unbidden, a memory of that last Christmas in Belfast surfaced. Sharon had wanted snow, and late on Christmas

Eve, the rain had turned to a sleety mix that frosted the rooftops.

A voice beside him broke into his reverie, and he turned to see a tall, green-eyed woman with a glossy plait of brown hair. She had a wide, sensuous mouth and the fresh pink complexion of a child. Something about her seemed familiar, but he couldn't place where he might have seen her. He saw her eyes widen as she read the name embroidered above the pocket of his lab coat, but as she started to speak, the employee choir, cued by a visibly perspiring Santa, broke into a loud rendition of "Frosty the Snowman."

His mind back on WISH, Martin started to move away, but she caught his arm. Tiny charms hung from the thin silver bracelet she wore: a baby's rattle, a gingerbread house, children's toys. Her nails were short and unpolished.

"Dr. Connaughton." She brought her mouth closer to his ear to be heard above the music. "Catherine Prentice. From Public Relations. Lucky coincidence, huh? I've paged you a whole bunch of times, left messages up in the unit and suddenly here you are."

"And here I am." He looked directly into the light green eyes of Catherine Prentice from Public Relations. "Will wonders never cease?"

Her face flushed pink. Arms folded across her chest, she returned his level stare.

"Actually, you mispronounced my name." Even as he corrected her, he wondered why it mattered. "It's *Conno*-tun not Con*naugh*ton. There's no accent in the middle."

"I'll remember that." A flicker of a smile. "Dr. *Connaughton*." This time she pronounced it correctly. "That's an Irish province, isn't it? Connaught?"

"It is," he said, surprised she knew of it, "Connacht in Gaelic. It's in the west. A bit of a barren place. Have you been there then?"

"No, but my grandfather's from County Sligo. He used to tell me all these stories. He said Connacht was so rocky and desolate that Oliver Cromwell's men gave prisoners the choice of death or exile there."

"To hell or Connacht," he said, inordinately pleased by the exchange. "That was the term." Her eyes weren't exactly green, more of an aqua. Unusual color. And there was something different about one— He realized he was staring.

"Anyway…" With one hand, she flipped the long braid of hair back over her shoulder. "You didn't get any of my pages?"

"I did, but I ignored them."

"Shame on you." She fixed him with a reproving look. "People like you make my job very difficult. Consider yourself lucky I've got the holiday spirit." As she brushed a strand of hair from her face, the silver bracelet slid down her arm, lodged at her wrist. "The thing is, I've also got a producer breathing down my neck. Do you have a couple of minutes?"

"No, I don't." If this had something to do with the press, he wanted no part of it. His one-and-only encounter with reporters still gave him nightmares, and he had no desire to repeat the experience. "I need to check on a new admission and after that I have to be somewhere else. Sorry."

Before she could respond, he plunged into the crowd and bolted for the elevator.

CHAPTER TWO

MARTIN LET the white noise of the Neonatal Intensive Care Unit wash over him, waiting for it to restore some degree of equanimity. All around him, the sounds and sights of technology. The gadgetry brought in to rescue when the natural process went awry. The hiss and screech of ventilators. Machines that pumped and pulsed and calibrated. Electronic monitors with their waves and spikes and flashing signals. Delicate, intricate and complex all of it, but a damn sight easier to deal with then human emotions.

Martin gazed at the jumble of lines that snaked in and out of the baby boy in the incubator, a 28-weeker who weighed slightly more than a carton of eggs, and tried to put the scene in the lobby out of his mind. He couldn't. What the hell was wrong with him anyway? If he'd deliberately set out to antagonize Catherine Prentice, he couldn't have succeeded more completely.

A voice broke into his reverie and Martin saw the baby's teenage father, his face anxious under a baseball cap turned backward.

"So, like, what are all those wires and stuff?" The boy looked from Martin to the baby.

"Well, this blue one in his mouth is the ventilator," Martin said. Then, seeing that the boy was on the verge of tears, he glanced around for one of the other physicians on the unit. He was all right explaining the technical side of things, not so good with the emotional side.

"So what does it do?" the boy asked.

"It's attached to a computer that regulates how fast he breathes, and how much oxygen he gets." As he looked up at the gangly kid, Martin thought of the responsibilities facing the boy, enough to daunt someone twice his age. He tried to think of something reassuring to say. Or do. Put your arm around his shoulder, for God's sake, he thought. Instead, he launched into an explanation of the various tubes and lines that he could see by the boy's dazed expression meant nothing.

"So do those IV things hurt?"

"Only for a second," Martin said. "After that, no."

"How come he's got those things over his eyes?"

"To protect them from those lights." Martin pointed to the bank of bright lights over the baby's warmer. "See how yellow he is? That's because his liver isn't working properly. Those lights will help lower the bilirubin."

"Kind of looks like he's sunbathing, huh?" The kid gave a nervous laugh. "So is he, like, gonna make it?"

"Probably. He's got some problems, but they're all fixable." Arms folded across his chest, he watched the boy watching the baby. Minutes passed, the years rolled away and it was a younger version of himself. The day he'd learned Sharon was pregnant. The image faded, and he looked up to see Catherine Prentice.

"Poor kid," she said after the young father had left. "He looks scared to death." Her bottom lip caught in her teeth, she shook her head as though clearing the image. Then she shot him an accusatory look. "How come you just took off like that? You didn't even give me a chance to tell you what I needed."

"I'm not really here." He started for his office next door to the unit. She followed him. "What you're seeing," he said as he moved over to his desk, "is an illusion."

"Tell you what then. Why don't I pretend you're there and explain what I need?"

"Make it quick then." Despite himself, Martin suppressed a grin. A quick comeback always appealed to him. But he wouldn't be distracted. Head bowed, he searched through a stack of folders on his desk, looking for the report he wanted to use in his presentation. "What is it you need?"

"An attractive, unmarried doctor."

His head snapped up. Then he saw the amusement in her eyes. Her reply had thrown him as she obviously knew it would, and he'd reacted just as she'd intended him to. Challenged, he let his gaze travel to her left hand, now on the doorjamb, linger on her bare fourth finger.

"Not for me." She looked him straight in the eye, but a faint blush colored her face. "For *Professional Match*. Every week they match up single men and women representing different professions. This week it's medicine. You've seen the show, I'm sure."

"Actually, I don't watch TV." He scribbled a note. *$60 a day for the WISH program* v. *$2,000 a day for a crack baby in NICU,* then looked up at her. It occurred to him that she was attractive. He liked the long, thick braid of hair and she did have a great mouth. No lipstick that he could tell, but an almost crushed look to her lips. The way a mouth that had been kissed for the better part of the night might look. *What the hell was he thinking?* He began to dig through the papers again. "I don't even own a TV."

"That's very admirable of you, Dr. Connaughton."

"Thank you very much." He met her eyes. Mocking him, he could see. Probably saw him as a stiff, humorless workaholic. Probably right too, but what did he care? "If you're going to ask me to be on the show though, the answer is no."

She looked surprised. "Why not? They've got doctors from three other hospitals, and we need someone to represent Western. All you have to do is answer a few questions, get in a plug for us. You're going to be really fabulous, I know. The women will love your accent. You might even meet the woman of your dreams." She smiled as though it were all settled. "Okay, it's tomorrow morning at ten. I can either drive you down myself or meet you at the studio."

"No thanks." Martin rose, walked around the desk to where she stood, signaling—he hoped—that the matter was closed. "I'm really busy and…"

"And?"

"And to be perfectly honest…" he hesitated, then decided to let her have it. Maybe this was one way to get rid of her. "I think this sort of thing…this puffery, is ridiculous. Empty-minded drivel. Rubbish. It has no place in medicine."

"Other than that, though," she said with a straight face, "you kind of like it?"

He resisted the urge to soften what he'd said with a joke or a crack; even to his own ears he'd sounded self-righteous. So what? He didn't care what she thought. He had more important concerns. "I believe I explained. I'm trying to get ready for a presentation. I haven't time for this."

"Western is right in the middle of a huge marketing campaign, Dr. Connaughton, and *Professional Match* has just the demographics we're trying to reach. It would be a perfect tie-in to have you on the show." She flashed another bright smile. "And besides, it's the holiday season. Goodwill to men and all that stuff."

"Yes, well…look, I've already explained my feelings."

"I know. But I wish you'd reconsider."

"Sorry." He looked at her. "And I do have work to do."

"Hmm." She frowned and bit her lip. "There's nothing I can say to change your mind?"

"Nothing." He leafed through a stack of papers.

"Well, sorry I wasted your time." Her smile gone now, she turned to leave, then, as though struck by another thought, took a step back into the office. "Since you don't have a TV, you probably read a lot, huh? Ever read Charles Dickens, Dr. Connaughton?"

"Of course," Martin looked at her, puzzled. "Why?"

"I was just thinking that there's a character in *A Christmas Carol* that you'd probably recognize." A tight little smile, a flutter of her fingers and she was gone.

Moments later the phone on Martin's desk rang. A secretary informed him that Edward Jordan, Western's president and chief executive officer, would like to see him. STAT.

GOD, WHAT WAS WRONG WITH HER? Face burning, Catherine left Connaughton's office and ducked into the nearest rest room. *Scrooge.* She'd called him Scrooge. Her hands on the washbasin, she stared at her reflection. You are definitely losing it.

You...*oh please.* Tell me this is a bad dream. Tell me I didn't...*forget to put makeup on one eye.*

Yep. Gary had called that morning just as she was brushing on mascara. By the time she'd finished telling him that it would be a cold day in hell before he got the kids, she'd been so rattled she couldn't see straight. *Grhhhhhhhhhhh.* Now her mirrored self stared back at her. One eye wide and perky, the other...not. No wonder Martin Connaughton had given her such a weird look. And now she'd called him Scrooge, which meant that even if he might have been a teeny bit inclined to do the show, which he obviously wasn't, but if he'd had a last-minute burst of Christmas spirit, well, she'd blown it.

Imagine your job riding on it. She left the rest room and started across the hall to the elevator. Derek couldn't really mean that. He couldn't fire her just because some surly, stubborn Scrooge of a doctor didn't want to be on a stupid TV show. And it *was* a stupid show. In a weird way she kind of admired Connaughton for turning it down. The other two doctors had practically kissed her they were so happy to be chosen. Not Connaughton.

Admirable, but it didn't make her job any easier. She punched the elevator button. With any luck, she'd get back to her office and fix her makeup without running into anyone. After that she'd figure out what to do about Connaughton.

"Catherine," a voice behind her said.

Nadia. Even before she turned, she recognized the voice. Why wouldn't she? She and Nadia went way back to junior high school where they'd both been in love with Brett Malley. Things cooled between them after Catherine started dating Brett, then got downright icy when Nadia stole him away. But they'd made up and, in the years since, had supported each other through various emotional upheavals including Nadia's divorce from her first husband. In turn, when Catherine's marriage had crumbled, she'd cried on Nadia's shoulder. And, when she'd needed a job, Nadia, who headed Western's marketing department, had recommended her for the public relations position. Unfortunately, she hadn't learned about Nadia and Gary's year-long affair until after she'd started working at Western. Encounters with Nadia were definitely one of the downsides to the job, but she was determined to stick it out. If only to prove that, although strings had been pulled to get her the job, she could keep it on her own merits.

"Gary said you were kind of upset when he called this morning." Nadia smiled and reached to touch Catherine's arm. "He can be *such* a brat sometimes, I told him not to spring things on you but he just *had* to get it off his chest. Are you okay? I mean you're not mad or anything?"

Nadia had a breathy, little-girl voice, guileless blue eyes and a cloud of wispy blond curls. Even in the strappy high heels she favored, she was barely five feet. Next to Nadia, Catherine felt like a lumbering ox. Now, as she looked at Gary's new wife, in her pale blue cashmere sweater and matching skirt, she imagined locking her fingers around Nadia's tiny neck, just above the heart-shaped locket Gary had undoubtedly given her, and squeezing very hard.

"You know what, Nadia? I don't intend to discuss this while I'm at work. And I especially don't intend to discuss it with you. Anything I have to say about my children, I'll say directly to their father." She forced a tight smile. "Understood?"

"Oh, absolutely," Nadia agreed. "You *should* talk to Gary, I've tried to stress that, but..." She smiled as if to say, *What can you do?* "Anyway, what I *really* wanted to talk to you about was that *Professional Match* show. We're trying to get our ducks in a row for the marketing campaign, and Derek said you were working with Dr. Connaughton. She smiled. "Lucky you. He is such a *doll.* So is he all excited about being on TV?"

HE'D NEVER BEEN KNOWN for sunny optimism, but as he headed for the executive committee meeting where he was to make his last-ditch effort to save WISH, Martin tried to think positive thoughts. It wasn't easy. He steered the Fiat north on Pacific Coast Highway. Past the taco stands, the auto-salvage yards and pawnshops, past the pink stucco apartment blocks where barefoot children spilled out onto threadbare patches of green. WISH territory, but a summons to Ed Jordan's office just as he was leaving the medical center had temporarily eclipsed thoughts of WISH.

The administrator had wanted to hear Martin's version of the altercation he'd gotten into with the teenage son of Western's chief of pediatric neurosurgery two days earlier. He'd caught the boy making a drug deal in the parking lot. Enraged, he'd grabbed him by the collar, hauled him up close then recognized his face.

"My dad's going to hear about this," the boy had said.

"I hope he does," Martin retorted. "There are babies up there fighting for their lives because of idiots like you."

"He'll get your ass."

"I'll look forward to it." He'd held him suspended for another moment, then let go so suddenly that the kid had staggered backward against a Mercedes. "You're lucky I'm giving you a chance," he'd told the boy. "It's a damn sight more than a lot of others get. Now take off before I call security and have you picked up."

The kid had mumbled something under his breath, then climbed into the Mercedes and drove off. Martin knew they'd never touch the kid, his father was too influential. According to Jordan, Nate Grossman was responsible for bringing in more patients to the medical center than any other surgeon on staff.

Sun beat down on the Fiat's canvas top, heating the car's interior. Mid-December and it had to be eighty degrees. In the three years he'd spent in California, he hadn't managed to overcome the feeling of strangeness at Christmastime. The merriment seemed as contrived as the artificial frost that glazed Western's lobby windows, only partially concealing the swaying palms outside.

A pulse in Martin's temple tapped a staccato beat, the familiar throb of anger. If the situation wasn't serious, the irony would make him laugh. While he tried to convince administrators to keep funding an antidrug program, the chief surgeon's son was out in the parking lot drumming up business.

Figure out what was making you so angry, Jordan had said. It wouldn't take long. Overprivileged punks selling crack in the parking lot; the kind of skewed priorities that poured money into salvaging infants but cut it off for prevention. And then, thinking again of Catherine Prentice, money lavished on fripperies like public relations.

It should have been easy to dismiss the exchange, but the memory of her standing there lodged in his brain like the fragment of a song. Something elusive about her, something he couldn't name. She reminded him of someone. A fleeting expression, the way she held her head.

Stifling in the Fiat's cramped quarters, he rolled down the window. A symphony of freeway sounds poured in. Latin rhythm from the low-slung cruiser to his left, a jangle of jazzed-up Christmas music from an adjacent Toyota. Buses, big rigs, all trumpeting out their presence. Acrid, coppery-smelling air filled his lungs. Ahead of him, a tan station wagon made an abrupt lane change, then, as Martin pulled into the gap, the car darted back. He slammed on the breaks and hit the horn, then noticed the sticker on the station wagon's bumper: Mean People Suck.

Jordan had actually suggested he apologize for roughing up the kid. Martin loosened the tie he'd worn especially for the presentation and wondered whether Jordan had actually been serious.

He switched on KNX, the all-news radio station. Someone had thrown a bomb through a living-room window in Northern Ireland, killing three residents. It had happened half a mile from the flat where he and Sharon had lived. He switched the radio off. Ireland was a distant memory. A faded picture in an album he seldom opened anymore.

A quick lane change brought him up behind a gravel truck. Pebbles, like buckshot, smattered the Fiat's windshield. With a glance over his shoulder, he changed lanes again. Red taillights began to wink on. He rubbed the back of his neck, readjusted his lanky frame in the car's cramped interior and flipped the radio back on. The traffic report told him something he already knew: the northbound Long Beach Freeway was jammed.

Two fifty-three. His presentation was scheduled for three. He drummed his fingers on the steering wheel. The traffic had ground to a complete halt. Up ahead, he saw a helicopter circling slowly, a metallic vulture above the sluggish body of traffic. He craned his neck out of the window, peered up into the grimy primrose sky. A second bird had joined the vigil, the call letters for a local TV station painted on its side.

Two fifty-five. Martin slammed his palm on the steering wheel, then, unable to tolerate the inactivity, pulled onto the shoulder, got out and started along the line of stationary cars. Traffic was completely immobilized on both sides of the freeway. He ran back to the Fiat and grabbed the medical bag he kept there. Maybe there'd been an accident.

Half a mile or so ahead of him, a crowd had gathered around a large beige clunker. As he drew closer, he saw a woman in a gray sweatsuit emerge from a Toyota. Carrying what appeared to be folded blankets, she made her way to the beige car and disappeared through the driver's-side door.

He pushed his way through the crowd, squatted on the asphalt next to the car's passenger door and looked inside. A woman, in her mid-to-late thirties, he judged, lay sprawled at an awkward angle across the seat, a blanket draped across her lap.

"I'm a doctor," he called into the car. "What's the problem?"

"She's having a baby," the first woman said without looking up, "And it's in a hurry to arrive." She placed a folded blanket behind the woman's head and eased out of the car, crawling backward across the seat. "You're a doctor, huh?" she said when she was back out on the freeway again.

"Right."

Her expression registered a brief battle between distrust and relief.

He met her eyes, but said nothing. If he'd stepped out of a Mercedes wearing a three-piece designer suit, he thought, he would have had no trouble convincing her of his profession.

"Hey, take over," she said finally, apparently deciding to take him at his word. "Her water broke. She's having contractions. Someone called the highway patrol, but it looks as though the kid will get here before they do."

He heard a moan from the car and crawled inside. Conflicting thoughts raced around in his brain. If he stopped to help her, he'd be more than just a few minutes late for the presentation, and the highway patrol would have an air ambulance dispatched, he reasoned, so she was in no real medical danger. As he considered what to do, the woman screamed and her body went rigid. He looked at his watch and noted the time. Three-ten. Right now he should be well into the presentation. He blocked the thought, waited for the contraction to subside and surveyed the interior of the car. Packing cartons and boxes were jammed into the back seat, clothes on and off hangers piled to a height that all but obscured the rear window.

"Right, then, I'm going to help you." He looked at her. A sheen of perspiration covered her face. Fine lines around her eyes and mouth put her age close to forty. "Martin Connaughton," he said. "What's your name?"

"Rita." The woman bit her lip and her eyes filled with tears. "Hodges. You'd think I'd know better after four kids, wouldn't you? I figured this one wasn't due for another two months."

"Have you seen a doctor?" he asked, but he'd already guessed the answer.

She shook her head. "My husband and me just got out here from Tennessee. He's got the other kids. I was supposed to be checking out some apartment in Downey, then this happens... Oh God—" her face contorted "—here comes another one."

Her scream filled the car, ricocheted off the windows.

He checked his watch again. Three minutes since the last one. Outside, the crowd of onlookers, faces up at the glass, jockeyed for a better view. Anytime now, he thought, there'd be vendors hawking soft drinks.

"You're the star of the Long Beach Freeway, Rita." He caught her in an awkward embrace and maneuvered her around until she was stretched across both seats. Then he tented the gray blanket over her knees. "Everyone wants a look."

She grinned weakly. "Yeah, a look up my crotch. Jeez, I hope they don't flash it on TV."

It wouldn't surprise him, he thought as he checked the make-shift delivery set-up. Since she occupied both seats, there was no room for him inside the car so he climbed out and stood on the asphalt. Like an old-time photographer covered by a black cloth, he peered into the tented area between her knees. Sweat trickled down his back.

"Okay, Rita, let's see what's going on here." A routine

task under normal conditions, the examination seemed surreal against the backdrop of freeway activity. He listened for a police siren, an air ambulance.

The air in the car grew stifling. Sweat dripped into his eyes. Wiping his face, he tried to remember the last time he'd actually delivered a baby. Eight years at least. In New Guinea or Ethiopia, he wasn't sure. All he remembered was that everything had been fine. Mother and baby okay.

Rita screamed again and pushed. A head appeared, black and slick as a seal. He heaved a sigh of relief.

"How's it going?" He emerged from his blanket tent and smiled at her, playing the combined role of coach and obstetrician. "Doing okay? Almost over. A couple more pushes and we're there."

She moaned. Her abdomen rose and tightened up into another contraction and she moaned again, a slow ascent into a full-pitched scream. The veins in her face and neck bulged. She screamed and pushed some more.

"Come on, Rita," he urged. "Now. You can do it. *Now.*"

She gave one last shrill cry and a baby girl emerged. The crowd at the car window, larger now, drawn by Rita's screams and the unfolding drama, broke into applause.

Martin looked up to a sea of grinning faces and waving hands. He took a deep breath, trying to slow his heart rate to something approaching normal.

With one glance at the baby, he realized that his relief, like the infant, was premature. About twenty-eight weeks, he guessed. A little over two pounds. Viable in that sense. Her dusky color wasn't good though, neither was her muscle tone. Less reassuring still was her single weak cry. As he cut the umbilical cord, he felt a prickle of fear. The feeble sound was hardly a declaration of life.

Where the hell was the air ambulance? He cleaned out

the infant's nose and mouth as best he could and handed her to Rita.

"A daughter." He forced a smile and a note of reassurance to his voice. "Hold her tight against you, inside your clothes. All right? Make sure she stays warm."

Rita looked from him to her new daughter. A range of expressions played across her face. She fumbled with the buttons of her shirt, got it open and yanked her bra away from her breasts. "Is she okay? She's not crying much. My others all yelled their heads off."

"We need to get her to the hospital." He pulled the edges of her shirt together so that they covered the baby. "The ambulance should be here any minute."

Fervently hoping he was right, he watched for a moment, then returned to the tented canopy. As he reached up inside her for the placenta, his hand caught a tiny foot. He released his grip, felt around again. No doubt, it *was* a foot. He shook his head. This couldn't be happening. Exploring, he found what had to be the shoulders of a *third* infant.

"Holy Mother of God." For a moment he couldn't move, his grip frozen on the tiny limb. Rita's scream galvanized him into action. "Where the bloody hell is the highway patrol," he yelled over his shoulder. "Tell them…"

A second, louder scream interrupted him.

CHAPTER THREE

"JOSH GILLESPIE, right." Catherine cradled the receiver between her ear and shoulder and consulted the scrawled jottings on her notepad. "Eight years old," she said, reading from a sheet of yellow paper. "Life-Flighted here about seven this morning. Hit by a car as he was crossing the road. We need a condition report for the media." She hesitated a moment. "A couple of reporters want to speak to the parents."

"Josh is in surgery." The voice of the nurse in the Pediatric Intensive Care Unit was abrupt. "He's—" She stopped, a hint of suspicion evident now. "Who did you say you were?"

"Catherine Prentice. Public Relations."

"I don't know your name."

Catherine drew a square around the boy's name. If she'd sounded more confident, would the nurse have questioned her? She pushed the thought away. Her head ached, her stomach felt as if she'd swallowed a lump of lead. And the *Professional Match* producer had called again. Now she'd have to go plead with Martin Connaughton to see if she could get him to change his mind. Which might have been easier if she hadn't called him Scrooge. All of this when what she really wanted to do was go and pick up her kids, start a new life somewhere where Gary and Nadia would never find them.

"I've just started working here," she told the nurse. "You can call me back to verify if you want."

"I'll take your word," the nurse said. "He's critical. On life support. The mother's here, but—" she lowered her voice "—she's pretty hysterical. Try back in an hour or so."

After she'd hung up the phone, Catherine stared at the small framed picture of Peter and Julie on her desk, wondered how *she'd* cope if anything happened to either of them. A sudden superstitious dread washed over her as though she'd tempted fate by even contemplating the possibility. She touched the picture: first Peter's face, then Julie's.

Like a tornado, the divorce had hurled her around, ripped away the sheltering protection of domesticity, battered her confidence and self-esteem. In the aftermath, she'd looked at the transformed landscape and recognized nothing at all that was familiar. Even now, she couldn't get rid of this image of herself, standing Dorothy-like on a Kansas plain, her two children sheltering under her skirts. Winds whipped around her and, off in the distance, was another tornado just waiting to strike.

She shook her head to dislodge the image and dialed the NICU. Connaughton was off-site, the clerk told her, so she left a message for him then called *Professional Match* to say she was still working on getting someone. After she hung up, she tried to focus on another project, but her thoughts kept drifting to Gary's demand for custody.

What she didn't know was just how far he would go. He had a habit of threatening her just to keep her a little concerned and insecure. Like the time when Julie was two months old and he'd gone on a white-water rafting trip with a couple of his buddies. He'd complained that he was unhappy and stifled, that she'd let herself get fat, that she cared more about the children than him. Without the trip to restore his spirits, he would walk out of the marriage, he'd said. The third time he used the same threat, she'd called his bluff, forcing him to find new material.

Office noises drifted around her. The low hum of conversation in the next room, the whoosh of a file drawer sliding shut, a burst of laughter from the reception desk. In the coffee area, a microwave oven pinged its readiness and, seconds later, the whiff of hot popcorn filled the air. In her first week at Western, she had decorated her office with pictures of the children, a couple of trailing green plants, a small amber lamp and a glass bowl which she kept constantly replenished with jelly beans. It was her thing, creating nests.

She stared at the computer screen, tried to think of a snappy lead for the release she was working on, but nothing came to mind. Somehow it was difficult to concentrate on promoting a bunch of wealthy, golf-playing doctors when she was worried about losing her kids. A movement in the doorway made her look up and she saw Derek, cellular phone in one hand, a bran muffin in the other.

"Forget about Connaughton," he said around a mouthful of muffin. "The producer called me just now, they've found someone else."

"Derek, I'm sorry, he just refused—"

"What about the kiddie on the trike?"

"Bike." Catherine corrected. "He's in surgery."

"There's a TV crew camped outside the E.R.," he said. "See if you can get mommy to talk."

"I already tried," Catherine said. "The nurse said to call back later."

"The nurse isn't on deadline." He finished the muffin, crumpled the paper wrapping into a ball and aimed it at her trash bin. It missed. "Reporters are. That's why *you're* here. Never mind, I'll take care of it." As he walked away, his cell phone rang and he grabbed a pen and yellow pad from her desk and started scribbling notes. Moments later, he clicked the phone shut and looked across the desk at her, an expression on his face she couldn't quite discern.

"Big media event. One of our docs delivered triplets on the Long Beach Freeway this afternoon. He stayed until the air ambulance arrived then took off like a bat out of hell. Said he was in a big hurry." He glanced at his notes. "Babies and mommy are on their way here. Security says the press are already swarming all over the lobby. I'm going to get them corralled in one of the conference rooms. Once the kids are stabilized, we'll arrange for some pool footage."

Catherine followed him out of the office, eager for an opportunity to redeem herself. "Do you want me to put some background stuff together?"

"Later. Right now, everyone wants to talk to this guy. What I need you to do is find him and get him down to the conference room, pronto."

"Sure," Catherine agreed. "What's his name?"

"Martin Connaughton," Derek said. "And don't drop the ball this time."

SHE GAVE HERSELF a pep talk as she made her way up to the NICU. You *can* do this. You will overcome Connaughton's resistance. You will prove Gary wrong about Nadia being the only reason you got this job. And tonight, to celebrate, you will take the kids out for pepperoni pizza without thinking about the calories. Then after they're in bed, you will have a bubble bath and, maybe, a glass of wine, because you will have deserved it. Go do it, girl.

Outside the unit, a dark-haired reporter with glossy red lips and a tightly fitting suit in matching crimson, flashed

Catherine a smile that appeared and disappeared as precisely as if a button had been pressed.

"Selena Bliss," she said. "I'm looking for Dr. Martin Connaughton."

"*Conno*tun." Catherine smiled as she corrected the reporter's pronunciation. "I'm looking for him, too." Not sure how Selena and her cameraman had managed to escape both security and Derek's corral, she figured that if you looked like Selena Bliss, a lot of things might be possible. "You need to be in the conference room," she said. "In a few minutes we'll be giving a briefing."

"I'd rather wait here for Dr. Connaughton," Selena said.

"I'll bring him down to the conference room." She maintained her smile. "That's where he'll be doing the interviews."

The reporter glanced at the cameraman standing nearby, then looked at Catherine. "You're new here, aren't you?"

"Yes, I am." The smile began to feel forced. "Ready?"

"Maybe you're not aware of it, but that's not the way I work." Selena Bliss smiled again. "Derek Petrelli said I could have an exclusive with Dr. Connaughton."

"Derek never mentioned an exclusive to me," Catherine said. "But I'd be glad to check it out with him. If that's the case, we can set something up. For now though, if you'll go down to the conference room—"

"I'm not hanging around a conference room waiting," Selena said. "I'll wait here."

Struggling for a way out of the impasse, Catherine heard a voice behind her and turned to see Nate Grossman, chief of pediatric neurosurgery. Ignoring Catherine, he stuck out his hand to the reporter, his face a beam of delight.

"Selena Bliss! Do I have a story for you! Have you heard about the new surgical technique that we've perfected here at Western to—"

"Actually, I'm here to interview Dr. Connaughton," Selena said.

"Connaughton?" Grossman's face darkened. "Why would you want to talk to him?"

"He's quite the hero of the hour." Selena summarized the freeway rescue. "So we want to talk to him about what he did. How he felt at the time. How the babies are doing, that sort of thing." She smiled. "It's a really nice heartwarming story."

"Tell you what," Grossman said. "How about I take you into the unit and let you get some shots of the babies? Meanwhile, I'll fill you in on the new procedure. It was written up in the *New England Journal*—"

"Excuse me, Dr. Grossman." Catherine felt the situation slipping out of her control. "We wanted to avoid having camera crews in the unit, so we've arranged for pool footage of the babies."

"Oh, Selena doesn't want pool footage." Grossman winked at the reporter as if to say he knew her lingo. "Come with me, I'll have someone get you a gown." He looked at Catherine. "If anyone complains, tell them to talk to me."

Selena gave her a triumphant little smile and followed Grossman into the unit. *May you go on the air with lipstick on your teeth,* Catherine thought as she tied on a protective cotton gown and made her way down to the end of the unit where Grossman was holding forth for the benefit of the camera.

"The tall one is Connaughton." He pointed to a figure in scrubs whose hair and lower face were covered by a surgical cap and mask. "Right now he's putting in a breathing tube. He's already wired up the other two."

"Everyone seems kind of tense." Selena looked at him. "Is the procedure complicated?"

"No, but it's kind of tricky—like threading a needle, but a lot more exacting. The baby can't breathe while it's being done and the heart slows down." He chuckled. "There's always the risk you'll get 'em properly tubed, but dead."

Posturing idiot. Angry, Catherine saw Selena's eyes widen, saw her scribble something else in her notebook. "Of course, that sort of thing doesn't happen here at Western," she added quickly.

"Of course it doesn't," Grossman agreed. "That was just a little joke. In our intensive care unit—" he tapped the reporter's notebook "—*we care intensively.* You can quote me on that."

God, this guy was truly insufferable. Catherine saw Connaughton look up and stare at the camera, then turn his attention back to the baby.

"Heart rate dropping," a voice said from the cluster around the bassinet. "Heart rate sixty—fifty."

The cameraman began filming.

"Heart rate *forty.*" The voice was urgent. "Come out *now.*"

Catherine saw a hand whisk something from the baby's face. Someone else started pumping a black rubber bag. Moments later people began moving away from the bassinet. Connaughton said something to a nurse, then pulled his mask around his neck and walked over to where she stood with Selena Bliss and Grossman.

The cameraman followed with his lens.

"Dr. Connaughton." As she moved toward him, Catherine felt the blood rush to her face. "Catherine Prentice. I met you this morning. I, uh…is the baby okay?"

"Turn that damn thing off." He gestured at the camera. As he wiped his forehead with his mask, he looked from the reporter to Catherine. "The baby's fine." His face darkened. "What the hell is going on here?"

"You've created quite a stir." She smiled at him. "There's a whole conference room full of reporters downstairs all waiting to talk to you. Including—" she nodded toward Selena still standing with her microphone outstretched "—this reporter here—"

"Perfect opportunity for a nice little plug for Western," Grossman said. "I've been telling Selena about some of the work we're doing." He winked at her. "Including, of course, some of our state-of-the-art neurosurgery—"

"Excuse me, Dr. Grossman." Catherine looked from the surgeon to Connaughton and saw the strain of the past few hours evident in his eyes. Empathy vied with demands of the job. She motioned Selena Bliss and her crew to stay put and drew him aside. "Are you okay?"

"Okay?" With a glance at the reporter and cameraman clustered out of earshot on the other side of the unit, he stared at her as though he'd forgotten why she was there. "Sorry?"

"You look kind of..." Self-conscious, she decided to take a different approach. "How are the babies?" It wasn't an idle question, she really wanted to know, but nerves made her plow on. "And the mother? I hear she's up on postpartum. God, what an ordeal. Lucky for her you were there." His eyes, a dark blue, were fixed on her, but she sensed his mind was elsewhere. Across the room, Selena Bliss pointedly glanced at her watch. "Look, I'm sure talking to the press is the last thing you want to do, but—"

"The press?"

"Every reporter in town wants to talk to you."

"Tell them I have nothing to say."

She smiled, although something told her he wasn't joking. "Dr. Connaughton, I realize that you probably thought the request this morning was, uh—"

"Frivolous?" The faintest flicker of a smile crossed his

face. "Well, I suppose you'd expect Scrooge to think that way, wouldn't you?"

"Ah." She tried to smile. "About that. I'm sorry. I shouldn't have said it."

"It's hardly the most damning thing I've ever been called." He pulled off his surgical cap, ran his hands through unruly reddish-brown hair. "Look, I can't discuss this now." He started off down the corridor at a fast clip. "I missed an important meeting."

"Okay then." She ran along beside him. "When would be more convenient?"

"Never." He reached the door to the emergency stairwell, pulled it open and started up the stairs. "Nothing's changed. I don't talk to the press."

"Look, Dr. Connaughton..." She tried another tack. "What you did this afternoon, delivering those babies, was a wonderful, humanitarian gesture. People are really interested in that sort of thing. And with the babies here at Western, it's really great public relations."

"That's what you said about *Professional Match*."

"Right." She thought quickly. "I know I did, but that was kind of fun PR. This is different. It's terrific exposure for Western's NICU. We could spend millions and not get better advertising."

"I'm sorry." He took the stairs, two at a time, glanced back at Catherine who trailed a step or two behind. "I don't want to do it. Humanitarian gesture or not, had I known that helping would create all this attention, I'd probably have stayed in my car."

"Just a minute, Dr. Connaughton." She reached him on the top landing. "People want to know how the babies are doing. Can't we at least do a brief condition update?"

"Two of them should be fine. I'm very concerned about the smallest one." He pulled open the stairwell door and

headed for administration. "If you want to relay that on
my behalf, feel free to do so." With that, he disappeared
through the polished wooden doors into Paul Van Dolan's
office suite.

"HOW THE BLOODY HELL can he be tied up?" Martin
looked from the chief financial officer's secretary to the
clock on her desk and tried to banish the image of Catherine's dismayed expression. Surely it was his right not to
talk to the press? "It's five past four," he told the secretary.
"My presentation was at three. It was supposed to last for
two hours. If I'd been there, we'd be right in the middle of
it at this moment—"

"But you *weren't* there, were you, Dr. Connaughton?"
The secretary bared her teeth in a tight smile. "So Mr. Van
Dolan made another appointment. He's a very—"

"Busy man. I know, you already told me." Later, he
would stop by Catherine's office and apologize, he decided.
Explain that he'd been under pressure. "When is he available?" he asked the secretary.

"He's tied up with budget meetings for the next two
weeks."

"All I need is half an hour, forty-five minutes."

"He's tied up with budget meetings for the next two
weeks."

"Are you telling me that from the time he comes in to
the time he goes home, he doesn't have thirty minutes to
spare?"

"Dr. Connaughton." The secretary sighed. "Mr. Van
Dolan is a very busy man."

"Did you check his calendar?"

"It isn't necessary, he's tied up with budget meetings for
the next two weeks."

After he left the administrative suite, Martin used a phone in the hospital lobby to call Van Dolan's secretary.

"Afternoon, ma'am," he drawled. "I'm Randolph Manwell with the Mallinkamp Foundation. As you know, Western's a top contender for the medical humanities grant—"

"Yes, Mr. Manwell—"

"Just flew in from Houston and *ah* know it's kinda last minute an' all, but *ah* sure would like to have a few minutes of Mr. Van Dolan's time this afternoon."

He heard a rustle of paper

"You're in luck, Mr. Manwell," the secretary said. "Mr. Van Dolan had a cancellation. If you could be here at, say, four-forty, he could talk to you for a few minutes."

"Why, thank you, ma'am, *ah* sure am obliged to you."

He hung up, called the NICU and asked for Tim Graham, another neonatologist.

"Is it all clear up there, Tim? No more bloody reporters?"

Graham laughed. "For now, but I'd take the back stairs if I were you. You've suddenly become a celebrity. Everybody's talking about what you did."

"Listen, Tim." He hesitated. "If that woman from public relations, Catherine her name is—"

"Long braid? Stacked?"

"I, uh…right. Anyway, if she stops by, tell her…never mind. I'll tell her myself." On the way back to the unit, a woman called his name.

"Dr. Connaughton. Mrs. Edwards, Parking Enforcement. I understand you failed to affix a sticker to your car. All cars parked in the physicians' lot must have a parking sticker affixed to the left side of the rear bumper. It's hospital policy, Dr. Connaughton. After tomorrow, security is instructed to tow away cars without stickers."

Martin gave her a blank look.

"Your parking sticker, Dr. Connaughton. Where is it?"

"I think I've lost it." Aware of the double meaning, he couldn't suppress a grin. With a what-the-hell abandon, he added, "The dog ate it."

"Dr. Connaughton, you might find this amusing—" the woman's tone made it clear she didn't "—but we have these rules for a reason. It makes it very difficult when people don't take them seriously."

"I'll go and have a look for the sticker." Martin wanted only to terminate the exchange. "If I can't find it, I'll come and get another one. Don't tow my car though, okay?"

Her pert little smile suggested the triumph that comes with having the last word. "As long as it has a sticker, Dr. Connaughton." She started to walk away, then called his name. "You know, I just thought of something." Her eyes narrowed. "Weren't you the doctor who delivered those babies on the freeway today?"

"No." He shook his head. "Different doctor."

"I'M WONDERING if you were aggressive enough with Connaughton." Derek gave Catherine an appraising look. "You've got to be tough with these doctors. Insistent. They'll sniff out any weakness, just like a dog, and then they'll walk all over you."

"He didn't walk all over me." Catherine pictured Connaughton's eyes as he'd refused her entreaties—eyes exactly the color of the cobalt blue in Julie's box of Crayola—and wondered whether he had, but then dismissed the thought as nonproductive. "Short of bodily dragging him down there, I don't know what else I could have done. He just plain doesn't want to talk to reporters."

After he'd eluded her for the second time, she'd achieved a temporary save by having one of the other neonatologists deliver a medical update. That, and an interview with the

triplets' parents, had mollified Selena Bliss and the rest of
the press corps. Derek, to her relief, also seemed satisfied—
at least he'd dropped no more hints that her job was in
peril. The problem was that everyone still wanted to talk
to Connaughton about his role in the rescue.

"So." Derek slumped down in the chair in front of her
desk. "What we need to do now is rethink our strategy.
Regardless of what he says, Connaughton wants to be on
TV. They all do. It's an ego thing. Sooner or later they all
succumb."

"I honestly don't think he will," Catherine said. "He
made it pretty clear what he thinks of talking to the press."

Derek shook his head. "He's no exception. Trust me.
You just didn't go about it in the right way. Here's what I
want you to do. Call a news conference for tomorrow morning around ten. Alert everyone that Connaughton will be
there ready to spill his heart out about his heroic deeds."

Catherine frowned. "I don't understand. He's already
said—"

Derek held his hand up. "But you didn't offer him an
incentive, did you?"

"An incentive?"

"Of course. Something he wants very badly and for
which he'll willingly pay the price."

"Talk to the press, you mean?"

"Exactly." Derek beamed. "Your learning curve is im-
pressive."

"But, Derek…" She watched him amble out of the of-
fice. By the end of the day, especially when she was tired,
Derek's theatricality got on her nerves. "Come back here.
How am I supposed to know what he wants?"

He glanced over his shoulder at her. "Well, that's what
you have to find out, isn't it?" A few minutes later, he
stuck his head around her office door. "By the way, the

holiday party at the Harbor House tonight? Are you going?''

"Oh Jeez." She ran her hand across her face, thought of the pepperoni pizza and the bubble bath. The two hours of quality time she'd actually penciled in on her calendar. "I wasn't really planning to be there. I thought you were going.''

"I am, but, politically, it would be a good idea for you to attend as well. Jordan takes it rather personally when he holds these bashes and people don't show up." He dug into the glass jar of jelly beans she kept on her desk, popped a handful into his mouth. "Anyhoo, I'm splitting. See you later.''

Catherine looked at her watch—five-fifteen. On days that Gary didn't collect the children from school, her mother picked them up and baby-sat until she got home, usually around six. Twice in the past week though, Derek had wanted her to attend evening meetings and she'd had to call and extend the baby-sitting hours, which inevitably prompted her mother to suggest that what she really needed to do was look for a husband so she could stay home full-time and be a proper mother.

With the tips of her fingers, Catherine massaged her forehead, tried to clear her brain enough to figure out what might get Connaughton to cooperate. And, while she worked that out, how to give her kids enough quality time that she could honestly believe they were better off with her than Gary. A moment later, as she picked up the phone to call, she noticed the pink message slip, half hidden under a stack of papers. Written in her secretary's neat round handwriting, the note said:

(1) Your ex called to remind you he needs a decision pronto. He said you'd know what he meant. (2) Your

daughter wants to remind you that you're supposed to go shopping for her ballet-recital dress tonight. DON'T BE LATE!!!

IN THE CORRIDOR outside the NICU, Martin pushed some coins into the vending machine. Two Snickers bars, a package of cheese and crackers and an orange. Lunch and dinner. The day before, one of the dietitians had caught him having a similar meal and hinted that a more balanced diet might improve his disposition.

Doubtful. Although he'd made it in to see Van Dolan, he could have saved himself the trouble. Essentially, he'd been told the chances of WISH funding were slim to nonexistent, which pretty much resolved the Ethiopia question. Tomorrow he would tell the group to count him in. Why stick around?

He watched a young couple walk hand in hand past the nursery windows, the girl in a cotton hospital gown stretched tight over her extended belly. As though it were yesterday, he saw his wife's heavy, late-pregnancy walk, the baggy blue cardigan of his that she'd worn because he'd still been in medical school and they couldn't scrape up the cash for maternity clothes, the way she'd smiled when…a thought flashed into his consciousness.

Catherine Prentice reminded him of Sharon.

CHAPTER FOUR

STRUCK BY the realization, Martin leaned back against the wall, playing images of his wife's face against those of Catherine's. It explained why he'd reacted to her as he had. As Catherine had stood in his office smiling at him, the resemblance was strong enough that he'd been angry with her for not being Sharon. Which, he thought as he finished the orange, was as good a reason as any to leave Western.

The loud ping of the elevator interrupted his thoughts. Martin watched as the doors opened and a stocky man with closely cropped hair emerged, pushing a woman in a wheelchair.

"Dr. C." The woman waved to him. "Just the person we were looking for."

Martin stared blankly at the woman before he recognized Rita Hodges. With her hair brushed and caught up in a pink ribbon and her mouth outlined in matching color, she bore little resemblance to the bedraggled woman he'd assisted earlier in the day. The man with her grinned widely, revealing a mouthful of even white teeth.

"Eddie Hodges, Rita's husband." He pumped Martin's hand. "The triplets' dad. Nice to meet you, Dr. Connor."

"Connaughton." Martin felt his hand caught in the man's vigorous grip. Short, but powerfully built, Eddie Hodges had blue eyes, so pale they seemed almost opaque. His tight black jeans were topped by an equally formfitting red polo shirt. The cream-color cowboy boots added a good two inches to the man's height. Martin imagined Eddie Hodges selling time shares of dubious market value.

"Just took Rita here to see our girls," Eddie said. "Now we're going back to the room to catch the whole thing on the tube."

"How come *you* weren't on TV tonight, Dr. C.?" Rita asked. "You did all the work."

"Publicity shy," he said. "I couldn't stand the thought of screaming mobs of fans chasing after me." Rita gave him a look that suggested she half believed him. "Actually, I'm glad I caught the two of you without any press around." He looked from Rita to Eddie. "I wanted to talk to you about the babies."

Eddie consulted his watch. "The news is gonna be on in ten minutes."

"I won't take long." Martin shoved his hands into the pockets of his lab coat, briefly described each baby's condition. "I think two of them will do fine," he said. "Frankly, though, I'm very concerned about the smallest one."

"Her name's Holly." Eddie seemed undaunted by the medical news. "We got all their names picked out. The other two are Berry and Noelle."

"Seeing as they're practically Christmas babies," Rita added with a wavering smile. "That reporter gal just had a baby herself, but it was a boy. She said if it'd been a girl, she was going to call it Holly Noelle."

"So she said we could have the names," Eddie grinned. "Pretty cool, huh?"

"About Holly though, Dr. C." Rita looked up at him. "She's going to make it, isn't she? I mean, she's not going to…"

"It's too soon to tell." Up close now, under the makeup, he saw the dark smudges beneath Rita's eyes and wished he had more encouraging words for her. "We'll know more in a day or two."

"She'll be fine," Eddie Hodges looked again at his watch. "*I* feel great about all of them. They've got my genes, if you get what I'm saying. And they're all going to make it. Holly, too."

Martin rubbed his hand across his jaw, refrained from comment.

"See, Dr. C., I'm real big on positive thinking. Me and Rita's been kind of down on our luck lately, but what I'm saying is, that's all changing. Things are looking up. It's going to be like those Siamese twins with agents and commercials and everything. What we don't need is negative energy, so I'd appreciate it if you didn't say nothing else about Holly not making it." He smiled. "Okay?"

"Got it." He decided that he wasn't at all keen on Eddie Hodges. If the next few days went as he expected them to, Rita was going to need a lot of emotional support. It was doubtful that she'd receive much from her husband.

"So that's dad, huh?" Tim Graham had come in at the end of the conversation. "I caught him on the news tonight. You'd have thought he pulled the whole thing off single-handedly."

"He sees the triplets as a ticket to financial freedom, I think," Martin said. "Doesn't want reality to mess up his rosy picture."

"Could be trouble." Graham dropped onto one of the chairs that stood around the bank of desks at one end of the unit. "Speaking of which, I guess you missed your WISH meeting, huh?"

Martin nodded, then recapped the less-than-productive meeting with Van Dolan.

Graham removed his glasses and rubbed them on the pocket of his scrubs. "You know something?" he said after a minute. "As much as I understand the need for programs like WISH, you can kind of see why administration isn't falling all over themselves to fund it."

Martin just stared at him.

"Think about it. Western depends on services like intensive care for revenue. Administration considers NICU a cash cow, for God's sake. Every time WISH succeeds in preventing an admission, Western loses another paying customer." Yawning, he flipped the carousel where messages for staff were written on pink notes and filed under each individual's name. "Let's see if Christie Brinkley or Demi Moore have been trying to reach me. Nope. I guess they finally took no for an answer." He gave the device another twirl. "Two love notes for you though."

Martin glanced at the slips of paper. Both were from Catherine Prentice in Public Relations. The last, marked Urgent, was sent nearly two hours earlier at 5:00 p.m. He crumpled the slips into a ball, tossed them in the trash.

"Press still hot on your heels, huh?" Graham shook his head.

"You'd think it was the Second Coming, wouldn't you? I'm a doctor, for God's sake. I just stopped to help out." Martin rubbed the heels of his palms into his eyes. "I should do a bait and switch," he said in jest. "Tell Catherine Prentice I'll talk to the press and then start yammering on about WISH and the need for prenatal care. That would thrill administration."

Graham laughed. "Try it. What do you have to lose? Actually, you could probably catch her at the holiday party tonight." He looked at the clock on the wall. "Right as we speak, the Harbor House is full of milling, fun-loving Western employees and doctors. Just apologize profusely for ignoring all her messages and tell her you've seen the light."

Martin pulled up a chair, swung the seat around and sat down, his arms around the backrest. "You think she'd be there?"

"Sure. She's in PR. Those people always hang out at social functions," Graham said. "They're social animals. Party people. It's their thing."

"WHAT WAS THAT, sweetie?" Catherine stood in the lobby of the Harbor House Hotel, the receiver jammed up against one ear, her palm flattened against the other, straining to hear what her daughter was saying. Behind her, sounds of revelry poured out of the ballroom where Western's holiday party was in full swing.

"Daddy called," Julie announced in her child's singsong voice. "Twice. He said if you don't have time to get my ballet dress, he and Nadia would take me to get it. He said they saw a real pretty one in the Little Ballerina shop. *And* Nadia's going to get me some new tights because mine have holes in them. *And* she's going to get Peter a new jacket because his old one is yukky."

Catherine's fingers tightened around the receiver. A rush of adrenaline made her pulse race. So this was going to be Gary's tactic. Keep the pressure on until she broke. "Listen, Julie." She tried to keep her voice slow and steady. "If Daddy calls again, tell him I said not to worry about it." *Tell him to stay the hell away and stop trying to buy you.* "*We* are going to get your dress, okay? Just you and me. I promise."

"Tonight?"

"No. Not tonight." Catherine closed her eyes. A band had struck up in the ballroom, the bass notes seemed to reverberate through her body. "I'm going to get away as soon as I can, but the stores will be closed by the time I get home. You'll be in bed, but we'll go tomorrow, okay?"

Silence on the other end. "Julie, sweetie, I know you're disappointed, I am, too. If there was any way I could have got out of this thing, I would have." More silence. "Tell you what, kiddo. How about we make tomorrow really special? We'll get your dress then go get a hot-fudge sundae? Brownie sprinkles, whipped cream, the whole works." She heard Julie's slightly mollified assent. "Good, now let me talk to Grandma, okay?"

She told her mother about the a tuna casserole in the freezer, tried not to snap as her mother launched into a rambling account of the dangerous things microwave rays could do to food, reminded her to be sure Peter took his asthma medication and, in a slightly wheedling voice, asked if she would mind very much just running an iron over the blue dress Julie wanted to wear for school tomorrow.

When her mother complained that stooping over an ironing board aggravated her back, Catherine urged her not to bother, she would do it herself in the morning. With a final reminder to be sure all the doors were locked, she hung up. Tomorrow night, she thought as she headed down the corridor to the rest room, she'd do the pot roast for dinner. Before she took Julie to Little Ballerina and thwarted Gary by spending money she didn't have.

Inside the rest room, she squinted in the bright white light, frowned at her reflection in the mirrored walls. Pale, drained and a little disheveled. Definitely not a thing of beauty. With everything else there was to juggle, how the hell did single mothers manage to date? Some of them did, she'd overheard a couple of nurses in the cafeteria discussing how soon it was okay to let a boyfriend sleep over. One of them said she always had sex at his house, never at her own if the kids were there. The other said she didn't bother about it, sex was a fact of life. Kids adjusted.

She leaned over the washbasin, splashed her face with

cold water. Sex and dating were the last things on her mind, especially now that Gary had started this custody thing. A man in her bed would be all the ammunition he needed.

Swept by a stew of emotions—fatigue, anger, frustration, self-doubt, she grabbed a paper towel from a dispenser, held it tight against her face. Life felt like one huge compromise. Worrying about finding Connaughton while she scrambled eggs for the kids this morning, standing in some stupid hotel bathroom when she wanted to be home, reading a bedtime story to Julie, helping Peter with his homework.

For a moment, the disillusionment and anger seemed to engulf her. She took a few deep breaths and splashed more cold water on her face. Tomorrow, she'd do something really special for them. Exactly what, she didn't know yet, but something. And then she would work on Dr. Martin Connaughton.

Five minutes later, she pushed her way through the shoulder-to-shoulder crowd in the ballroom looking for Derek. At one end, a small forest of bleached, tumbleweed Christmas trees twinkled with tiny white lights. In the middle of the room, dancing couples swayed and grooved to "Jingle Bell Rock." Administration reportedly spent big bucks on the annual holiday party and this year was obviously no exception.

She spotted Derek at one of the buffet tables, paper plate in one hand, a plastic glass of wine in the other. He had changed into black linen slacks and shirt and his hair was combed straight back off his forehead.

"*Gawd*, what a day it's been." He speared a piece of bacon-wrapped shrimp. "One damn thing after another. D'you reach Connaughton yet? Selena Bliss paged me twice tonight. Says I owe her a favor and she has to talk to him, or she'll never give us any decent coverage again.

What are these things?'' He gestured at a silver chafing dish. ''Alpo balls?''

''Swedish meatballs, I think.'' Catherine piled some celery and carrots on her plate, doused them with a scoop of diet ranch dressing. ''No luck with Connaughton. I'll go up to the unit first thing in the morning. The babies should have all stabilized by then, so maybe he'll be more receptive.''

''Good.'' He ladled meatballs on his plate then stopped to inspect a silver tray. ''Keep trying. There's been a new development, and we need to be sure Grossman and Connaughton are singing out of the same hymnbook.'' He lowered his voice. ''There's no love lost between the two of them.''

''So I've heard.''

''Grossman thinks he's God and so does everyone else at Western, except for Connaughton. Now Grossman wants to try this new surgery that's never been tried on a kid this size, but Connaughton thinks the kid's too sick and he's not making any secret of it.'' He dug a toothpick into a meatball. ''The problem is, I want to promote this teamwork concept and...what are these little numbers?''

''Rumaki.'' Catherine dipped a carrot stick in dressing. ''Teamwork concept?''

''Exactly.'' Derek winked at a passing reveler in form-fitting black leather pants. Face flushed with wine, he poked a toothpick into a wedge of cheese. ''What was I saying?''

''Teamwork.''

''Right. The Freeway Triplets and Western's team of miracle workers. Connaughton who delivers them, cares for them in our state-of-the-art NICU. Grossman who performs this miraculous, life-saving surgery. Fabulous PR. Jordan loves it.''

Catherine watched a conga line form a few feet away. A

man she recognized as one of the lab techs, motioned her over to join him. She shook her head, then leaned closer to hear Derek's voice over the noise. A wave of wine-scented breath forced her back.

"What makes this whole triplet thing particularly timely—" Derek brought his face closer "—is that Ned Bolton has been nosing around lately—"

"Ned Bolton?" Catherine frowned. "The medical writer with the *Tribune?*"

"The same." Derek nibbled a piece of cheese. "Bolton's specialty is striking fear into the hearts of public relations people. I suspect he secretly wants to bring every hospital in his circulation area crashing down in an avalanche of scandal. Anyway, last month we had a couple of, uh, surgical mishaps that Bolton thinks we're trying to cover up. He hinted—not very subtly—that the incidents were a result of underlying management difficulties." Derek drained his wine. "Jordan nearly hit the roof when he heard that one."

She nodded. Although she hadn't yet dealt with the chief of administration directly, she had attended executive meetings with Derek and, on occasion, had seen Jordan's sudden bursts of temper. "Is there any truth to the allegations?"

Derek waggled his hand, palm down. "Yes and no. It's a long story. The point though is to divert Bolton and the rest of the pack with this triplet thing. That's why we need to milk it for all it's worth." He glanced at his watch. "Listen, I've had about all the holiday cheer I can handle for one night. Jordan gives his speech at eight. We need to get something in the newsletter. Stick around for it, will you?"

Catherine opened her mouth to speak, then closed it, silenced by the thought of how much she needed her job. Another half hour seemed like a life sentence, but she dragged up the phony smile she'd perfected during her marriage and sweetly agreed to stay. In need of a stimulant to keep her going, she started over for the coffee urn at the far end of room and collided with a tall blond man. He introduced himself and, in amazingly short time, regaled her with details of his stock portfolio, real estate and assorted collection of cars and boats.

"I ski Mammoth," he rambled. "Got a condo up there, all exposed beams and glass, hot tub, wet bar. Ski all day, party all night."

Catherine smiled politely and considered possible avenues of escape. Her head ached and the smell of overheated bodies and reheated food was making her feel slightly sick. Even if she had the time or inclination to date, she reflected, if this was an indication of what was out there, she'd go without.

He flashed dazzling white teeth and moved a little closer, his eyes appraising. "So, what do *you* do for fun?"

"Not a whole lot." She inhaled a cloud of aftershave, took a step back to avoid nose-to-nose contact and searched her mind for a sufficiently unexciting activity. "Gardening," She took another step backward. "Cooking." In this way, she could eventually backstep her way out of the room. "Work."

He shook his head and moved a step closer, continuing their little pas de deux. "Y'know what they say about all work and no play, don't you?"

"Yeah, but I don't care."

"Hey, babe." He looked into her eyes. "Want to split this place, go get a drink somewhere?"

As she formed the words of refusal, she heard a male voice behind her.

"Excuse me, I need to talk to Catherine."

A male voice with an Irish accent. She knew without turning that it was Martin Connaughton.

CHAPTER FIVE

THE MARKETING MAN, caught momentarily off guard by the intrusion, rallied quickly. "Hey, that's cool. No sweat, I'll just mosey over there and check out the munchies." He shot Catherine a parting wink. "Catch *you* later."

Catherine watched him disappear into the crowd, then turned to Connaughton. A beer bottle in one hand, he wore a battered tweed jacket, some sort of collarless shirt under it and jeans. His reddish-brown hair fell untidily over his forehead, and his eyes were lined with exhaustion. But as she looked at him, all she could think of at that moment was how attractive he was—not handsome, or conventionally good-looking, but attractive: sexy, slightly disheveled, more than a little weary and, she suspected, completely unconcerned about the way he looked.

"Martin Connaughton," he said as though perhaps she'd forgotten. "You're looking for me?"

"I *was* looking for you. About four hours and five messages ago. You didn't answer your page or your messages. Again."

"Well, now I'm here."

"How do you know you didn't just barge into an important conversation?" A vestige of irritation lingered. *Now* he was ready to talk. "That guy might have been...I don't know, the love of my life."

He raised an eyebrow. "In that case you were managing to conceal it remarkably well. I've been watching you from across the room for the last..." He glanced at his watch. "Ten minutes. You looked bored stiff. Actually, I thought I'd do you a good turn by rescuing you."

"You did?" Surprise deflated her anger like air from a balloon.

"I did." A faint smile played across his face.

She stood there, momentarily robbed of words by an intense awareness of his physical presence. His height, the way his jacket fit across his shoulders, the slight shadow of beard. Maybe he'd come straight from the hospital, just changed from his scrubs. She felt weird, breathless almost. Everything around them seemed distant and unconnected.

"So?" His smile grew wider.

"So." She felt her face color. "We need to talk."

He caught her arm, shepherded her to an empty space by the door. "I suppose that this is the part where I throw myself on your mercy and tell you that it's been a hell of a day so please accept my abject apologies for my earlier behavior."

The remark, with its teasing undertone, once again caught her off guard. The cool, distant doctor had metamorphosed into a sexy guy who had a definitely disconcerting effect on her heart.

"You don't really seem too abject." She matched his tone. "I like a lot of groveling before I forgive."

"Unfortunately, groveling isn't one of my strong suits," he said solemnly. "But supposing I did want to grovel my way into your good graces. How would I go about it? Could I redeem myself by talking to your pals out there?"

"My *pals*. You make it sound so frivolous." She suppressed a smile and an errant thought: she could fall for him, big time. Her face felt warm. "As a matter of fact, you can meet them tomorrow. I've scheduled a press conference at ten."

"You've already set it up?" Dark blue eyes widened slightly. "How did you know I'd do it?"

"Just a hunch." She realized she was beginning to enjoy the exchange. "Can you be there?"

"There's nothing I'd rather do. Just tell me what you want me to say."

"We can work on that in the morning." She leaned her shoulders lightly against the wall, her arms at her sides. Relief, but more than that, something about Martin Connaughton had completely transformed her mood. "Back to groveling though."

"Yes?"

"Just this morning, I seem to recall you making some sort of comment about public relations. How did you put it?" A hand cupped to her chin, she pantomimed deep thought. "I think the word you used was *puffery.*"

"Temporary insanity on my part," he replied with an obvious effort to maintain a solemn expression. "I retract everything I might have said. Public relations is a calling of the highest order."

"You know something?"

"You don't believe me?"

"Not for an instant." She smiled into his eyes. "So what produced the dramatic change?"

"I've got a project that's very important to me." The laughter left his face. "It's called WISH. I'd like to talk to you about it." He glanced around the crowded room. "Maybe we can find somewhere a little bit quieter."

"So that's really what WISH is all about," he said after he'd given her the overview of what he was trying to do. "Drug counseling and adequate prenatal care can go a long way toward preventing tragedies like Kenesha Washington."

Music and laughter from the hotel floated out to where they sat on a low stone wall. Above them a smattering of stars, ahead a narrow strip of beach and the dark ocean. What surprised him was how easily the words had flowed. The emotions that just that morning Dora Matsushita had urged him to unlock were right there as he explained, and he knew by Catherine's expression that he'd touched her.

"And you're hoping that administration will be so pleased with your glowing tribute to Western's NICU that they'll change their minds and decide to fund WISH after all? Is that your strategy?"

"Something along those lines." He smiled. "As the PR expert, how does that sound to you?"

"As the practitioner of fluff and puffery you mean?"

"I already apologized for that, remember? Besides, you called me Scrooge."

"And I apologized for that," she replied. "Although you *did* seem kind of dark and gloomy this morning." She glanced at him from under her lashes. "I figured that maybe it was typical Irish behavior. You know, all brooding and melancholy."

He laughed. "That's a myth. The truth about the Irish is that at any given time in history, half of them were starving. If they'd had enough to eat, they'd have been as bright and cheerful as yourself."

"So you missed breakfast this morning? That's your excuse?"

"There's no excuse for me. I'm just cantankerous."

"Yeah, I'd heard that," she said. "A loose cannon was the way someone described you."

Martin laughed again, well aware of his reputation at Western.

"About WISH though," she said after a moment. "I'm

kind of low on Western's totem pole of influence, but I'll do what I can to put in a good word.''

"Thanks.'' Tempted to shift now to the personal and ask her more about her family, Martin reminded himself he was here for a purpose. And, if he'd read her correctly, she understood his concerns. In fact, her face, which seemed to register the slightest emotion, made her a fairly easy read. And if that didn't give her away, he thought with amusement, her hands did.

"What's the joke?'' she asked. "You're sitting there smiling to yourself.''

"I was just thinking that perhaps you had Italian somewhere in your ancestry.''

"Oh, the hands?'' She grinned and her face colored slightly. "I know, everyone teases me about it. If I ever get rheumatism, I probably won't be able to talk. There's no Italian though. Irish on both sides.''

He said nothing, struck by an odd sense that he'd come home, that he knew this woman with her long plait of hair and blushing smile. Years away from Ireland had done little to dilute the strain of Celtic mysticism in his veins, and the feeling awed him. "Your children?'' he said, finally giving in to his need to know. "How old are they?''

"Peter's ten and Julie was six last week.'' She grinned. "For her birthday cake, she wanted carrot and pineapple with chocolate frosting.''

"God.'' He pulled a face. "That sounds revolting. Did she get it?''

"Yeah, I baked it myself. Birthday cakes are kind of my thing. Any cakes actually. Chocolate, apple, cheesecake, you name it. Don't tell Ed Jordan—'' she brought her face closer "—but I'd rather be home with my kids, frosting a cake, than doing public relations.''

"But then we wouldn't be sitting here talking.''

"True."

"How long were you married?"

"Nearly twelve years."

"That's a long time for a California marriage, isn't it? I thought they all self-destructed after five years."

She smiled. "It takes work, I guess. You both have to want it. In our case, I guess I wanted it more than he did. We had this really terrific house and sometimes I'd sit in the kitchen and the sun would be pouring through the windows, and there were cookies or something like that in the oven and the kids would be playing. I just remember feeling so happy. I mean, who needs a career? That *was* my career."

"The perfect wife and mother, huh?"

"I guess not so perfect since we're now divorced."

"You didn't want the divorce?"

"You could say that. When he told me he wanted to end it, I felt as though I'd been fired from the only job I'd ever wanted." A quizzical smile on her face, she turned to look at him. "Do you have any idea why I'm telling you all this?"

"Probably because I'm asking."

"But it's all one-sided. What about you? Have you been married?"

"A long time ago."

"Any kids?"

He shook his head. "So would you try it again?" he asked. "Marriage, I mean?"

"Probably not." She frowned at her hands, folded in her lap. "It was a pretty powerless time in my life. I had no real stake in anything. Unfortunately, I couldn't see it then. I just deferred to him without really thinking about it. Sometimes I'd decide I was tired of living under a dictatorship and complain. Then he'd do something really sweet and generous and I'd feel like a bitch.''

He laughed.

''It's true. I don't think I started out that way, it just happened gradually. A little compromise here, another one there.'' She shrugged. ''It's an insidious thing. By the time we got divorced and I really looked at myself, I barely knew who I was anymore. I guess in a weird sort of way, I'm grateful to him for forcing the issue. It's probably the only thing I *am* grateful to him for—except the children, of course.''

''And I was going to ask if it had left you embittered.''

''It shows, huh? Embittered and embattled. But wiser. I'll never let myself be dependent on someone like that again.''

''But surely it doesn't have to be all or nothing.'' He wondered why it seemed important to convince her. ''Marriage doesn't have to mean giving up all your autonomy.''

She shrugged. ''Maybe not. But I'm kind of gun-shy.''

A moment passed and neither of them made a move to leave. A breeze blew a wisp of hair across her face. He watched her push it away. Watched the silver charm bracelet she wore slide down her arm as she did. *Leave,* he told himself, but she was smiling at him and the breeze carried a whiff of her floral perfume. *You've accomplished what you came here to do,* he told himself, but the sky was sprinkled with stars and the moon was a pale crescent suspended above them. *Leave.* But each time he looked at her, he felt a yearning for a time when the future had seemed bright and full of promise and a small voice in his head asked, *Well, why not again?*

''This morning when I saw you in the lobby,'' he finally said, ''you reminded me of someone I used to know. Now though I can see that you're not really like her, it's just an expression you get.''

She watched his face. ''Old girlfriend?''

''No.'' He shook his head, felt her waiting for more. ''No,'' he said again.

Moments passed. The oleander bushes that lined the lawns trembled in the breeze.

He watched her face. She'd moved slightly so that she now sat in profile to him. Back rigid, bottom lip caught in her teeth. Vulnerable somehow. A wave of fierce protectiveness swept him, stunning him with its intensity. He wanted to put his arm around her, to pull her close, to promise that he'd prevent anything bad from ever happening to her. Sure, a voice in his head scoffed, like you promised Sharon. He glanced at his watch.

''It's getting late.'' She turned to face him. ''I should probably go back in.''

Laughter floated out from the hotel, heels clattered on the flagstone pathway. Words clattered in his brain. Inside, the band started up again.

''Listen, Catherine,'' he finally said. ''I think you need to do something crazy.'' He stood, held out his hand to her. ''Let's dance.''

She laughed. ''I'm the world's worst dancer.''

''Second worst. I guarantee.''

''Ed Jordan's probably looking for me. I was suppose to listen to his speech.''

''Is that going to be a problem for you?''

''It might be. Tomorrow.'' She took his hand. ''Come on, let's live dangerously.''

IF YOU HAD ANY SENSE, Catherine thought as she whirled around the room in Martin's arms, when this dance is over you will thank him very nicely and make a quick exit. That would be the safe thing to do. The sort of thing that Julie and Peter's mommy would do. The sort of thing that the Catherine Prentice she thought she knew would have done. But his arms were around her, and her chin rested on the rough tweed of his jacket and her lips were tantalizingly close to the skin of his neck, and the Catherine Prentice she thought she knew, the cookie-baking, homework-checking, PTA president Catherine, had gone AWOL. In her place was this strange, barely recognizable woman. A woman whose body turned into mush every time she looked into Martin Connaughton's eyes.

"What do you think?" He pulled away slightly to look at her. "Pretty bad, aren't I?"

"The worst." She smiled up at him. "My feet will never be the same again."

"Do you want to stop?"

"No." *Never,* she thought as couples glided around them, shadowy and indistinct in the spangled light. She was bewitched. The evening had become this magical shimmering thing that much later she would unwrap and slowly examine like a precious gift. He pulled her closer, his long body hard against hers, hummed softly in her ear. Outside, as he'd asked about the children, the real Catherine had briefly returned to issue warnings, but he'd taken her hand and the words had melted like snowflakes in the sun. The music played on and, caught up in the dreamlike spell, they danced and danced. When the band played its last number and the lights were raised, she felt as though she'd awakened from a trance.

Minutes later, they were back out in the dark night, the air cool on her overheated skin. Reality slowly returned. As they stopped beside her pale blue Plymouth van, she felt like Cinderella. Her magic coach had turned back into a pumpkin.

"Very glamorous." She grinned at Martin. "Probably couldn't guess I had kids, huh?"

"What have you got in there?" He peered inside the window. "Toys and bikes?"

"Pretty much." She unlocked the door and slid it open. On the carpeted floor were red and blue plastic crates of toys. One marked Julie, the other Peter. Two smaller cartons contained books. Pegs on the wall of the van were hung with jackets. She watched his face as he looked around, his expression rapt.

He turned to her. "It's all so...organized."

Catherine laughed at his interest. "Well, it's easier that way. Keeps them occupied when we're driving." She reached under the seat and pulled out two smaller cartons. "See. Cookies. Pretzels. Sodas. Helps cut down on impromptu fast-food visits," she said with a grin.

"You go on a lot of outings, do you?"

"We go to the beach. Camping. Sometimes we go up to the mountains. My mother has a cabin in Big Bear."

"And do you have campfires? Cook marshmallows? That sort of thing?"

"Uh-huh. Sing songs, the whole shtick." She laughed, suddenly self-conscious.

"What?"

"I'm just surprised that you find it interesting. I love doing this kind of thing, but..." She bit her lip, already sorry she'd embarked on the story. "Their father always made me feel that it was the only thing I was capable of doing. He used to call it my Becky-Home-ecky stuff. I guess it never seemed particularly interesting or valuable."

"You're wrong about that," he said.

A moment passed and they stood together looking at each other and she realized she was holding her breath. The Martin Connaughton she'd first seen that morning was not the man with whom she'd spent the last few hours and she wondered who exactly the real one was. If it was the man standing before her now, with this look of tenderness on his face, she could be in big trouble. Very big trouble.

But a moment later, as if a curtain had been drawn, the look was gone.

"Ten o'clock tomorrow?" Unsmiling, he inclined his head slightly. "I'll see you then."

As she pulled out of the parking lot, Catherine felt as dazed as if she'd been hit on the head with a baseball bat.

BY THE TIME Martin drove into the Long Beach Marina, the bewitched feeling he'd had with Catherine was mostly gone, dissipated by the two messages he'd had from the unit. One was a new admission, the other an update on Holly Hodges, whom he'd twice caught himself calling Kenesha. Nothing about her condition reassured him. He had called for a neurological consult because he suspected that, in addition to all her other problems, she was bleeding into her brain.

Still a glow lingered, a small pinpoint of light in the dark. He stopped at the row of marina post office boxes to collect his mail and strode down the wooden gangway whistling.

Fog had fallen like a gray shroud over the water, cocooning the dense thicket of sailboat masts. Among them was his own dwelling, an old forty-foot Coronado sailboat. It had once provided diversion for weekend sailors on jaunts to Catalina and Mexico and needed some cosmetic work, but it suited his needs just fine.

It occurred to him as he jumped aboard that the way he'd felt as he'd talked to Catherine, he would have agreed to speak to the press, WISH or no WISH. The thought both exhilarated and unnerved him and was still on his mind as he bent down to put the key in the padlock. Then a movement behind him made him look up and do a double take.

Valerie Webb stood in the shadows watching him, a small smile on her face.

"Greetings." Valerie moved into the marina light's cool glow. A silvery veil of moisture covered her red hair and pale trench coat. "I was hoping you wouldn't be too late. It's a touch chilly out here."

"Val." Martin pulled himself up, the padlock still in his hand. "What the hell are you doing here?" His mind scrambled for an explanation, then he remembered that she'd done the press briefing. It seemed an unlikely reason for her visit, but he thanked her, apologized for not having done so earlier.

"*Da nada.*" She waved away his apology. "It's no hardship smiling for TV cameras. Good way to score a few political points. Jordan was tickled pink. But that isn't why I stopped by." A gust of wind blew her hair and she drew her trench coat tight, hugged herself. "God, it really is cold up here. Can we go inside?"

Still baffled, he looked at her for a minute, then turned and climbed down into the small galley. Valerie followed close behind. He flipped on the lights and dropped his mail on a Formica-topped ledge. "Okay, shoot." He shrugged off his jacket. "What's this all about?"

"I was talking to Nate Grossman before I left tonight. "About the surgery he's planning for Holly Hodges."

An image of Holly as he'd last seen her ran through his mind. Bruises from her birth that morning covered her head; her skin had the purple, glistening look of a peeled plum. Holly was what staff privately referred to as a "train wreck of a child," at risk for every disease and complication in the book. The idea of surgery was ludicrous if not immoral. He said as much to Valerie.

"Tell that to Grossman," she said. "He's holding a press conference tomorrow to announce it. I stopped off at the holiday bash tonight, I was going to tell you then." A smile flickered over her face. "I looked all over the place for you, then I saw you outside talking to the PR gal. You seemed quite engrossed. I'm surprised she didn't tell you. She must have known."

Martin shrugged. His interest in discussing work-related topics had diminished in direct proportion to his increasing interest in Catherine.

Valerie stood in the middle of the cabin watching him, one hand cupped around her chin, her expression thoughtful, as though he were an interesting piece of abstract art she hadn't quite figured out. Their eyes met for a moment, then something drew his eye to the small silver spider on a chain around her neck. Suddenly he knew why she was there. He let the silence lengthen.

"I want to know what I've done," she finally said.

"Done?" He shook his head, feigning confusion. "What do you mean?"

"You know damn well what I mean, Martin. You've been avoiding me for the past week. Whenever I see you on the unit, you act as though nothing happened between us." She picked up a piece of junk mail he'd set on the desk, glanced at it, then looked up at him again. "I'm sorry, but I'm really bothered. I had a great time. I kind of thought you enjoyed yourself, too. Sooo…"

"I'm not sure how I'm supposed to act, Valerie," he said, impatient now. An hour or so ago, he could have stayed up all night, now all he wanted to do was sleep. "I'm sorry, I thought we were on the same wavelength. If I was wrong—"

"No, no. *No.*" Her expression softened. She touched the tips of her fingers to his mouth, held them there a moment.

"It was mutual. You didn't exactly have to drag me kicking and screaming into the bedroom."

Weary—and wary—he brushed a hand across his face. "So what's the problem then?"

"I guess I don't feel as casual about what happened as I thought I would." She frowned, looked down at her feet for a moment. "I know about all the noninvolvement stuff and I really meant it then, but now...I can't stop thinking about you. We just seem right together." Her face animated, she caught his arm. "Seriously. Think about it. Obviously we know there's good chemistry, right? We're both professionals, both in medicine. We're both lonely—"

"Maybe *you're* lonely." He went to the sink, ran water into a glass. "I'm perfectly satisfied with my life." He swallowed the water in one gulp, put the glass down and turned around to her, arms folded across his chest. "Except for the fact that I'm exhausted and want nothing more than to fall asleep, I'm fine. So, at the risk of being rude, I'm going to say good-night and—"

"Listen to me. Please." Her eyes filled. "You have no life outside of Western. Neither do I." Her voice softened. "Didn't it feel wonderful to wake up in the morning together?" She moved over to where he stood, put her arms around his neck and lightly kissed his mouth. "I care about you, Martin. I think we could be good together."

"It won't work, Val." As he disengaged her arms, he felt the throb of a pulse in his temple. "My only interest right now is in getting WISH funded. That's why I've agreed to talk to a horde of reporters tomorrow even though the thought appalls me. A relationship, with you or anyone else, is absolutely the last thing on my mind."

For a moment, Valerie didn't speak. Then she laughed, once, a wry laugh that twisted her mouth. She slowly shook her head. "Your problem is that you don't really know what you want. Maybe if you let someone actually get close to you, it might make you happier than all your goddamn causes. Think about it sometime.''

HE WAS TIRED ENOUGH after Valerie left that he thought he would sink easily into dreamless sleep, but hours later he lay on the bed, kept awake by her accusation, by the events of the day. By what to do about Ethiopia. About Holly. About Catherine.

He punched the pillow into a more comfortable shape, turned to lie on his other side, but the worries continued their endless assault. In the past year, Western had become increasingly political and marketing oriented, qualities that turned him off completely. And while there were gratifying moments in the NICU, the increasing reliance on sophisticated technology often made him feel more as though he were tinkering with an automobile than a baby. Around and around his thoughts went, but always returned to the inescapable conclusion that without WISH, his life had little meaning.

Outside, he heard the mournful call of the foghorn, the groan of the boat against the moorings. An eerie sound that always made him think of tortured spirits fighting to break free. He put the pillow over his head to block out the sound, closed his eyes, but sleep still eluded him. Amidst the jumble of thoughts that flowed through his brain came a realization. Although he wouldn't admit it to Valerie, she was right, he *was* lonely. Talking to Catherine Prentice had made him realize something. What was missing from his life, what he craved with an almost painful intensity was the kind of closeness that he had once known with his wife.

He wanted someone to understand him again. He wanted to matter to someone. He wanted to be needed.

One of the songs Sharon used to sing likened life to an

ocean and love to a boat. "In troubled waters," one of the lines went, "It keeps us afloat." The song had become a metaphor for their marriage. They would talk of the rough seas they might weather, the crew they would one day create. The memory saddened him, heightened his feeling of loneliness. Sharon's death had wrecked their boat and he had drifted aimlessly and alone ever since. His relationships with women were like the one he'd had with Valerie Webb, brief and superficial, little more than fulfillment of a physical need. Except for Valerie, none of the women had professed any deep feelings for him and he had certainly never felt any for them. But he was tired of being alone. Tonight, he'd glimpsed the possibility of something more.

Catherine's face swam slowly into focus, her wide mouth and pink cheeks, and he recalled the almost-eerie sense of familiarity about it. Away from her, the idea seemed fanciful and sentimental, but also very comforting. He finally fell asleep, the image still in his brain...

Martin is back home. Rain is falling, a heavy gray Belfast rain. It's as if the sky is weeping. Someone calls his name in an Irish accent. The voice—Sharon's voice, he realizes—seems to be coming from behind a brick wall. He runs back and forth along the length of the wall. Sharon needs him, but he can't reach her. Breathless and frantic he keeps trying to get past the wall. Sharon's cries become more desperate and then from far off he hears a police siren, a shrill sound that gets louder and louder until it finally wakes him.

Heart pounding, he sat up. After a moment, he realized the phone beside the bed was ringing. A resident calling to say that Holly Hodges had coded.

CHAPTER SIX

THE ALARM ON Catherine's bedside table buzzed at five, and Martin's name popped into her head before her eyes even opened. For a moment, she lay in the warm bed and let her thoughts drift lazily. His arms around her as they'd danced, the way he'd looked at her as though he'd been about to kiss her.

And then, just like that, a curtain had come down and he'd seemed as remote and cool as he had when they'd first met in the lobby. Of course. *He's a man.* That's the way they all are. You never know where you are with them. Don't ever expect anything else.

"What time did you finally get home last night?" Her mother poked her head into the room. "I sat up watching TV till ten and you weren't home then." She frowned. "Feeling okay, sweetie? You look a little peaked. Are you taking those antioxidants I gave you? They've made a world of difference to the way I feel, I'll tell you. Want me to put some coffee on?"

"Sure, that would be great." Catherine pulled on her old yellow robe and followed her mother into the kitchen. She couldn't afford to think about Martin Connaughton in anything but a professional connection. Besides, she'd probably bored him silly yakking about the kids all night. Bringing out the toys like some demented den mother. He probably couldn't wait to get away.

"What kind of work were you doing until ten o'clock at

night?'' Her mother, in a pale blue taffeta quilted dressing gown, glanced over her shoulder as she measured coffee. Her short, graying hair clung to her scalp in wispy tendrils. ''Will you get paid overtime?''

''I'm on salary, Mom. I don't get overtime.'' With her foot, Catherine pushed open the door to the laundry closet and dumped a load of white clothes into the machine. It was one of those stackable units, much smaller than the one she'd had in the house she used to live in with Gary. Sometimes the drier didn't work properly, and she had to drape damp clothes around the kitchen and bathroom. Better that though than going to Gary for more money, something her mother constantly urged her to do. She wanted independence, whatever the price. ''I was talking to this doctor. The one who delivered the triplets.''

Still groggy with sleep, her hair hanging loose down her back, she padded into the kitchen and opened the refrigerator. Milk. Margarine. Martin. *Stop it.* Even if she hadn't turned him off with all the kid talk, she didn't want a relationship, especially with someone she worked with. Everyone knew that was a big mistake. She pulled out the Tupperware container of pancake batter she kept made up and set it down on the counter. But last night had felt so…magical. There was no other word for it.

''Well, not to tell you your business, sweetie, but if Western expects you to stay up till all hours talking to doctors, they need to pay you more money.'' She reached into the cabinet for mugs. ''Is he married?''

''Married?'' Catherine stared at her mother. ''No…I mean, what difference does that make? We were talking about this program he runs for pregnant women who are addicted to drugs. He's very interesting…great accent. Irish. From Belfast.'' *And I thought he was going to kiss me, but he didn't. Unfortunately.*

"You're blushing," her mother said. "Unless it's early menopause and you're having a hot flash."

"I'm thirty-four, Mom. I think that's a little young for hot flashes." Maybe she'd read something into the evening that wasn't there. Maybe he'd only wanted to ask about WISH and she'd started yakking and he couldn't get away. Maybe he'd only asked her to dance to shut her up.

She grabbed a carton of milk from the refrigerator and stood, holding it as she stared through the window at the morning traffic on Second Street. The hoots and squeals of horns and brakes filtered into the kitchen, blended with the slosh of the washing machine, the gurgle and drip of the coffeemaker. The traffic noise had taken a while to get used to. At first the hum had kept her awake at night. Now she hardly heard it. Amazing all the adjustments, big and small, she'd made in the past year.

"They say it's a mistake to mix business and pleasure." Her mother tore open a pack of Sweet'n Low and poured it into her coffee. "If you see him again though, ask him if it's true this stuff gives you brain tumors."

"Sure, Mom. Why don't I call him right now?" Catherine poured coffee for herself. If her mother's endless obsessing about health matters didn't irritate her until she wanted to scream, it would be comic. "Anything else you'd like me to ask him?"

"Don't be sarcastic. Someone has to worry over these things."

"So give someone else a turn." The fear that she, herself, had the same genetic predisposition, scared her. Gary was always accusing her of worrying too much and then he'd give her something to worry about. *Like threatening to take the kids.* She shivered in the cold kitchen, got her fuzzy slippers from the bedroom and turned up the heater so the place would be warm when the kids got up. Then

she busied herself at the sink where her mother couldn't
see her face as she thought about Martin.

Okay, he *was* attractive and no matter why he'd asked
her to dance, she'd enjoyed it. In fact the memory still made
her hot inside. And even though he'd first struck her as
cold and unfeeling, he obviously cared about WISH. And
a man who cared about children could definitely find his
way into her heart. And she loved the way his accent faded
in and out so that even ordinary words sounded exotic.

"Your washing's done," her mother said. "You didn't
hear the buzzer go off? Maybe you need to get your hearing
checked. Your aunt Rose on your father's side was deaf as
a post at forty."

"I heard it, Mom. I was thinking." Catherine dumped
the whites into the drier, loaded coloreds into the washer.
For a moment she stood and watched as the water sloshed
over the clothes. But what if she *hadn't* imagined it all?
What if he asked her out and things went really well? What
about the whole sex thing? Where would they do it? Her
bed? And what about the kids? Would she tell them, or just
go to his place when they were at Gary's?

Oh for God's sake, you spent a couple of hours with the
man. Did he say anything about seeing you again? Did he
put any moves on you? Even a little good-night kiss? And
what was that Derek said about Valerie Webb? Need more
reasons? You're still on probation at Western. Gary's trying
to get custody of the kids. Anyway, when have men ever
done anything but screw up your life?

She went into Julie's room, looked at her sleeping daughter, all tangled up in the Big Bird sheets. "Hey, sleepy-
head." She sat down on the edge of the bed, kissed her
daughter's soft, sleep-warm faced. "Rise and shine."

After her mother left for a doctor's appointment, Catherine went into action like a speeded-up 16 mm film. She

woke Peter, ran another load of laundry, ironed Julie's blue dress, took a shower and set out some clothes to wear. While the kids were getting dressed, she put on her makeup at the bathroom sink, double-checking to make sure she'd done both eyes. Then, just for the hell of it, she added a spritz of L'Aire du Temps and went into the kitchen to start breakfast.

"Mommy!" Julie's scream rang out from the bedroom. "Get in here quick."

"What is it, honey?" Fork in hand, her heart racing, she spun around. As she did, the floppy sleeve of her robe hit the bowl and sent it clattering to the floor. She stepped over the spattered pancake batter to find Julie standing on her bed, hands clutched to her chest.

"A mouse!" Julie squealed. "There was a gigantic mouse on my bed. Get it away, Mommy, I hate mice. "

"Yeah, well, I'm not too thrilled about them either." Catherine's heart went into overdrive. Mice terrified her, they always had. She dashed into the kitchen for a broom, then had another thought. "Let's go see if Peter can catch it."

Half an hour later, the tiny field mouse had been caught and dispatched by Peter who carried it by the tail to the end of the street and set it free, while he muttered under his breath about stupid females. The scare made Julie throw up on the dress Catherine had ironed and complain that she was too sick for school. She didn't want pancakes and they were out of her favorite juice. Peter was wheezing again, and Catherine discovered that she only had black tights, which didn't go with the red skirt she'd planned to wear. As she rummaged through the dresser drawer for another pair, the phone rang. Julie pounced on it, and Catherine heard her relay the mouse story.

"We never had mice in the old house, Daddy," Julie sobbed. "How come they have to come to this house?"

"THE HOUSE IS NOT vermin infested, Gary." Catherine downed her second cup of black coffee for the morning and glanced at the clock on the office wall. Seven-forty. Martin was supposed to meet her at ten. Gary's call—as she'd walked into the office—had temporarily blocked all thoughts of Martin, but she had a job to do.

"Look, I don't have time to talk about this now," she told him. "I've… No, *I'm* buying Julie's ballerina dress. I don't care what Nadia promised her. We're getting it tonight. So please drop her off in time for me to get to the mall. Peter, too. Six, okay? No later."

She slammed down the phone. Today was Gary's day to pick up the kids from school and she just knew he was going to somehow screw up her plans to take Julie shopping so that Nadia could save the day by buying the dress. *Along with her kids' affection.* Anger and caffeine made her heart race so hard, she felt dizzy. Okay, she couldn't deal with Gary stuff right now. Where was Martin? No, not Martin. Dr. Connaughton. She took some deep breaths, gulped down more coffee and wrote out half a dozen sound bites for him to use at the press conference. After that, she took her hand mirror from her desk, checked her makeup and paged him.

He still hadn't answered thirty minutes later when Nate Grossman dropped by to find out how many stations were covering his announcement. Every station in town, Catherine proudly told him. Ten minutes later, he was back to inform her that a medical emergency had come up and he either had to talk to the press immediately or he couldn't do it.

At nine, Derek came in and took over arrangements for

Grossman's announcement. Catherine paged Martin again. Ten minutes later when he still hadn't responded, she was on her way up to the unit to find him when she ran into Ed Jordan who wanted to know whether she had finished the piece on his speech the night before. He would like to see a draft by four that afternoon, he told her.

There is a lesson to be drawn here, she thought. She pressed the button for the elevator. Never think you have things under control. The minute you think you do, you will, without a doubt, be proven wrong. Make that two lessons. Daydreaming about tall, blue-eyed Irish doctors is a bad idea.

MARTIN LOOKED DOWN at Holly. A tube, held in place with adhesive tape, ran from her mouth into her lungs. The tube was connected to a ventilator that kept her lungs open. More tubes in her umbilical cord carried water, sugar and other nutrients into her body. Electrodes on her chest measured her heart and breathing rates. Another on her stomach measured the oxygen that passed through her skin. Alive thanks to technology.

"Hey, Martin, there's someone from public relations looking for you," a voice behind him said. He turned to see Tim Graham, eyes crinkling above his surgical mask. "Seemed a little rattled. Something about a press conference at ten"

"Watch her legs." His attention was on the baby. "Not much movement, is there? It doesn't look too good." Then Graham's words registered. "Oh Jesus, the press conference. It went right out of my head." As he started to leave, he noticed the white spot on Holly's leg, left where his finger had been. It meant she was retaining too much carbon dioxide and not getting enough oxygen. Her color wasn't so hot, either.

"Let's bag her," he told the respiratory therapist.

The therapist unplugged Holly from the ventilator, started pumping oxygen with a black rubber bag. Seconds ticked away. The baby's chest heaved mechanically each time the bag was squeezed.

"Dr. Connaughton." The unit secretary spoke at his shoulder. "There's someone from public relations to see you."

Martin watched Holly for signs of improvement. Any positive change would be a temporary solution at best. For now, all they could do was buy time.

"Dr. Connaughton. She said it's urgent."

"Let's see how she does." He watched the baby for another minute, then turned suddenly, startling the secretary who had her hand raised to touch his shoulder again. He pulled his surgical mask around his neck, went out to find Catherine. She stood in three-quarter profile, a cellular phone to her ear, long brown hair pulled back with a gold barrette.

Whether it was lack of sleep or too much on his mind he didn't know, but he couldn't focus. Jumbled images flashed through his brain. Holly with her panoply of hardware. Her fool of a father with his cowboy boots. Catherine's green eyes, her hair brushing his face as they'd danced last night.

Life was like a kaleidoscope. All the different pieces fall into place to make a pattern. Then a slight movement and some of the pieces change and a new pattern begins to emerge. Another movement and… Catherine looked up and saw him. The spots of color on her face matched the red of her blazer.

"DEREK, I KNOW they're all waiting." Her heart racing, Catherine looked away from Martin. "I'm up here in the unit with him right now." A pause. "Yes, I *know* that. Look, I'll be down in just a minute. Okay?" Another pause. "I *know* that. Bye." She flipped the phone closed.

"Dr. Connaughton," she said. "You have a press conference in five minutes."

"Right." He ran his hand across his face. "The press conference."

"Don't tell me you forgot." She smiled her PR smile, wide but short on sincerity. "We were supposed to meet at ten. It's five to."

"Right," he said again. "Look, I'm sorry, I don't think I...tell me what you want me to say."

What did she want him to say? Catherine put her hand on the small of his back, then withdrew it as if scalded. No touching. Touching was trouble. They started for the elevator. What *did* she want him to say?

"Just answer their questions," she finally managed to say. "Try to avoid medical jargon. Get in a plug for Western if you can."

In the elevator going down to the conference room, she tried to deliver a media crash course, but kept losing her train of thought. Martin, his back against the wall, seemed oddly detached, as though part of him was still up in the unit. They got off the elevator, headed down the corridor at a fast clip.

"Don't let them intimidate you." She continued her tuition. "Don't answer questions you don't know the answers to."

"Such as?"

Such as, why *didn't* you kiss me last night? Did I really read you wrong? Such as, can I possibly act normal around you? Such as, what would I do if you tried to kiss me now? She bit her thumbnail. Martin pulled her hand from her mouth.

"Listen, Catherine. About last night—"

"Okay, here's a hypothetical question…" She fixed her eyes on Martin's face. *Last night didn't exist. Your interest in this man is purely professional.* "A hypothetical question," she said again. "Such as… 'Are all the babies going to make it?' Well, that was a bad example, we know they will all make it, but—"

"Actually, that's not true. I'm not at all sure Holly will make it."

She looked at him, suddenly focused. "The father was really upbeat when I saw him this morning. In fact, he was talking about some surgery that Grossman wants to do."

"The father's an idiot. Surgery isn't going to save her life." His face darkened. "It's going to bloody well *condemn* her to life."

"Martin…" All other thoughts eclipsed by his remark, she closed her eyes for a moment. "Please, *please,* don't say that. Look, everyone is saying this surgery is the one hope Holly has. Jordan's calling it a chance at a miracle. In fact, that's the theme of our publicity campaign."

She watched his face. Eyes dark now, troubled. He inhaled, slowly let out his breath. From inside the conference room, she could hear the muffled voices of the press. The chirp of beepers. A phone rang somewhere.

"I'm sorry, I can't do it," he said. "Yesterday, you told me all I had to do was talk about delivering the babies and do an update on their condition."

"But that was yesterday. Before Dr. Grossman decided that Holly was a candidate for surgery."

"The surgery is a publicity stunt. It can't possibly help her."

"The parents are really upbeat about this, though. Especially the father. I mean, put yourself in their place. I know you don't have children so—"

"So I couldn't possibly understand?"

"I didn't say that." Startled by the anger in his voice, she frowned at him. "All I'm saying is, maybe you're wrong about the benefits of surgery. This is a new procedure, it hasn't been tried yet. Medicine is art not science, right? Maybe it *will* help Holly."

"It *won't* help Holly."

She took a breath, trying for calm, but she could imagine the expressions on the faces inside when she told them Dr. Connaughton would have no statement.

"Look, I'm sorry," he said. "I didn't want to do this in the first place, I just agreed because…because of you, quite frankly."

"And I'm asking you to help me again." Her heart raced. "There's a lot riding on you doing this." *Like my job, for instance.* "I don't know what else to say except that I really *need* you…need your cooperation."

For a moment, they stood together in the dimly lit corridor. She couldn't tell whether she'd managed to convince him, didn't know what she'd do if she hadn't. Then something flickered in his eyes.

"You owe me one, Catherine," he said.

Two MINUTES LATER, still in his green scrubs, Martin stood before a bank of microphones in the administrative conference room. Nervousness knotted his stomach, his mouth felt like cotton. The feeling reminded him of a piano recital he'd been in as a boy. He wanted to do well, but wasn't sure he could get all the notes right.

He located Catherine in the sea of faces. Arms folded across her chest, a frown of concentration creasing her forehead. As they'd stood together in the dimly lit corridor, she'd looked up at him through her lashes, and he'd seen the ghost of Sharon and had known right then that he couldn't let her down. *I need you.* He had to get a grip. He ran his hand across his face. Catherine wasn't Sharon. And now he was ready to sell out his principles.

A reporter who wore a cluster of tiny red Christmas bells at each ear asked him to describe his feelings as he'd delivered the babies. Another asked if he'd been nervous. Someone else wanted to know whether he'd ever done anything like this before. Eventually, the questions moved on to the status of the babies' health.

"Berry and Noelle are doing well," he said. "We'll probably be able to get them off the ventilators and have them breathing room air very soon."

"How about Holly?"

"Holly's condition is a bit more serious." Stopped by the understatement, he tried to gather his thoughts. "None of her systems—her lungs, her heart, her kidneys—are functioning well. Each one places a strain on the other. She's also at risk for a number of complications, any one of them potentially life threatening."

"You don't seem particularly optimistic, Dr. Connaughton."

"It isn't a question of optimism. At this point with Holly, it's too soon to tell." He started to feel a little frantic. How many variations could he come up with on the same theme? "We're racing against the clock, but we don't really know the deadline. What we do know is, if she doesn't start to do better after a while, she probably *won't.*"

"Well, let me put it this way," the reporter interrupted with a frown. "Dr. Grossman and Holly's parents both seem considerably more upbeat about her prospects—"

"Dr. Connaughton." Another reporter waved her hand. "About the surgery Dr. Grossman is proposing for Holly? Some medical experts feel the dangers outweigh the possible advantages. What's your opinion?"

Martin ran a hand across his face. His eyes searched the crowd for Catherine. Her smile had disappeared.

"Are you opposed to it on the grounds that it is considered experimental, Dr. Connaughton? What are your feelings?"

"Would you say your approach to treatment is more conservative?" It was the reporter with the Christmas-bell earrings.

"What I think," he slowly started, "is that we need to accept the fact that some problems probably shouldn't be treated." He stared at his hands on the lectern. A pulse tapped in his eyelid. "I believe that we make a mistake when we look at every medical problem as a nail to be hammered away at with technology." Lord, that didn't come out right. He needed to correct it. "Just because we *can* do something."

A bead of sweat rolled down his back. Again, he searched the crowd for Catherine. *I need you, Martin.* God, it had sounded so bloody fantastic. Even at the expense of selling out. Someone shouted another question, and he thought about just walking away and then suddenly Catherine was beside him on the podium.

"Sorry to do this to you guys." She smiled at the reporters, "but Dr. Connaughton has an in-studio interview downtown, and I've got exactly ten minutes to get him there. We'll have to get back to you later." Before they could respond, she'd hustled him out of the conference room and into the corridor.

Outside they stared at each other.

"Studio interview?" he asked.

"I wanted to get you out of there." She nodded her head in the direction of the conference room. "Look, they're going to be swarming out of there any second now. It might be more convincing if we weren't hanging around here."

One hand lightly held his arm. "We can go up to my office. You look as though you could probably use some coffee."

IN CATHERINE'S OFFICE, he stared through the window at the parking lot. Rain had started to fall, a mild drizzle that in Belfast would have been described as a bit overcast. Umbrellas had sprouted like mushrooms, a kaleidoscope of shifting hues and patterns. He followed the passage of one striped in red and blue and tried to understand what was happening to him. Half an hour ago, Catherine had stood in a dimly lit corridor and looked up at him through her lashes. The years had fallen away, and Sharon was talking to him, giving him another chance.

Impatient, he banished the image. The reality was that he'd allowed himself to be dragged into a publicity gimmick and then done a half-baked job that would do nothing for WISH and didn't even have the saving grace of honesty. What he should do now was cut his losses and take the Ethiopia post. Leave before he got sucked in any deeper and actually started endorsing Grossman's surgery.

He heard Catherine's voice behind him and turned to take the disposable cup of coffee she handed him. She had braided her hair, he noticed, and reapplied lipstick, a shade of red that matched her jacket. Odd, now she didn't look at all like Sharon. Just that shadow of resemblance every now and then. When she smiled he realized he'd been staring at her.

"Are you sure you're okay?" She gave him an appraising look. "You seem kind of shell-shocked."

"It was a bit like having grenades lobbed at me, now that you mention it," he agreed. "But I'm not sure I did a very good job of dodging them."

She sipped her coffee. "To tell you the truth, I doubt that it did much for WISH, but I have some other ideas we can talk about. I think some media training would help you with ongoing press contact. There's a former TV anchor who gives one-day sessions to some of our doctors. If you let me know what dates would work, I can set it up."

He looked at her and couldn't imagine anything he would hate more. Then she caught her braid in one hand and flipped it forward. Distracted by the sensuousness of the gesture, the way the braid fell just below the swell of her breasts, he tried to think of Ethiopia but heard himself mumble something about Tuesdays being best.

"Great." A smile lit her face. "I'll set something up." She moved to the desk, motioned him to a chair on the other side. "I know this morning was an ordeal, but I really appreciate you going along with it. For a moment I thought you were going to back out. What made you change your mind?"

"Your air of desperation, I think it was," he said solemnly. *You needed me.* There was a beat of silence then Catherine laughed, a loud hearty laugh that made him laugh, too, and wonder briefly why he needed to go to Ethiopia.

"God, I was panicking." Catherine shook her head as though recalling the moment. "I thought I might have to drag you in there bodily."

"That might have been interesting." He watched her face color, a flush that started at her jaw and moved slowly up her cheek, then he leaned across her desk to pick up a framed picture. A dark-headed boy and a girl with blond curls posed against a backdrop of autumn leaves. "Your children?"

"Uh-huh." Catherine looked at the picture in his hands then smiled up at him. "Little monsters most of the time. This morning, Julie just had to wear this blue dress that naturally needed ironing. I got it all ironed and she threw up on it. She found a mouse on her bed, and Peter..." Her face colored. "Here I go babbling again." She took a couple of oranges and a bag of cookies from a desk drawer. "Help yourself. The least I can do after what I put you through is feed you."

Martin grinned at her, intrigued by the account. He took an orange, rolled it under his palm for a moment. "When I was a kid in Belfast, these were a luxury that we could only afford at Christmas."

"You've come to the right place for them, then." She smiled at him. A moment passed as though she was sorting through questions to ask him. "Do you miss Ireland, I mean do you get back very often?"

"No... I lost my return ticket a long time ago." He saw her look up from the orange she was peeling but he didn't elaborate. She wore the silver bracelet he had noticed the day before. He imagined her with her children, engaged in all the little rituals of a household. Bustling them off to ballet lessons and soccer practice. He could also see her with her braid undone, hair spread across a pillow.

He stared at the white membranous skin under the orange peel, then nicked it with his thumbnail. The words were all there, clamoring to be said, but trapped behind the protective wall built up over the years. Seconds ticked away, and he felt his silence become a wedge between them. A spot of juice from the orange dribbled like a tear onto the desk.

Catherine handed him a tissue, gave him a long look then lowered her eyes. A moment passed, and suddenly she was all brisk action. He watched as she whisked pieces of orange peel from the desktop, her charm bracelet clinking with the movements.

"On the issue of surgery for Holly," she said in a businesslike voice. "Who will win do you think, you or Grossman?"

"Grossman, probably." Relieved to be on familiar ground, but taken aback by an odd sense of loss, he took a moment to collect his thoughts. "When there's a difference of opinion, surgeons usually prevail. It's the power of the knife. Not only that, but Eddie Hodges wants the surgery and the parents' wishes are usually followed."

She nodded and started to speak, then her telephone rang. A reporter asking about the triplets, he surmised from her end of the conversation. As she talked, her neat round handwriting filled up the lines of a yellow tablet. After a few minutes, she hung up and stared at her notes for a moment, tapped the pen against her teeth.

"Hmm. Not good news." She looked across the desk at Martin. "That was Ned Bolton, the medical writer with the *Tribune*. He's, uh…intrigued by your remarks this morning, particularly by the fact that you and Grossman seem to disagree on surgery for Holly Hodges." Her eyes met his for a moment. "He wants to talk to you, but we need to establish some ground rules first."

He folded his arms across his chest, listened to her explain once again the team concept Western wanted to portray. She chewed her lip, frowned, paused, started again. Would it be possible, she wanted to know, for him to agree with Grossman, at least publicly? Could he live with that? They could work together on some remarks that would— she drew quotation marks in the air—"clarify" his earlier comments. How would he feel about that?

He got up and walked to the window behind her desk and glanced outside. The rain had intensified; the wind spattered drops against the glass and whipped at the palms and eucalyptus. He turned away, leaned his shoulders against the sill. In the dim, gray light of the room, the scent of the oranges they had eaten hovered like an exotic perfume.

After a moment, Catherine swiveled to face him. She sat forward on her chair, heels spread wide on the lower rung, knees together. The black skirt she wore had ridden slightly up her thighs to reveal a faint run in her tights that began at her left knee, worked its way up and out of sight.

"You're very quiet." She pushed the sleeves of her sweater above her elbows, and studied him for a moment. "What's the problem? Is it this reporter, or the whole press thing in general?"

"I'm not sure." He turned back to the window and the wet parking lot. His answer should be obvious. No, he couldn't perpetuate this charade that he knew was morally wrong. It *should* be obvious, but something about Catherine made him question his convictions.

He heard the scrape of her chair, and then she was there beside him, close enough that he could feel the warmth of her arm through the cotton of his lab coat. Last night he had identified what was missing from his life, now she brought it all into focus. He saw himself making love to her, stunned by the intensity of his need. A moment later, he saw with equal clarity the wall he had built. He wanted her physically, but he wanted her emotionally too, and only he could tear down the wall.

"I was just thinking about what you said last night about the myth of Irish melancholy." Her voice was soft. "That was your theory, that the Irish were gloomy because they didn't have enough to eat?"

He nodded, turned to look at her. In the light from the window, her eyes were an emerald green, her skin almost translucent.

She grinned. "Well, from the looks of you, you must be starving." When he didn't respond, she touched his arm, left her hand there for a moment. "Seriously, it can't be that bad. Whatever it is we can work it out. Talk to me."

"Actually, I've come to a decision." He moved away, picked up his empty coffee cup from her desk and tossed it in the trash. Then he checked the pager at his belt, glanced at his watch. Anything to avoid her eyes. "I've been trying to decide whether to join this medical group that's going to Ethiopia in two weeks," he said finally. "All things considered, I think I'd be able to do more good there than I can here."

CHAPTER SEVEN

CATHERINE PUSHED at the green beans on her plate, oblivious to the cafeteria noise all around, and tried to convince herself that Martin's decision to go to Ethiopia meant nothing to her. Why *would* she care? It was pretty clear that his interest in her was strictly professional. No matter how magical last night had seemed, today was another story.

"Instant spuds." Derek regarded his plate of food with disdain. "The saving grace is that it's free." He looked across the table at her. "You did bring your camera with you?"

Catherine pointed to the camera, clearly visible on the table, and tried to drag her thoughts away from Martin.

"Eat." He pointed his fork at her plate. "How did Jordan's speech turn out?"

"Still working on it." She shifted the food around with her fork. If she hadn't been staring into Martin's eyes like a lovesick teenager instead of listening to Jordan, she wouldn't have had to resort to begging the secretary for his notes. "There are some points I need to clarify."

"Good." He speared a piece of turkey off her plate. "Perhaps you could also clarify what impact you had in mind with Connaughton's press conference this morning. I distinctly remember discussing with you the concept of teamwork."

Catherine took a deep breath, she'd expected his reaction. "I know what we discussed, Derek," she said slowly.

"And I understand the message you want to get out, but Mart…I mean Dr. Connaughton is a doctor not a puppet. He's got his own professional opinions of what's right and wrong. Holly Hodges is medically unstable, her prognosis is poor. She's not a candidate for surgery.''

"You're not here to parrot Connaughton's opinion." Derek eyed her across the table. "Your job is—"

"I know what my job is. You asked me to explain why he said what he did at the press conference." She put her fork down. "And that's what I'm trying to do. He did the press conference because…" A recollection of the exchange with Martin about her air of desperation made her face flush. "What I'm trying to say is, he didn't want to talk to the press in the first place, but he thought it might help get WISH funded.''

"He doesn't have a snowball's chance in hell of getting WISH funded.''

"Maybe administration should reconsider WISH." Catherine thought of the look on Martin's face as he'd told her about Kenesha Washington. "Just the cost of caring for one baby in the NICU—"

"I appreciate that you're new to this job." Derek dabbed at his mouth with a napkin. "So I'm willing to allow that perhaps you don't fully understand that we have an extremely good story here." He looked at her. "Are you with me so far?''

"Yes, Derek." She suppressed a surge of irritation at his tone, which recalled memories of her father patiently explaining why she needed to be a good girl.

"Good." He smiled. "Well, we now have another new development. Ed Jordan wants Western to absorb the costs of Holly Hodges's surgery." He glanced over at Catherine's untouched plate. "Are you finished with that?''

Catherine slid the plate over to him, watched as he demolished the food.

"Ed wants it announced in a special ceremony with all the principals in attendance, of course. Eddie and Rita Hodges, the triplets, Grossman, naturally, and..." He gave her a meaningful look. "Connaughton."

Catherine said nothing.

"Now, if we play this right, Western will look bighearted and wonderful and, more importantly, it will further our reputation as the local leader in neonatal care. Still with me?"

"Yes, Derek. You're saying that—"

"I'm saying that the very last thing we need is Connaughton out there muddying the waters as he did this morning." His face darkened slightly. "He's managed to create controversy where there should be none. I've had already had three reporters beeping me, wanting to talk to him about his difference of opinion with Grossman."

"Good Lord, Derek, you sound as though he deliberately set out to be controversial." She heard her voice rise. "It's a professional difference of opinion. You can't see that?"

He ignored her question. "What I need you to do now is get Connaughton to clean up the damn mess he made. And from now on when he talks to the press, he sticks to our script."

"There probably isn't going to be a next time." She looked at him. "Today was just a last shot for WISH. In fact—" She stopped, not sure whether Ethiopia was common knowledge. "Well, he's just not going to do it. I mean he's really appalled at the idea of surgery for Holly. He's not going to reverse himself because it's good PR for Western."

"Bull." Derek stabbed at a piece of turkey and looked

up at her. "Should I remind you that you also didn't think he'd do the press conference this morning?"

"That was different. He wasn't compromising—"

"I want him to clean up his mess," Derek repeated. "If you need to, dangle WISH like a carrot. Tell him Jordan's favorably reconsidering the whole thing."

"Lie to him, you mean? Or is there really an outside chance?"

He laughed. "WISH is deader than anything down in the morgue. But if that's what it takes to convince him to toe the line, use it. Jordan will back me up. By the way," he said as he picked up his tray, "a word to the wise. Medical centers are like small towns for gossip. The big buzz was the two of you dancing last night, and then someone saw you both in the parking lot."

"Derek—"

"Look, maybe it's none of my business, but of all the men to screw around with—"

"Excuse me?" She looked at him. "Screw around with?"

He shrugged. "Figure of speech. I'm saying if you're looking for a little action, you're out of your depth. Valerie Webb got to him first."

EVEN IN THE UNIT, where he could usually block out external concerns, Martin couldn't keep thoughts of Catherine from his brain. Why *had* he told her about Ethiopia? Fear? The consequences of letting someone get close again?

Something old has to die, Dora had said, for something new to be born.

Lost in his musings, he saw the jagged green line on Holly's monitor go flat.

Rita, in a rocking chair at the bedside, gasped. Her hand flew to her mouth.

"It's all right." He reached across to silence the alarm, then reattached the monitor, which had fallen off the baby's chest. Rita's face had gone white. In contrast to the day before, when she'd spruced up for the TV cameras, she looked haggard and tired with dark smudges of fatigue under her eyes. "Really," he assured her. "Just a false alarm."

"Every time that happens, I think it's for real." Tears ran down her face, dripped onto her blue-and-white hospital gown. Her shoulders began to shake. "I look at her and I never know if it's going to be the last time."

Five minutes later, the alarm went off again. Martin glanced at the monitor. This time it was for real. The oxygen in Holly's blood had suddenly plummeted. In a flash, a respiratory therapist unplugged her from the ventilator and began pumping oxygen into her lungs with a black rubber bag. Without looking up, he reached for the transilluminator, trained its blue beam on Holly's chest wall.

"He's looking to see if there's a hole." Holly's nurse held Rita's hand. "One of her lungs might have collapsed. It happens sometimes."

"Doesn't look as though that's the problem though." Martin straightened up. "I think it's the respirator. The lungs are just falling apart."

"Should we try the oscillator?" the resident asked. "It might be easier on her."

Martin thought about it. Western owned a couple of the state-of-the-art units, but there were side effects. He looked at the respiratory therapist.

"Your call. What do you think?"

The therapist pursed his lips. "We usually try to reserve them for kids who aren't this bad."

"Just for the record," a nurse added, "They've got two high-risk deliveries in the L&D."

Martin thought for a moment, drew a deep breath. "If it would help, I'd go for it, but I don't think it's going to work for her. She already has lung damage. Given all her other problems, I think it borders on heroics—"

"Yeah, well, I've got a problem with that." Eddie Hodges had arrived unnoticed and now stood across the bassinet. "This is my kid we're talking about, and I want her to have the ossywhatsit. I don't give a shit who else needs it."

"The issue we're discussing is whether it will help Holly," Martin said. "And I don't believe it will. I think it will cause more suffering without offering any real hope for long-term survival."

"I want her to have it—"

"Eddie." Rita grabbed her husband's arm. "Listen to Dr. C. He said he doesn't think—"

"I don't damn well care what he thinks." Hodges's eyes locked on his face. "You stay out of it, Rita. You don't know what you're talking about."

"But—"

"Rita." Eddie gave her a threatening look. "Shut the hell up, I said."

"She has as much right to her opinion as you do." Martin glared at Hodges, his pulse quickening. "You might even try listening to her yourself." After a moment, he turned to Rita. "I'm sorry, what was it you were saying?"

"I was just saying that if it's not going to help her..." Her voice trailed off and she cast a nervous look at Hodges who stood with his arms folded across his chest. "Still, I suppose we should try everything first."

"Right then." Martin addressed the respiratory therapist. "Since Rita would like us to try it..." Another pause. "Let's give it a shot and see what happens."

He stood off to the side and watched as the respiratory

therapist unplugged Holly from the ventilator and attached her breathing tube to the oscillator. The baby's body shook with the force of the new machine's rapid-fire movements. At this point, he knew they'd just about reached the limit, both technically and ethically, of what could be done to save her life. All they could do now was wait.

He squeezed Rita's arm, then, ignoring Hodges, left the unit. Minutes later, the man confronted him out in the corridor.

"You know, Doc, I don't think you'd like that TV gal to hear what I just heard in there."

Martin stared at him, unsure what the remark was supposed to mean.

"The way it looks to me, you got money you get treated one way," Hodges's eyes narrowed. "If you don't, tough shit. Forget about the fancy equipment—"

"Oh, for God's sake." Comprehension increased his irritation. "This has nothing to do with money. Maybe if you paid a little more attention."

"Hey, I know what I heard." Hodges tapped the pocket of his polo shirt. "And I got a tape recorder in there that catches everything that's being said—"

"Good. Do yourself a favor and listen to it sometime."

"I bet you don't have any kids yourself, right?"

"No, I don't."

"I knew it." Hodges's face was triumphant. "If you had kids of your own, you'd understand—"

"If Holly were my daughter—" Martin fought to control his temper "—I wouldn't want her to suffer needlessly."

"Yeah, that's easy for you to say, but you don't know, do you?" Hodges took a step closer. "'Cause she's not your kid, right? So I don't want to hear nothing about not treating her, or every goddamn reporter in town's going to hear about it. Got that?'' He stuck his index finger in Martin's chest. ''Huh, Doc?''

''HEY, I THINK I saw your doctor on the news tonight. Irish accent. Tall, reddish hair. Dark blue eyes. Intense. Looks like he needs a shave.'' Darcy, Catherine's neighbor on the other side of the duplex, sat at the kitchen table drinking raspberry tea while Catherine folded laundry. ''Cute though.''

''I hadn't noticed.'' Catherine pulled open the drier door. ''You think so?''

Darcy worked as a waitress at the Jolly Roger in the marina and was quite expert at summing up men. Thirty-five, divorced and childless, she also took drama classes at Long Beach City College where she'd been a student for at least twelve years. A succession of different men moved quickly in and out of her life. All seemed wealthy in a vaguely shady way and after a week or two always turned out to be jerks.

Catherine glanced at the clock. Eight-thirty. She'd told Gary to have the children back by six. Phone lodged between her ear and shoulder, she tried calling him again while she surveyed the contents of the refrigerator. When his message machine came on, she hung up, took out cheese and a couple of eggs from the refrigerator. Quiche and a salad, she decided, and then it occurred to her that Gary wouldn't be content with just thwarting her plans to buy Julie's dress, he was probably stuffing both kids with junk food so they wouldn't be hungry for whatever she'd cooked.

''So what's the story on this guy?'' Darcy asked. ''Is he married?''

''What guy?' Her mind still on Gary, she glanced over

at Darcy, who wore a long black skirt, black lace-up boots, a black vest and what looked like a rosary.

"*Hellooo.*" Darcy cupped her hands to her mouth. "Earth to Catherine. What's with you tonight? It's this doctor guy, right? Come on, drop the act. Every time you mention him, you blush."

"I do not." Catherine ran her fingers through her bangs, glanced up at the clock again and mentally rehearsed what she was going to say to Gary. If she didn't kill him first.

"You're really hot for him, huh?"

"Hmm?" She bit her lip, looked at Darcy. "I'm sorry, I missed that."

"Jeez. You're more absentminded than this college professor I dated. He used to walk out of the house, I kid you not, with the labels still on his clothes." A pause. "Ten minutes after we screwed, he couldn't remember whether we had or not…"

"Come on," Catherine protested.

"No, that one was a joke, I just wanted to see if you were listening." Darcy grinned, leaned across the table, stuck her face under Catherine's. "I think we need to work on your doctor guy."

"He's not *my* doctor guy." She checked the clock again. "He's someone else's doctor guy. This incredibly beautiful pediatrician. Long red hair and white skin. And really tiny. I hate her."

"Hey, Cath, you're not exactly chopped liver."

"Listen, we're not even in the same league." She started grating a block of Monterey Jack cheese. "I mean, I can fix myself up, but…I still have this high-school yearbook picture in my head. Big feet, big teeth." She stuck out her teeth in a bucktooth grin. "I looked like a big goofy horse. Even a long mane of hair."

Darcy laughed.

"I'm serious. Ask my mom. Well, no, don't ask her because she'll tell you if that I'd just watched my weight I could have had any boy I wanted. And then being something of a masochist for that sort of thing, I married Gary, who told me I had hips like a peasant. I'd always be baking cookies and stuff, but I never ate them because I was scared of getting fat." She sipped her tea. "But I got fat anyway."

"Well, you look good now, Cath. Really. Don't put yourself down." Darcy's eyes glimmered with interest. "But tell me about this guy. What is it about him?"

"Martin?" She traced a pattern on the table with her forefinger. "Nothing. You think I should get my hair cut?"

"No and quit changing the subject. He's really hot, huh?"

She shook her head at Darcy. "You are relentless."

"So tell me."

"Okay." Actually, it was kind of a relief to finally unload. "Last night when we were talking, he looked at me and…"

"And?"

"Well, I actually felt weak. I swear, I've never felt that way before. I thought it was all a myth."

Darcy grinned. "Poor sheltered Catherine."

"Yeah, I know, what can I say?" She reached for the carton of Little Debbies, hidden behind cans of corn and green beans on the middle pantry shelf so that the children wouldn't find them. It had been a Little Debbie kind of day. She threw the box onto the table and thought about how to describe Martin. "He's got this reputation for being, I don't know, kind of—"

"An asshole?" Darcy's expression was disapproving. "Just what you need."

"No." Catherine ripped the plastic wrapping from the cake, surprised by the vehemence of her defense. "No, sort of an outsider. He's very intense. Serious. At first I thought he was really cold, but he cares, I can tell. Not in some superficial way, but really deep down.'' Blood rushed to her face. ''God, listen to me. I hardly know him.'' She bit into the cake. ''Drop it, Darcy, okay?''

''I'm going to fix you up.'' Elbows on the table, Darcy regarded her. ''You gotta have something else besides kids and work. This Martin guy probably comes with a load of baggage and you don't need that. Listen, there's this friend of Brad's, I've met him. Nice-looking. He's a lawyer.''

A HORN HONKED, a car door slammed and Catherine glanced at the clock. Ten. No chance of her buying Julie's dress tonight. Gary had won this round. As she went outside, she caught a fleeting glimpse of his blond hair as the black BMW sped off into the night. The children stood on the grassy patch by the curb, their arms filled with packages. A faint drizzle beaded their parkas. In the glow of the street lamps, loaded down with their bundles, they seemed small and very vulnerable, their skin and lips a bluish hue, eyes huge and dark. Like little refugees, Catherine thought, shipped from one place to another. A chill ran through her, and she gathered them both to her sides. The bastard couldn't even stick around until they were safely inside the house. Some father.

''Mommy.'' Julie tugged at Catherine's hand, her voice shrill with excitement. ''Let's go in. I've got to show you something. You can't look though.'' Inside, she disappeared into her bedroom. ''Don't peek.''

''Okay. I'm not moving.'' Catherine looked at Peter who had immediately dropped on the floor in front of the television. ''Hi, sweetheart.'' She planted a kiss on the top of his head. ''How did everything go? How was your day?''

"Fine." Peter didn't move his eyes from the TV. "My bike got a flat tire. Dad fixed it."

She bit back an anger-fueled response. The divorce hadn't been his fault. As she started to ask about his homework, Julie's voice came from the bedroom.

"Okay. Close your eyes," she called with a squeal of excitement. "I'm coming out."

Catherine obeyed, heard a rustle of fabric, then her daughter's breathless laughter. She felt her mouth curve in a smile. Felt overcome suddenly with a rush of tenderness. Whatever else went on in her life, she knew where her center was.

"Okay. Now."

She opened her eyes. Julie, six, all blond curls and dimples, stood before her, a confection of peach-colored gauze and satin. For a moment Catherine couldn't speak. Kneeling down on the floor, she hugged the child, kissed her face then leaned back on her heels to get a better look. "It's beautiful, sweetheart. You look like, I don't know, an angel."

"It's my new ballet dress, for my dance thing at school on Friday." Julie executed a wobbly pirouette. "Isn't it pretty?"

"Dad and Nadia bought it for her," Peter said from his seat by the TV.

Catherine swallowed, felt her pulse quicken. She watched as Julie began a series of leaps across the room, arms flung wide, fingers and toes pointed. A final leap brought her down beside her brother.

"Show Mommy what they bought for you." She looked at Catherine, her eyes wide. "It's *soooo* neat."

"Shut up, Julie." Peter pushed her. "It's not that big a deal."

"You shut up." Julie jumped onto the couch then leaped

off and bounded back across the room. She stood in front of her brother, flapping her dress up and down. "Peter has a girlfriend," she chanted.

"Mom, make her shut up." He scowled at his sister. "You're lame."

"Am not." She stuck out her tongue. "Not. Not. Not. *You* are. You said the F word. Four times."

"Julie." Catherine caught her daughter's hand. "Come and sit down with me."

"But he did, Mommy. I heard him."

"That's enough, Julie."

"I like Nadia." Julie regarded Catherine. Her face turned sullen. She curled a strand of hair around her finger. "Nadia's nice. She said she's going to take me shopping a whole lot of times. We're going to do girl things. Daddy says she's real pretty and smart."

Catherine met her daughter's guileless blue gaze. A wave of anger washed over her, left a bitter taste in her mouth. Once again she felt her hands encircling Gary's neck.

"Watch, Mommy." Julie broke away from her grasp and leaped suddenly across her line of vision, a blur of peach satin.

Catherine looked away. The dress seemed to taunt. It wasn't fair. She wanted to stomp and protest. She and Julie were supposed to buy the dress. She wanted to tell the child to take it off. Instead, she got up and walked over to the TV set where both children, now suddenly quiet, were watching a car chase. She sat on the floor between them, put an arm around each of their shoulders and pulled them against her.

"I love you guys a whole lot, you know that?" They both nodded, their eyes glued to the screen. Catherine sat with them for a while, tried just to be with them, not spoil the present with negatives thoughts. She took a deep breath and began to feel calmer. Then she remembered the time and got up and switched off the set.

"Come on, Mom," Peter said. "Just let me watch this one show."

"Nope." She kissed his nose. "It's ten-fifteen and way past your bedtime. Come on." She poked his ribs. "Up and at 'em." After she'd got Julie to bed, hung the hateful ballet dress in the closet and kissed her good-night, Catherine went into Peter's room. He was already undressed and in bed, his eyes wide open, fixed on the ceiling. She could hear the faint asthmatic rattle of his breathing.

"Are you okay, sweetie?" She sat down on the bed next to him, smoothed his hair back from his forehead. "Do you need to use your puffer?"

"Yeah, I guess." He reached under his pillow, pulled out the blue plastic inhaler. "That little puppy Dad bought Nadia? It's supposed to not cause allergies but it kind of makes me wheeze."

"You didn't have your inhaler with you?"

"I guess I forgot it." He exhaled, closed his lips around the plastic mouthpiece, depressed the metal top and inhaled. "Anyway," he said after he'd let out a breath, "Dad said I should try to control the wheezing myself and not just rely on medicine."

"Well, since Daddy doesn't have asthma, maybe he doesn't know what he's talking about," Catherine snapped, unable to hold back the words. "And maybe he shouldn't have a dog in the house when he knows you're allergic to them."

Peter toyed with the inhaler's metal cylinder, his eyes downcast.

"God, Peter, I'm sorry." Filled with remorse now, Catherine bit her lip to stop the tears she could feel welling up. "It's just that Daddy..." *Is the world's biggest jerk.*

"Well, we don't exactly get along too well lately and...look, I didn't mean to bring you into this. I'm sorry, really."

"It's okay Mom." He patted her arm. "Dad gets kinda...well it's like he's always bragging about how much money he and Nadia have and all the things they've got. Don't let it get to you though. I like it better here, Julie does, too. Dad keeps asking if we want to live with him, but we both want to stay with you."

Catherine looked at her son's pale face with its delicate bone structure, the still ragged movement of his breathing through his blue cotton pajama top. She saw the man he would one day become, imagined the other women who would think they loved him and the children he would one day sire and she knew that no one would ever love him with the fierce intensity she felt right then. Her throat closed and she reached over to hug him.

"Thank you Peter," she said finally. "You can't possibly know how much that means to me."

"S'all right," he said with a grin. "It's kind of like I'm the man of the house now, huh?"

THE LEATHER JACKET Gary had bought Peter probably cost the equivalent of what she made in an entire month, Catherine thought as she hung it in the hall closet, an exotic bird amidst the flock of inexpensive parkas and nylon windbreakers. Hours after both the children were asleep, the expensive jacket and Julie's equally costly ballet dress seemed like demons sent by Gary to torment her. And, despite Peter's reassurances, they had succeeded.

Her head propped up on pillows, feet dangling over the armrest, Catherine lay on the sofa and tried to analyze the anger that was pulsing through her blood. Segovia played on the stereo, a vanilla-scented candle flickered on the coffee table and cast an amber light on her glass of Chardonnay. Along with bubble baths, they were her usual remedies for relaxation, but tonight they weren't helping. Over and over, like a stuck record, she replayed the words she would say to Gary. *I'm doing everything I can to provide for the children, and you're undermining my efforts by buying them expensive gifts I could never afford. Not only that, but you're dishonest. It's not even your money. It's Nadia's.*

Over and over, the demented recording in her head played on. Every time she forced herself to think about something else, her brain eventually returned to the Gary sound track until she wanted to scream in frustration. When the Segovia piece finished, she padded over to the stereo, flipped through the CDs for something else to play, then decided she couldn't be bothered. What was the point when it didn't drown out the mental clamor?

What really bothered her about Gary's gifts and his campaign for the kids, she decided as she turned off the stereo, was that she, herself, somehow equated financial security with happiness. She blew out the candle, took the wineglass into the kitchen and rinsed it under the tap. Gary, or Nadia, had more money than she did and, Peter's reassurances aside, she worried deep down that Gary was right, that perhaps he could somehow give the children a better life.

Intellectually, she knew that they didn't need expensive gifts to make them happy. But that didn't stop her from feeling somehow inadequate. She hated the thought that Gary could afford to buy the children the kind of things she wanted to but couldn't. Take him to court for more child support, her mother kept urging. A solution that would only give Gary more control. That definitely wasn't the answer.

She wiped off the counters, rinsed out the few dishes in the sink and stacked them in the drainer. The whole money thing went back to her own childhood. After her father walked out, there was never enough to go around. Her mother would buy clothes for her from thrift stores. Once, when she was thirteen, her mother had bought her a dress to wear to a birthday party. To this day, she could remember it. Pale green polished cotton patterned with tiny white flowers. The color brought out the green in her eyes and the cinched-in waist flattered her budding figure. She'd felt great until one of the rich girls at the party recognized it as one of her own castoffs, a discovery she'd announced to everyone.

The memory of that dress still made her cringe. Even though thrift stores were kind of trendy now—Darcy always shopped in them—Catherine couldn't bring herself to go inside one.

She locked the doors and turned off the lights in the kitchen. In the bedroom, she flipped on the bedside lamp, one of her mother's garage-sale acquisitions. A hideous yellow frilled number, but it had been a birthday present and Catherine didn't have the heart to get rid of it. Same with the orange velvet couch her mother had purchased, although fortunately not as a gift. "It only cost fifteen dollars," she'd said. Catherine had maintained a tactful silence. These days, her mother's salary as an office manager didn't require the sort of penny pinching she'd had to do after her husband walked out, but she still fretted endlessly over money. Her other advice to Catherine was to, "Find someone else as soon as you can. It's too hard to make it without a man bringing home some money."

Ironically, marriage to Gary had only reinforced the notion. His income had allowed Catherine to create the kind of home life she felt children should have. And which she herself had always wanted. Then he'd walked out on her and the money problems had started all over again.

She pulled off her jeans, shoved them in the closet, unclasped her bra, let it drop to the ground and unbraided her hair. Struck by a thought, she sat on the edge of the bed. If financial security equaled happiness, and you couldn't be financially secure without a man, then maybe the answer *was* to find another man.

At first, she dismissed the idea as ridiculous but after a while she began to reconsider. Despite Gary, the happiest she'd ever been in her life was when she'd been a full-time mother to her children.

By contrast, her life these days was one giant compromise. However hard she worked, she would never be able to provide for them in the same way that Gary and Nadia could. And the problem wasn't just the material things, it was having enough time to be the kind of mother she wanted to be. That she couldn't be under the present circumstances.

So why not marry again? The children aside, what would be so bad about sharing her life with someone else once more? Waking up next to a warm body instead of cold emptiness? She lay back on the bed, watched the rise and fall of her breathing. Restless with her thoughts, she got up and walked over to the dresser mirror.

In the shadowy light of the bedside lamp, she stared at her reflection. Her unbraided hair fell around her shoulders and breasts like a cloak, the ends reached the cotton band at the top of her panties. When she moved, the long dark strands parted to reveal the tips of her nipples. While her breasts weren't the gargantuan wonders they'd seemed in high school, they were still big enough to make her feel self-conscious in a formfitting sweater and, her stomach, even before childbirth, had never been completely flat. Would a man find her desirable?

Hands cupped around her breasts, she tried to imagine a

man's mouth on them. Martin's face floated into her mind. The image made her heart race, her breath come in short bursts. In the next instant, embarrassed and furious with herself, she jumped up from the bed, and yanked on her bathrobe.

God, she was a fool. Her face hot, she tied the bathrobe tight around her middle. Who the hell was she with her big boobs and untoned body to think she even had a chance with him, when right at that very moment he was probably banging the petite and perfect white body of Dr. Valerie Webb? Angry at herself, at men in general, at women who looked like Valerie Webb, she went into the kitchen and microwaved a cup of hot water. When the timer pinged, she took a chamomile tea bag from the canister and dropped it into the cup.

Of all the men to develop a crush on, why the hell did it have to be Martin Connaughton? Darcy was probably right, he came with a load of baggage she didn't need. Actually the lawyer Darcy had mentioned might be a really good idea. A little pro bono legal advice on how to fight Gary—with a side order of sex. She didn't need marriage for that. And the kids didn't *need* expensive clothes.

Besides, the financial security her marriage had offered had also exacted a considerable price. She'd paid by giving up little bits of herself: pride, self-esteem, independence. From the day they were married, she hadn't made a single decision about her own life that didn't revolve around Gary or the children. For fear of annoying him, she'd never taken a stand, never disagreed with him.

He'd been the bright star and she'd wobbled around in his orbit, the good and unselfish wife, always deferring to him. No, marriage definitely wasn't the solution.

She took her tea into the living room, flipped on the TV,

ran through the channels and stopped when she heard the words Western Memorial.

"...Holly, the smallest of the Freeway Triplets remains in critical according to her neonatologist, Dr. Martin Connaughton, who delivered the babies during rush-hour traffic on Interstate 710. But a difference of opinion on the prospect of neurosurgery for Holly may have created a rift among members of the medical team. While Dr. Connaughton believes Holly is too medically fragile to undergo the complex procedure, Western's chief of pediatric neurosurgery, Dr. Nate Grossman, and Holly's father, Mr. Edward Hodges, are both upbeat about the baby's prognosis and say the surgery is needed to save her life."

Eddie Hodges's image flashed on the screen. "Holly's doing real good," he said. "She's hanging in there. We all feel real positive that the surgery's gonna fix her right up."

The remote still in her hand, Catherine stared at the screen in dismay. During the morning's press conference, she'd been too anxious to really hear his comments. Now in the context of Grossman's and Eddie Hodges's optimism, she understood the potential for controversy. When the phone rang, she knew it was Derek.

"Goddamn it." He didn't bother with a greeting. "I've been watching this crap all night and every damn segment is the same. One of the stations even got another medical expert who says he agrees with Connaughton. This whole story is going to go south unless we get him to backpedal."

"I just caught Channel 5—"

"Connaughton's out of control." Derek interrupted. "I ran into him tonight as I was leaving. He came up to see you about something and went off the deep end. I've just got off the phone with Jordan. If Connaughton isn't willing to cooperate and publicly endorse the surgery, administration wants to cut him loose. If we get media—"

"Hold on a minute, Derek, I don't understand. What do you mean by cut him loose?"

"I mean that he's always been enough of a renegade that if anyone asks us about his difference of opinion with Grossman, all we need to do is drop a few hints that suggest his credibility is in doubt. Just for starters, there's the whole issue of him attacking Grossman's kid in the parking lot. A little hint that perhaps his opposition to Grossman is based more on personal animosity than clinical judgment."

"That's not true, though." She leaned her head against the back of the sofa. "We talked about this at lunch, remember? I mean, there's a genuine difference of professional opinion. We can't deliberately set out to ruin a doctor's reputation just because he disagrees with Grossman. It's…unethical."

"Connaughton's a loose cannon. Everyone knows that."

"If he were such a loose cannon, they wouldn't have kept him around." She pulled her robe tight, the room suddenly felt cold. "You said yourself he's a brilliant doctor. Doesn't it occur to you that maybe he is right, and Holly shouldn't have the surgery?"

"For PR purposes, that's irrelevant," Derek said. "Grossman wants to do the surgery, and Western wants to pay for it. Our job is to arrange the publicity. If Connaughton's going to stand in the way of making this a good story, then it's his fault if he gets mowed down. We all do what we have to do."

"Listen, Derek—" she took a deep breath, tried to organize her thoughts "—before you say anything else to the press, let me talk to him first, okay? Maybe I can work something out."

"Are you willing to put your job on the line for him?"

Catherine swallowed, felt her stomach contract. "I'm not sure what you mean…"

"It's quite simple. You've accused me of being unethical. I don't think that's the case, but I'll give you the benefit of the doubt. We'll wait. If you can guarantee that the next time he talks to a reporter, what he says is in accordance with what we're trying to do, we'll all be happy. But if he says one more damn thing that causes any grief, he's set loose and so are you. That's what I mean." He paused. "Do you want to take the risk?"

CHAPTER EIGHT

ONE OF THE NURSES said it had to be the full moon. It wasn't a theory Martin subscribed to, but whatever the reason, the unit was suddenly flooded with so many admissions that for a couple of days he had time for little else but thoughts of ventilators and respiratory rates. Holly lingered on, her prognosis no better. He hadn't seen Catherine and despite what he'd told her, the Ethiopia decision was still hanging.

When he left Western, just before twelve on Sunday night, the temperature had dropped. Damp drafts seeped through the Fiat's canvas top, and he turned on the heater, held his hands to the vents. After the exchange with Eddie Hodges, he'd gone immediately to his office and started to call the fellow who was organizing the Ethiopia trip, then put down the phone and tried unsuccessfully to catch up on paperwork. Now—two days later—he was gripped by an illogical thought. He had to talk to Catherine.

"I don't know what's going on," he imagined himself saying, "but I can't stop thinking about you and the thing is…well, I know I told you I was going to Ethiopia but Eddie Hodges said my judgment about Holly would be different if I had children of my own and since you do have children, I wondered whether you thought me cold and detached and…well, whether you cared if I went to Ethiopia or not and, if I stayed, whether there was any possibility that we might see each other, outside the hospital, I mean."

Fortunately, he didn't know Catherine's address or phone number.

At Lucky's market in the marina, he stopped to pick up a newspaper and some beer. One corner of the parking area had been cordoned off as a Christmas-tree lot and strung with lights that shone down on the spruce and firs. When he'd picked up the paper the day before, the trees had seemed wilted under the blazing sun. Now, in the damp air, they looked bedraggled and forlorn. He walked into the brightly lit market, vaguely depressed by the sight. Those that weren't purchased would be ignominiously dumped. The chosen would be festooned with tinsel, bask in the spotlight for a day or two, then those, too, would be dumped. Either way it seemed a sad waste.

The whole Christmas frenzy couldn't be over soon enough to suit him, he thought as he headed back to the car again, purchases under his arm. The holidays somehow underscored his solitary existence, created this sense of always being on the outside looking in. In other years, he'd seldom given it much thought. Now as he walked down the gangway to the boat, he felt like a seaman with his bundled belongings. Walking alone down to the port, prepared to sail out into the dark, but not without a wistful glance over his shoulder at the lights on shore.

When he climbed into the galley, the flashing red light on his phone machine turned his thoughts to more immediate concerns. Three new messages. The first was Ed Jordan telling him to be in his office first thing in the morning. He didn't sound happy.

The second message was from one of the organizers of the Ethiopia expedition reminding him that they still needed his decision. The third was from Dora Matsushita wanting to know whether he'd evaluated the fifteen-year-old prospective WISH client she'd mentioned.

He ground the heel of his palm into his eyes, then made a note to call Dora tomorrow. In defiance of Jordan's warning not to take on new clients, Martin had set up an appointment for the girl, but she hadn't kept it, or even called to cancel. He thought of Dora's comment about the young mothers being on the edge. WISH could help, but the desire to change had to be there first.

Hungry now, he scanned the refrigerator for possibilities. He grabbed a couple of eggs and a package of bacon, broke the eggs into a frying pan and tore off four strips of bacon. While the food was cooking, he went back to the machine, replayed the Ethiopia message and jotted down the number. Even as he did, he wondered whether this was really the sort of change his life needed.

The sound of the bacon sizzling and the smell of hot grease reminded him of the food cooking on the stove. With the spatula, he broke the egg yolk, let it solidify over the bacon and sandwiched the whole thing between a couple of slices of bread. Then he popped a beer, carried it with his food, the newspaper and the day's mail into the bedroom.

Sprawled across the bed, he scanned the paper until he came to an update on the Freeway Triplets, as the press had dubbed them. The focus was mostly on Holly. An upbeat quote from Grossman in which the neurosurgeon went on at length about the proposed lifesaving surgery was followed by his own pessimistic remarks about Holly's prognosis. Not that it changed his opinion, but he could understand Jordan's concerns. His own gloomy prognosis was like the thundercloud hovering over a picnic. As he turned the page, he wondered whether the administrator had made his dissatisfaction known to Catherine. Tomorrow, Martin decided to see Catherine.

Catherine. Struck by an idea, he put the paper aside for

a moment, briefly considered calling the hospital operator for her number. When he looked at the clock, he saw it was eleven-thirty, probably too late for an out-of-the-blue call from a man who had announced he was going to Ethiopia.

The paper slid to the floor and he reached down to pick it up. Even in the turmoil of the past few days, Catherine was a constant presence in his head. There in unguarded moments; her face, her voice, a certain expression. And, despite himself, he couldn't help thinking…what if… He took a swig of beer, leaned back against the pillow, hands folded behind his head.

Conflicting forces tugged at him. On the one side, the tremendous pull of everything that had shaped his life until now. On the other, little more than an ephemeral vision of what the future might be. While the force of the past weakened a little each time he saw Catherine, it still exerted the greater strength. If he let go, if he were *able* to let go, the sudden release would send him hurtling into uncharted territory. The thought unnerved him enough that all he could do was hold on: unable to let go of one side, unwilling to let go of the other.

With a deep intake of breath, he turned back to the paper. If Catherine's feelings were mutual, and she had any idea of what was good for her, she'd give him a wide berth. He bit into his sandwich. In world news, the headline Embattled Northern Ireland caught his eye. A story about the bombing in Belfast along with a grainy black-and-white picture of a narrow street of houses. People stood clustered about, arms folded across their chests. A woman in an apron and head scarf. Men in cloth caps.

A pang of nostalgia made him pick up the phone. He calculated the time difference then dialed his father's number.

"It's you, is it, Marty?" the old man asked a few minutes later. "Sure and it's about time, too. Just having a cup of tea we were. Funny thing you should call right now. I was just after saying to Joan that it's been a while."

Martin closed his eyes and listened to his father's voice, remembering the anger that used to fill that voice. Age had softened the dour sternness, or perhaps it was the physical and emotional distance that now separated them. In his mind he saw the dark narrow kitchen of the house he'd grown up in. His mother—who'd died when he was twelve—would joke that she could stand by the gas stove, cook dinner, wash clothes, scrub her feet and face without moving from the spot.

"I saw Sharon's mam yesterday down at the fish shop and she asked after you," his father went on. "She always does. Down at the cemetery every day she is, putting flowers on the girl's grave." When he didn't answer, the old man said, "Well now, your sister's here. Shall I put her on?"

"Sure."

"Martin," she said after they'd exchanged greetings. "You sound like a Yank."

He grinned through a mouthful of food. Joan said the same thing every time he called. He pictured her face, her hair, much the same color as his own. Three years older than him, she had a large and rambunctious family. At last count, he was Uncle Martin to three nephews and two nieces.

"You've probably got one of those big, smart cars—"

He thought of his battered Fiat and laughed. "Oh right. Great big Cadillac. I smoke cigars, too. Come over and visit me and see for yourself."

"*Och.* It's too far away. What with Sandra and all. She's just gone eighteen, can you believe it? All that she has on her mind is going to the discos. And then there's the wee one. Four, he is.'' She chattered on for another few minutes. "Ah, but you don't want to hear all this rubbish, do you now?'' A pause. "What about yourself? Are you seeing anyone?''

"Sure. A different woman every night.'' Prepared for the inevitable question, he finished his sandwich, licked bacon grease off his fingers. "They're attracted to my money and good looks. But I'm heartless—''

"Get on with you. You need to settle down and get married. Start a family. You've punished yourself long enough—''

"Joan, for Christ's sake.'' He paused, tried to think of something that would send her off in a different direction. "Actually, I'm thinking about going to Ethiopia.''

"Ethiopia.'' The scorn in her voice was evident. "For God's sake, why? Is there not enough to keep you busy where you are? What about this WISH thing you were so fired up about?''

"That's not the reason, Joan. WISH is…well, it's a long story.'' He hadn't expected he'd have to justify leaving, wasn't in fact sure he could. "They've a need for pediatric specialists and—''

"Enough. I don't want to hear your nonsense. If you had a wife and family, you wouldn't have the need to be running off all the time. You can't keep your defenses up forever, you know. We all need people close to us. You might tell yourself otherwise, but you're wrong and—''

"Sorry about this,'' Martin interrupted. "But I thought I was talking to my sister. Apparently I've reached a psychiatry hot line.''

"It's because I'm your sister, Martin, that I'm saying this.'' She paused for a moment. "Let me give you a little parallel. You remember Paddy Murphy, don't you? The way his mind was always stuck in the past, nursing the old grudges, reliving ancient battles as though they were fought yesterday? Now what if everyone in Ireland had that same sort of attitude? The country would never move into the twenty-first century—''

Martin laughed aloud. "I'm a bit confused, Joan. Is it Paddy or Ireland you're comparing me to?"

"Sure, you can laugh if you want to." A note of indignation had crept into her voice, "But you need to move on, Martin, and I'm not talking about Ethiopia."

When he said nothing, she started on another topic. As they chatted back and forth, he finished the newspaper, then leafed through the mail he'd put on his bedside table. Little of it held his attention, a few bills and the latest issue of *Western World*, the medical center's quarterly staff publication. Idly, he leafed through the pages until he came to a section called Recent Additions: pictures and short profiles of employees who had joined Western in the last quarter. On the top row, between a lab tech and an optometrist, was a picture of a woman with a braid of dark brown hair and a slightly bemused smile. The caption underneath said Catherine A. Prentice, Public Relations. He stared at the picture.

"Martin. Have you fallen asleep? Did you not hear what I just said?"

"Sorry, no, I'm wide awake." He reached in his bedside drawer for a pair of scissors. "What was that again?"

"I said that maybe the next time I spoke to you, you'll tell me that you've met someone and are planning to settle down and raise a family." Silence. "It was a joke, Martin," she said after a moment. "Like saying you expect pigs to fly."

"Ah well, you never know, do you?" Martin finished clipping out Catherine's picture and propped it against the lamp, so that she seemed to be looking at him. "One of these days I might surprise everyone."

"SOMETIMES I THINK I'd rather sleep in for an extra hour, than drag myself out here every morning." Catherine, in an old red sweatshirt and black warm-up pants, jogged along Second Street beside Darcy. Clouds of vapor poured into the cool morning air. "Are you sure this is worth it?"

"Listen, when we're all skinny and gorgeous..." Darcy stopped suddenly, clutched at her turquoise-spandexed side. "Jeez, I'm dying. Maybe you have a point." She arched an eyebrow. "Winchell's?"

"No." Catherine grinned. "We can't give up that easily. Come on. Let's just go over the bridge and circle the marina. That's about two miles. Then I've got to get back and get the kids off to school."

As they crossed the Alamitos Bay Bridge, she thought of the day ahead. A press conference with the Hodges family at ten. The Ned Bolton interview to set up. Then she needed to talk to Martin. Her stomach tightened. The agreement she'd struck with Derek had kept her awake for the last couple of nights. The challenge scared the hell out of her but in a strange way it also exhilarated her. She'd taken a stand, held out for something she believed in. The old Catherine would never have had the confidence to take such a risk.

"I heard the parents of those triplets on the radio this morning," Darcy said. "The dad was yakking away, the mom hardly got a word in."

"I think he overshadows her a little," Catherine said.

"Yeah, I kind of got that feeling."

"She kind of reminds me of how I was with Gary. The way she sort of tiptoes around him, like she's scared to say anything to upset him."

"Why the hell do women put up with jerks like that?" Darcy checked the traffic and sprinted across the street.

"Hey, I did it for twelve years." Catherine ran beside her. "That's the weird thing. You can spot the problem in other people, but you don't always recognize it when you're in the same situation."

They jogged into the marina, quiet but for the creak of boats against the moorings, the occasional slam of a car door or an engine starting. Gulls wheeled and circled, scavenged over trash cans. True, there were days that she'd rather stay in bed, but she loved the twice-a-week early-morning jogs. It was even worth the stress of having her mom sit with the kids, although she had to pay the price of hearing dire warnings about the dangers of excessive running and how it could lead to anorexia. *Fat chance.*

Eyes narrowed against the light coming off the water, Catherine looked out at the bobbing boats, some of the masts decorated with Christmas greenery and ribbons, and felt her spirits lift. Despite some lapses—like the other night when she'd seen marriage as a rescue—the changes she had started to see in herself were definitely positive. Every day she seemed to shake off a little more of the old Catherine and she liked the way that made her feel.

As they made the lap around the marina parking lot, something familiar about the loping stride of a tall man in a leather bomber jacket and khakis diverted her thoughts. He headed toward her, briefcase in one hand, a couple of heavy binders under his arm. As he drew close, she saw the flash of recognition in his eyes. *Martin.* The sudden acceleration of her heart had little to do with jogging.

"Hi." She felt her face color. "I didn't expect to... What—"

"I live on one of those boats down there." He pointed to a gangway a few yards away. "Third one along."

Disconcerted by his obvious pleasure at seeing her and by her own erotic fantasies, she looked away. He's just another a doctor at the hospital, she reminded herself. Involved with someone else. Leaving the country. All you need from him is a little professional cooperation. Next to her, she could feel Darcy's avid interest. She tucked her hair behind her ears, made the introductions.

"We're practically neighbors," Martin said.

"True." Catherine smiled, at a loss for words. He smiled back. His hair was slightly damp and tousled. Under his open jacket, he wore a heavy knit sweater, almost the same dark blue as his eyes. Behind him, traffic rumbled on the bridge. He moved the folders under his arms. She shifted her weight to the other foot. Then they both spoke at the same time. He'd started to ask a question, just as she voiced hers.

He grinned. "You first."

"I wanted to…uh, there's a few things I need to talk to you about. Holly Hodges, specifically. I guess you've seen the press coverage?" He nodded, seemed about to speak, then stopped, an expression on his face she couldn't read. "Anyway, we need to develop a more coordinated press plan. What's your schedule like today?"

"We could have lunch."

"Lunch?"

"Lunch," he said with a laugh. "You look as though I'd suggested we spend an illicit weekend together."

"No, I'm just…" Distracted by the sudden image his words conjured, she felt her face color. God, she was never going to pull this off. "Lunch would work," she said. Briskly, she hoped. "How about the cafeteria around noon?"

"Actually, I was thinking of fish and chips."

"Fish and chips?" Now she sounded like a parrot.

"I called back to Ireland yesterday." A smile broke across his face. "My father mentioned the fish shop. I've been thinking about it ever since. There's a place on the pier. If you come up to the unit around noon, I'll drive us down there."

She looked down at her running shoes, up at him. There was no real reason she could think of to object. At least none she could bring up. "I'll see you at noon." Then she remembered his question. "You had something you wanted to ask me?"

"Well, I'd wanted to ask you out to lunch," he said with a smile. "You do still owe me for the press conference. Remember?"

"He's hot for you," Darcy said as they jogged away.

"Oh, come on," Catherine protested, but she couldn't stop smiling.

CATHERINE WATCHED a couple of reporters vie for a closer spot to the stage where Eddie and Rita sat in rocking chairs. Each parent held a sleeping infant, tiny red faces barely visible above the swaddled wrappings. Holly was still too sick to be moved from the nursery. Eddie grinned and shifted his bundle to allow a TV cameraman to get a better shot.

"This one's Berry." He glanced at Rita. "Right?"

"Noelle," she said with a smile. "This is Berry."

Laughter broke out among the assembled reporters. Cameras flashed. Heads bowed toward rapidly filling notepads.

"Are you going to dress them the same?" a reporter shouted.

"She better not," Eddie retorted, "or I'm gonna have some big problems." He paused. "Just wait till they start dating."

"Jeez, he laps this stuff up, doesn't he?" Derek stood at

Catherine's side. Arms folded across his chest, he had the thoughtful expression of a gallery browser. "I wish the mother were a tad more animated."

"I think the whole thing is much harder on her." Catherine watched Rita Hodges blink in the glare of the TV lights, recalled the painful time when her own son had been in the NICU. "*She's* worried about Holly. *His* main concern is how many reporters he can talk to."

"Mmm." Derek narrowed his eyes. "I still think we should have put Santa hats on the kids," he said. "It would have been much more visual."

"We couldn't get any small enough—" Catherine broke off to listen as Rita answered a reporter's question.

"All I mean is positive thoughts are good and everything—" Rita glanced at Eddie "—but sometimes you've got to, like, face up to things... I mean if Holly's not going to get better..." She bowed her head for a moment. "Well, I'm just saying that maybe it's something we should think about."

Catherine heard Derek groan.

The Channel 7 reporter looked from Eddie to Rita. "So do I take it that the two of you have different ideas on what's best for Holly?"

"No, that's not it," Eddie said quickly. "Rita feels the same as me—"

"No, Eddie—"

"Rita." He glared at her. "It's just like that ossywhatsit breathing machine she's hooked up to. I mean, they weren't even gonna try it—"

"But it's not helping her," Rita broke in. "Dr. C. said it wouldn't and he was right."

"Dammit." Derek shook his head. "It's not enough that Connaughton shoots his own mouth off, now he's got the mother singing the same song.'' He looked at Catherine. ''When are you going to talk to him?''

''After this.''

''Okay.'' He moved toward the platform. ''I'm going to get this damn thing wrapped up before she says anything else I don't want to hear. You go find Connaughton. For God's sake, get him to stick to the script and tell him he'd better make the mother see the light, too. If he can't do that—''

''Derek.'' She caught his arm. ''I'm not comfortable with this. The mother has a right to decide what's best for her child—''

He sighed. ''Look, the mother's opinion is Connaughton's opinion. If he told her snake oil would cure the kid, she'd want snake oil.'' The only thing that's of any concern…*any* concern to us is the publicity, and we need everyone singing the same song from the same hymnbook. And that song is 'Hallelujah for Surgery.' If that offends your moral principles, let me know and I'll do it myself.''

Catherine said nothing and he headed toward the platform where Rita Hodges stood surrounded by reporters. Then he glanced over his shoulder at her.

''I just thought of something,'' he called out. ''There's an administrative meeting at two. I can't make it. You'll need to attend for me. You can fill Ed Jordan in on what you're doing with Connaughton.''

WHICH WAS a good question to ponder, Catherine thought as she left the office and headed up to the NICU to meet Martin. What *was* she doing with Connaughton? An hour earlier, she had gone to the rest room, brushed her hair loose, carefully redone her makeup and rolled up the waistband of her dark green pleated skirt so that the hem skimmed her knees rather than hanging dowdily around her calves. When she returned to the office, one of the secretaries did a double take and asked if she had a date. The question brought her to her senses and she'd rebraided her hair and pulled her skirt down to its original length. It was a professional meeting, she reminded herself, not a date.

At the bank of elevators, she pushed the button for the fifth floor. The problem was that no matter how many reminders she issued, the message didn't quite sink in. Every time she thought of Martin, things got totally confused. Last night she'd dreamed that Peter was about to have surgery and she'd woken sobbing because Martin was trying to take him from her. She took a deep breath, flipped back her braid and signed in at the NICU main desk.

She found him bent over a bassinet, his eyes intent on a nurse who was drawing blood from a baby's heel. The card over the bassinet bore a rosy-tinted sketch of a chubby baby who bore no resemblance to the bed's scrawny occupant. The hand-lettered name on the card read Hodges, Holly.

The stout, gray-haired nurse gripped Holly's foot and pricked it with a needle. The baby flinched and Catherine turned her face away, unable to watch. She saw Martin reach for the syringe.

"Let me give it a try," he said, his eyes on the baby.

The nurse gave him a withering look. "Listen, Dr. Connaughton, I was doing this sort of thing while you were still running around in diapers. I can manage without your help, thank you very much."

Martin looked up then and saw her, but he didn't return her smile. Both he and the nurse seemed tense, an edginess to their banter. He reminded Catherine of an engine idling, ready to spring into action in an instant. His eyes darted from Holly to the monitor each time the nurse pricked the skin.

"Did you come here to talk to Dr. Connaughton?" The

nurse held the baby's foot once again and glanced up at Catherine. "Because if you did, you'll need to speak up. He'll forget you're even here."

"In case you haven't picked up on it," Martin said, "the consensus around here is that I'm losing my objectivity with this baby."

The nurse looked at the vial of blood she'd finally managed to draw and rolled her eyes. "*Losing* it?"

"Lost it," he amended.

The nurse grunted. "He's like an anxious daddy and a doctor all rolled into one. A bad-tempered one, to boot." She gave a sigh. "Trust me, it's no day at the beach around here lately."

"Ah sure, anyone would think you didn't like me at all." Martin put his arm around the nurse and grinned. The earlier tension seemed to lift. "I only hope that Catherine's opinion of me is a little more charitable," he said with a wink at her.

Catherine just smiled. Had she really seen him as cold? Sure. That's the way men were. In the blink of an eye, they could just change so that you never knew where you were with them. Which was why she didn't need one in her life.

"We're off to lunch," he told the nurse. "We'll be gone about an hour and I have my beeper—"

"Go." The nurse fluttered her hands. "And make sure he gets some decent food," she added with a glance at Catherine. "He lives on oranges and black coffee and candy bars, which do nothing for his disposition. What he needs is someone to take care of him."

CHAPTER NINE

"I LIKE CALIFORNIA beaches in the winter," Martin said as they walked briskly along the Long Beach pier to the small kiosk at the end. "They remind me of Irish beaches in the summer."

Catherine laughed, and turned for a moment to look at him. The beach stretched endlessly on either side of them, a pale field of sand edged by a distant strip of steel-blue water. Straight ahead lay the palm-tree fringed oil islands and beyond them tankers like toy boats. Gulls wheeled and circled overhead, filling the air with their raucous sounds.

"It's the truth." He dodged a bait bucket set out in the middle of the pier. "I remember our holidays. We'd all sit on the sands, bundled up in our coats and blankets, drinking tea out of thermoses to keep warm." He shot her a sideways grin. "And that was July."

"No danger of sunburn, huh?"

"Frostbite more likely," he said, and shot her a sideways glance. Her green tartan skirt, navy blazer and long braid made him think of a schoolgirl. Which, he reflected, was perfectly in accordance with the way he felt. As though they were playing truant from classes. They took their food to a wooden bench and sat with the paper plates of fish and chips between them. Nearby, half a dozen men in parkas and boots fished, their lines propped against the railings. Catherine started to open a package of ketchup, and he took it from her.

"Vinegar." He handed her the bottle he'd taken off the counter. "It's the only way to eat fish and chips."

"But these are the same as French fries—"

"Shh." He put his finger to his lips. "You're indulging me. I want to think they're exactly like the chips I had at home, so they have to have vinegar on them."

"What if you were eating a hamburger?"

"Then it would be okay to use ketchup."

She grinned. "It sounds pretty complicated."

"It is," he agreed. "And that's only part of it. Really good chips have to be soggy with vinegar and wrapped in newspaper."

She wrinkled her nose.

"It's Martin Connaughton's Law of Fried Potatoes." He doused his food. "Have you never heard of it?"

"No, indeed I haven't." Catherine imitated his accent.

"Ah well, there are very serious penalties for breaking it," he said. "One of them is being forced to hear nonstop renditions of 'Danny Boy.'"

She laughed and he told her that one of these days she should go with him and listen to some real Irish music. She smiled and said she'd like to do that. The breeze from the ocean blew their hair and the sun warmed his back. He smiled at her for a long moment. All the problems at Western seemed to melt away, and he wanted to stay right where he was forever.

Catherine took a chip from the bag, tossed it onto the pier. Immediately, a flock of seagulls swooped down to fight over it.

"Watch that one." He pointed to a gull that had separated itself from the flock and was strutting toward them.

"He's going to demand that we hand over the rest of the chips," Catherine said. "I think he's got a little revolver under his wing."

"One of the local gull thugs." He stretched his legs out in front of him, tipped his face up to the sun and closed his eyes. "I have an idea," he said after a few minutes. "Call Western and tell them we've resigned to lead lives of sloth and indolence. We'll sleep on the benches and eat fish and chips all day, then when the money runs out, you can catch fish."

"Oh sure." She pushed his arm. "While you're doing what?"

"I haven't decided yet, but I'm actually quite keen on the idea of doing nothing at all." He kept his eyes closed, soaked in the warmth of the afternoon sun. Christmas in California might seem bizarre, but there was a lot to be said for sunshine in December. They sat in easy silence for a little longer, Catherine's shoulder touching his, then she shifted slightly and he sensed a change in her mood. When he opened his eyes, he saw her watching him.

"What is it?"

"Reality suddenly intruded," she said with a frown. Wind blew strands of hair across her face, and she brushed them away with the back of her hand. "Work. I'm supposed to have a talk with you. Get you to shape up and sing out of the same hymnbook everyone else is using."

Martin nodded. Jordan had given him a similar lecture. As though a trapdoor had opened, all the other problems at Western now crowded in. He stretched and yawned. God, he didn't want to think about all of this now. What he wanted was to talk to Catherine about the decision he'd reached the night before, but something had crept into the air between them and it made what he wanted to say seem all wrong.

"At the press conference this morning, Holly's mother mentioned something you'd said." She crossed her legs, clasped her hands around her knees. "But Eddie disagreed and—"

"I'm not surprised," he broke in. Back slouched against the bench, he tipped his face to the sun again. But its warmth had gone, and the wind felt suddenly cold. "The two of us don't exactly see eye to eye," he told Catherine. "Hodges listens to Grossman. Rita listens to me."

"The ideal situation," Catherine said slowly, "would be for everyone to agree, at least publicly, about what should be done. From a public relations standpoint, this is a really good story, especially with Western picking up the tab. But if you, and now Rita Hodges, openly oppose the surgery, it obviously puts a different slant on things."

"Messes up your PR plan, is that it?"

"Thank you."

"Sorry." Contrite, he gazed at Catherine's legs clad in navy tights, knees demurely pressed together below the folds of her tartan skirt, then forced his thoughts back to the subject. A pulse in his temple started to throb. There was something wrong with a system that put public relations benefits before the patient's best interests. Something absurd about the expectation that he would ignore his clinical judgment and lie for PR's sake. This fiasco wasn't her fault. She had a job to do and he wasn't making it any easier for her, but he wished to hell she worked in a different department.

"As a mother, I can relate to what Rita is going through. Peter spent two months in the NICU."

He heard the emotion in her voice, fought the inclination to put his arm around her. "I'm sorry if I'm making it more difficult for you," he finally said.

"No." She shook her head. "The thing is, Peter had to have all these procedures, but no one knew for sure if they would really help him." Her eyes downcast, she traced her index finger over the weave on her skirt. "And he was being put through so much pain. But it would have been very hard not to try everything that might help."

Martin watched a couple of seagulls drag an empty Doritos bag across the ground, a few yards from where they sat. Both birds tugged at the bag and then a gust of wind blew it away. "I don't know all the details about your son," he said, "but I'm guessing his problems were nowhere as severe as Holly's. Of course, you'd want to do everything if there's any chance at all. Anyone would. Sometimes though, you just have to admit you've done all you can."

"Grossman seems to think more can be done."

"He wouldn't if the media weren't watching. What we should be doing, what we would be doing any other time, is just making her comfortable and letting nature take its course. That's what Rita wants, but she's up against Grossman and Western's PR machine."

Catherine dug her fingernail under a loose chip of paint on the wooden table. "The problem is…" Bottom lip caught between her teeth, she stopped to examine the pad of her index finger.

"The problem is you've got a splinter." He took her hand, held it in his palm and with his thumb and forefinger gently squeezed the end of her finger, then he flicked away the sliver of wood. "There, lunch and major surgery, what more can you ask?"

"I'll tell you that when I get your bill," she said.

"Look, I know you have a job to do." Her hand was still in his. "And if it helps, I'll mouth the platitudes to the press. But I'm not going to be party to railroading Rita. I've explained the situation to her as I see it and that's all I can do. The surgery is her choice."

As THEY PULLED into the doctors' parking lot, Martin seemed miles away, lost in his own thoughts. Preoccupied herself, Catherine hadn't really felt like talking and they'd driven back to Western in silence. Of course he wouldn't railroad Rita, she didn't want him to. But how much did her feelings about him influence what she believed about surgery? If Holly were her child, would she be so ready to accept that they'd done all they could?

She glanced over at him. He sat with one hand still on the steering wheel, his right arm extended over the back of her seat. His reddish hair, thick and coarse, just brushed the collar of his blue-and-white checked shirt. This close, she could see the faint dusting of freckles on his face, the twitch of a muscle in his jaw.

Earlier, during the ride to the pier, the cramped space of the small car had enforced a physical closeness that had charged the air. As he'd maneuvered into the parking space, his knee had brushed against hers and she'd felt her stomach do a slow roll. Now, while the physical proximity was still there, a dense curtain of silence separated them. The tension—his and her own—felt palpable. She cleared her throat to speak, and Martin turned to look at her. Their eyes met and held.

"I just want you to know that administration could make things difficult for you." She described Derek's threat to use the press to sabotage him if he didn't cooperate. "Although, if you're going to Ethiopia—"

"I'm not going." His voice was flat, uninflected.

"You're not? Why…when did you change your mind?"

"Last night, I think. I'm not sure. I'd been going back and forth on it." He looked down at the keys in his hand. "But last night I reached a major decision…a kind of turning point, I suppose. I want to stay and fight to keep WISH alive. If Western won't fund it, I'll keep looking until I find an agency that will." He looked down at the keys again. "But there's something else," he said without looking up.

Catherine waited for him to continue. Behind her she felt the pressure of his right arm across the seat back. The silence lengthened, and she glanced over at him.

"This will sound odd," he finally said. "We hardly know each other. I'm not exactly a model of stability and you have children..." He ran his hand across the back of his neck, then frowned at the keys in his hand as though he couldn't imagine how they'd got there. "I can't stop thinking about you. You're on my mind all the time."

She watched him. He hadn't looked at her at all as he spoke and now he sat with his head back against the seat, eyes straight ahead as though scared of what he might see if he turned to her. Moved by what the words had obviously cost him, she couldn't speak for a moment. In his silent refusal to look at her, he'd revealed more about himself than he could have with days of explanation. Words jangled around in her brain, the silence between them lengthened.

"I didn't want to go to that holiday party," he said, "and then we started talking, and I didn't want to leave. The same in your office. Same right now. There's so much I want to say, I don't really know where to start." With his forefinger, he slowly traced the pattern on the knob of the gearshift column. "I'd like to see you...outside of the hospital, I mean. We could take it very slowly. There's an Irish band at Mulligan's I'd like to hear. Perhaps we could have dinner first."

Catherine pulled at a loose thread on her skirt. Was she dreaming? *He couldn't stop thinking about her?* And she couldn't stop thinking about him. It seemed incredible, like something in a movie. *And about as realistic,* the voice in her head warned. *Look, you're finally getting your life to-*

gether, the voice continued. *You don't need a man to blow it all apart. Don't risk everything you've worked for.*

"I don't think that would be a good idea, Martin."

"Mulligan's?"

"Seeing you."

"Why?"

"Well, for one thing, we work together, which complicates everything. I mean, you didn't want to do the press conference, but then you did because I asked you to. If Grossman does the surgery, the situation will get even more difficult. The whole idea of compromising what you really believe just because—"

"What's the real reason?"

"The real reason?"

He nodded. "I realize that working together is a potential complication, but I don't think that's the problem. I think there's something else."

She folded her arms across her chest, stared at the tiny run in the left knee of her tights. "I just can't, that's all."

"I can see why you're in public relations," he said. "You explain things so well."

"Yeah, I guess that wasn't one of my better efforts." With a weak grin, she tried again. "See, my family is like this little boat bobbing around on the ocean. We're all fine as long as we stay in calm waters, but storms could be a problem and we don't have room for any other passengers."

"So what do I represent? The storm or the passenger?"

The question took her by surprise and she looked at him for a moment. "Both."

"That's very picturesque, Catherine, but I'm not asking to come aboard."

She felt her face color. God, what an idiot she was. He's talking Irish music and she's assuming he's after commitment. "I realize you weren't," she lied. "And of course, I'm not either. I mean, a relationship's absolutely the last thing I want, and anyway our lives are very different. You're unencumbered and I'm…" She bit her nail. Please God, stop me babbling. "All I'm trying to say is…"

Laughter played across his face. "Yes?"

"Actually, I don't know what I'm trying to say. I figured I'd bored you silly going on about my kids and baking cakes and now I'm just kind of blown away."

"Actually, I'm only interested in the fact you like to cook. It's been ages since I had a decent meal."

"Ulterior motives. I knew it."

He laughed, his eyes intent on her face. Logic told her not to get involved. Logic told her they were too different. The Becky-Home-ecky thing might appeal now, but he'd tire of it. Right around the time she started really needing him, he'd be gone. But what if she didn't *let* herself need him? What if they kept things friendly and casual? Like Darcy said, maybe she did need something in her life besides work and the children. And as long as she held the reins, why not? But then a thought occurred to her.

"You're not…I mean, are you involved with someone else? If you are, I'd rather know right now."

He waited a moment before he answered. "I've no commitments," he said.

She thought of the rumors about Valerie Webb. Maybe he didn't consider it a commitment, but if he and Valerie had something going, she didn't want to get caught in the middle. "What about—"

"Valerie Webb?"

She nodded. "You know the hospital rumor mill."

"I've no commitment," he said again. "To Valerie or anyone else. Valerie knows that. Whatever else you might have heard.'' With his finger he traced a pattern on the back of her hand. ''I'd tell you if it were otherwise.''

''I don't mean to give you the third degree,'' she said. ''I mean, we're talking…well, we're not talking anything serious, but I don't have much tolerance for fooling around and…'' Again her face went hot. *God, she was a veritable light show.* She looked up at him. ''Obviously, I also don't have much practice with this sort of thing.''

He laughed. ''Well, let's give you some practice. Tonight after work? We can leave from the medical center. That way if you decide I bore you silly, you can easily get up and go.''

''How about lasagna instead? I don't like to leave the children with a sitter unless I have to.''

''Lasagna? So that's a yes then? *Whew!*'' He laughed aloud and wiped a hand across his forehead. ''I haven't been that nervous since I was twelve, and Sister Mary caught me out walking with Sinead O'Malley.''

Amused, she waited for him to go on.

''It was after dark, and we were holding hands,'' he explained. ''Pernicious night walking, it was called. A very serious offense.'' A moment passed, and his face turned solemn. With one hand, he caught her braid, pulled it slightly. ''You might have just done a very foolish thing, but I'm glad you did.'' His palms on either side of her face, he kissed her softly on the mouth. ''That's just a down payment, all right?''

Friendly and casual, she reminded herself, but she couldn't keep the smile off her face or tear her eyes away from his. She wanted to touch him again just to be sure she wasn't dreaming. And then she remembered the administrative meeting. *''Omigod.''* She checked her watch. ''Derek's going to kill me.''

"AH, PUBLIC RELATIONS deigns to honor us with its presence." Ed Jordan, at the head of a long mahogany table, stood as Catherine walked in fifteen minutes late. Heads around the table swiveled to look at her.

Jordan waited until she'd found a seat.

"Since this is your first meeting—" his voice and face were stony "—I'll just warn you. For future reference, we take punctuality very seriously. Everyone in this room is extremely busy. No one has time to sit around waiting for those who can't be on time. Understood?"

"Yes, Mr. Jordan." It occurred to her that the last time she'd been late was the night of the holiday party when she'd missed Jordan's speech because she'd been talking to Martin. And now it had happened again, for the same reason. She crossed her fingers and made a silent prayer that it wasn't an omen. Windswept and still stunned by what Martin had said, she smoothed her hair and tried to compose her thoughts. In her haste to get to the meeting, she'd left her folder with the agenda and details of the week's media activity back in her office. Now she'd have to wing it, she thought, angry with herself. This was the first time Derek had asked her to attend an administrative meeting and she'd wanted to make a good impression. Being late was not the best way to start.

"When were you planning to do the Hodges surgery, Nate?" Jordan addressed Grossman, who leafed through a leather-bound appointment book.

"I'm going to Greece the end of next week. I'd like to do it before I go." Grossman pulled a pair of half glasses down his nose and returned his gaze to the calendar. "Let's see. Today's Monday. It would have to be…no, that won't do—it's going to have to be Thursday. I'm booked full until then." He glanced at Catherine for a moment. "If we leave it any later, the press will be too busy with Christmas stuff.''

Catherine listened with a sense of disbelief. Surgery, it appeared, was a foregone conclusion, regardless of who opposed it. She glanced across the table at Valerie Webb who had just started to speak.

"We've still got the problem with the mother, Ed." Valerie looked at Jordan. "She's as much opposed to the surgery as the father is for it—"

"Connaughton has brainwashed her," Grossman said. "However, I have a proposal that might be of interest to him. I'll talk to him later today."

"I can also talk to him," Valerie offered. "We work together closely in the unit. I understand some of his concerns."

"Good." Jordan's smile lingered on her face. "I think if you can make him understand—"

"Have you ever tried to *make* Connaughton do anything?" Paul Van Dolan rolled his eyes. "It's an exercise in frustration."

A smile spread slowly across Valerie's face. "Ah well, there's a secret to it." A tip of pink tongue darted between her lips. "You just have to know the right buttons to push."

Catherine saw the eyes of every man in the room turn to Valerie Webb. Each one, she guessed, speculating on the buttons involved. *I've no commitment. Whatever else you might have heard.* She realized she'd missed Jordan's question.

"I'm sorry." Her face flushed. "Could you repeat that, please?"

Jordan's expression suggested extreme displeasure. He let a moment pass. "I was saying—" he paused again "—that I'm a little concerned by Mrs. Hodges's remarks at the news conference this morning."

"Unfortunately, there isn't very much we can do—"

"Did you approach any of your media contacts about not running her remarks?"

Catherine shook her head. "I'm not sure that would work—"

"Did you try?"

"No, I didn't, but…it's not something we would typically do."

"I could cite a number of instances in which Petrelli has intervened."

"I'm sorry. I'm not personally aware of—"

"Never mind." Jordan made a notation on the pad in front of him. "I'll talk to him myself." He studied her for a moment. "We need an aggressive news media policy. It's of no value if you just roll over and play dead."

Caught off guard by Jordan's hostility, Catherine stared at him, at a loss for words. All eyes were directed at her. A tense silence seemed to use up the air in the room.

"Do we have fact sheets prepared about the surgery?" Jordan asked her.

"No, we don't." Always ready to blame herself, she started instead to get angry. At Jordan for publicly humiliating her. And at Derek who had said nothing to her about fact sheets. "I thought the surgery was still under discussion. I didn't realize it was definite—"

"You do have Dr. Grossman's curriculum vitae and background information for the press kits?"

"No. As I said, we weren't aware that surgery—"

"Do you customarily leave things to the last minute?"

"Mr. Jordan. We've been extremely busy the past few days."

Jordan glanced around the room. "May I see a show of hands, please. Anyone here who hasn't been extremely busy this week?'' A slight smile played across his face. "I don't see any hands.''

Catherine fixed her eyes on the table's wood grain and bit her bottom lip hard enough to taste blood. Either he was having a bad day himself and taking it out on her, or he had some personal animosity toward her, which seemed unlikely since he hardly knew her. She looked up and met Valerie Webb's eyes across the table. Valerie slowly winked. Then Jordan addressed her again.

"Perhaps you would update us on other media efforts related to the Hodges triplets.''

She summarized, as best she could from memory, the media activity of the past week. "Ned Bolton, the medical reporter with the *Tribune,* wants to do an in-depth piece on surgery for Holly. He'd like to talk to Dr. Grossman and Dr. Connaughton.''

"And you've given Connaughton media training on handling sensitive and controversial issues?''

"Well, not exactly. We did—''

"What does 'not exactly' mean?''

"I've spoken to him.'' She composed herself for a long moment, thought about the idea she had formed in the last ten minutes. "We discussed the issue this morning and he's adamant about his position. He doesn't believe that surgery is appropriate for Holly. He feels that she is medically unstable and her prognosis for complete recovery is poor. Unless he can honestly express his opinion, he doesn't want to talk to the press.'' She paused, made eye contact with those around the table. To her relief, she saw a few nods. "Since we're trying to build on the team concept,'' she said, looking again at Jordan, "I recommend that Dr. Connaughton does no further press interviews, and we designate another NICU physician to do updates on Holly's progress.''

Jordan motioned to the secretary taking minutes of the meeting. "Make a note that I want Petrelli to attend these meetings in future." He looked at Catherine. "Let me be sure I understand you clearly. You're telling me that you've done absolutely nothing to prepare for press coverage of the surgery—"

"Mr. Jordan—"

"May I finish, please?" He paused. "And you've allowed Connaughton to walk all over you—"

"That isn't what I said, or what I meant." Her face burned. "I'm trying to explain Dr. Connaughton's position and—"

"It's not your job to explain Dr. Connaughton's position. Your job is to present this medical center's position. I suggest you keep that in mind for future reference."

"SO HOW WERE the fish and chips?" Holly's nurse asked when Martin returned to the NICU from lunch.

"Very good." Whistling, he picked up a chart and flipped through the pages. "Very good indeed."

"Fish and chips?" Tim Graham looked up. "They had fish and chips in the cafeteria?"

"No." The nurse arched her eyebrow at Graham. "Dr. Connaughton went out to lunch."

"It's a beautiful day out there." Martin turned back a page to double-check a lab report. "Sun shining. Birds singing. Makes you feel good to be alive."

"Carol." Graham snapped his fingers at the nurse. "Look at him. I think he's running a fever or something. He's got this strange expression on his face."

She squinted at Martin. "I think it's just a smile."

"Maybe you're right. Sure is odd-looking though." Graham moved his glasses to rub his eyes. "He actually went *out* to lunch? Was he alone?"

"Nope." The nurse shook her head. "With a female."

"Does anyone know whether we've got the CT scan results back on Holly?" Martin fought to keep a straight face. "I don't see them here."

"A female?" Graham's jaw dropped open.

"Uh-huh. Kind of cute, too."

"Call the public relations department," Graham said. "Tell them Dr. Connaughton's discovered the existence of life outside the medical center. They'll probably want to alert the press."

"God, you're like a load of nattering fishwives," Martin said. "Worse in fact—"

"Dr. Connaughton." The unit secretary tapped him on the shoulder. "Dr. Grossman's secretary is on the line. She wants to set up some time for the two of you to meet. Today if possible."

"Sure." Martin turned to her with a smile. "Put the call through to my office and I'll check my calendar."

"Okay. That proves it," Graham said in a stage whisper as Martin walked away. "See how he agreed. Just like that. Even smiled. Something's definitely come over him."

CHAPTER TEN

"MOM, for the last time, it's not a date," Catherine insisted when her mother stopped over at six to drop off some multivitamins she'd picked up at Wal-Mart and found Catherine getting ready for Martin's arrival. "What do you think?" She held up a red sweater. "This with jeans, or my white shirt? Peter," she yelled into the living room. "You need to get started on your homework. Julie, pick up your Barbie dolls and take them into your room. Damn…" She looked at her mother. "I forgot to defrost the sausage."

Her mother followed her into the kitchen. "Well, if it isn't a date, I'd like to know why you're running around the house like a chicken with its head cut off—"

"Okay, maybe I'm a little scattered…" She opened the freezer, took out the Italian sausage and dropped the package onto the floor. "But it has nothing to do with Martin." She stooped to retrieve the meat. "I invited him to dinner. Period."

"And last week you were out all night talking to him."

"I wasn't out all night. Anyway that was mostly about work. This is…" What? Whatever it was, she didn't want to think about it. Any more than she wanted to think about the repercussions from Jordan's meeting. Tomorrow would be soon enough for that. She stuck the sausage in the microwave to thaw. "I'm just making dinner for him. He said he misses home cooking." Even as she spoke, she knew how lame the words sounded, and when she glanced over at her mother, she saw the knowing smirk.

"One thing leads to another, that's all I'm saying on the subject."

"Not in this case."

"Men are all the same, Catherine." Her mother took a pair of glasses from her purse and scanned the nutritional information on the back of the lasagna box. "They want one thing and one thing only and they don't stop until they get it. And then they're gone, just like your father. Lasagna, huh? Do you know how many calories there are—"

"No and I don't want to." Catherine dumped a carton of ricotta into a bowl. Right now she felt so tense at the prospect of Martin sitting across the dinner table from her, she couldn't imagine being able to eat a thing.

"I hope you're at least using turkey sausage," her mother said.

"Nope. The other kind, all loaded with fat. Want to stay and eat with us?"

"And drop dead from a heart attack? I don't think so." Her mother threw a furtive glance over her shoulder at the kids in the living room. "Make sure he uses protection," she said in a stage whisper.

"*Mother.*" Catherine felt her mouth drop open. "For God's sake."

"They're all the same. Mark my words. Even doctors," she added ominously.

Catherine bit back a smile. If nothing else, her mother's presence provided a little comic relief. As far as she could tell, Helen's social life centered primarily around the Rite-Aide prescription counter where she'd struck up a friendship with the elderly pharmacist, but things never seemed to move beyond discussions of antacids and pain relievers. And now she was offering safe-dating tips? "So Mom…"

She couldn't resist it. "You've had some firsthand experience with this stuff?"

"Actually, I have, Miss Smarty-Pants. But I don't kiss and tell. By the way, did you ask him about the Sweet'n Low?"

"Huh?"

"About whether it causes brain tumors. I told you to ask him about it."

"Yeah, I know. I forgot. I was too busy fighting off his advances."

Her mother pursed her lips. "Julie. Peter," she called into the living room. "Come and kiss Grandma goodbye." She took off her glasses, slipped them back into her purse and snapped it shut. As for you, young lady," she addressed Catherine. "You can smirk, but if you think this fellow is after anything more than a good time, you're fooling yourself. Your problem is you've had no experience with men except for Gary and…well, I rest my case."

"Hey, Mom." Catherine kissed her mother's cheek. "I'm in control, okay? I know what I'm doing."

MARTIN ARRIVED at Catherine's with a bunch of pink tulips under one arm, a bottle of Chianti under the other and books for the children. The wine had been easy—she'd told him they were having lasagna—and he'd enjoyed selecting the books. The flowers had thrown him into an agony of indecision. His first inclination had been roses, but then he'd worried that red was coming on too strong, and he couldn't remember what the other colors were supposed to signify, so he'd settled on tulips, which now seemed an odd choice, and sweat was breaking out across his upper lip, and he felt as nervous as a kid on a first date.

Catherine was in the doorway when he pulled up. Barefoot in jeans and a billowing white shirt, her hair in a loose braid down her back. The light from inside shone like a nimbus around her head and shoulders. At her side stood a small blond girl, one arm wrapped around her mother's leg.

"This is Julie." She disentangled the child's arms, crouched beside her and smiled up at Martin. "And this is Dr. Connaughton. Martin. He works with me at the hospital. Remember, you saw him on TV?"

The child nodded. "With the little babies."

"Right. *Really* little babies." Catherine motioned him inside and shut the door, shivering. "Brrr, it's chilly out there."

"Mommy," Julie tugged at Catherine's hand. "I have to tell you something important. We have to put the cheese stuff in the lasagna."

"I know, sweetie." Catherine ruffled the girl's hair, "We're going to in just a minute." She took the wine and flowers, smiled at Martin. "These are gorgeous. I didn't know tulips grew in December."

"Only in greenhouses," he said, and they both stood there smiling at each other until a boy's voice called out from the kitchen. Catherine gave an apologetic little shrug.

"Be right there, Peter. Chopping onions isn't his idea of a good time," she said with a glance at Martin. "Make yourself comfortable, okay? We've entered a critical stage in the lasagna operation, and I'm desperately needed."

He pulled off his leather jacket, sat down on the couch. The room was comfortable. Multicolored rugs on the hardwood floors, flowered curtains. Flickering lights from the Christmas tree glowed on and off, the lights almost mesmerizing. From the kitchen, aromas of onions frying, oregano. Kids' voices. He leaned his head back against the couch, closed his eyes and let it all wash over him like a soothing balm.

Someone tapped his knee.

"Are you taking a nap?" Julie studied him, her eyes as round as marbles.

"Not really." He returned her gaze. "Just closing my eyes."

Julie gave him a knowing look. "That's what my mommy says sometimes, but then she starts snoring." She climbed up on the couch beside him. "Hey, do you know what my teacher's name is?"

"Um—" he thought for a minute "—Fred."

She giggled. "No. Guess again."

"Toffee nose."

She grinned and smacked him on the arm. "No. That's dumb. It's Mrs. Harris."

"What's her first name?" Martin asked.

"Uh." She stuck her finger in her mouth, thinking. "Harris?"

"Harris Harris?"

"Nooo, silly. *Mrs.* Harris." She squealed, hit him again and climbed onto his lap, wiggling around until her face was almost touching his. "Are you my mommy's boyfriend?"

"Julie." Catherine reappeared, her face flushed from cooking. She wiped her hands down the sides of her jeans. "You were supposed to be helping make the lasagna, young lady." She looked at him and shook her head. "Is she driving you crazy?"

"No." Julie's voice was indignant. "We're having a conversation. "

Martin laughed. Both mother and daughter were looking at him with almost identical expressions. One a miniature of the other. Charmed, he impulsively caught Julie in a hug, then looked over the child's shoulder and winked at Catherine.

"Come help me in the kitchen," she said to him.

He followed her and was introduced to a small, dark-haired boy who stood at a butcher-block table stirring something with a wooden spoon.

"This is Peter." Catherine ruffled the boy's hair. "And this is Martin."

"Hello, Peter." He leaned into the doorway, his weight on one foot, arms folded across his chest. The boy scowled and returned to his task, evidently unhappy. Martin decided not to push. The kitchen was bright and warm and smelled of simmering tomato sauce. Dozens of hanging plants trailed green leaves and tendrils. Dried herbs, gleaming copper pots and a garlic braid hung from hooks above the window, cookbooks overflowed two shelves along one wall. A large blue ceramic pot contained assorted spoons, knives and whisks.

"Just a wild guess." He watched Catherine move around the kitchen, supervising the children's efforts, stopping to stir a pot of sauce. "I'd say you like to cook."

"You'd be right." She stood at the stove, wooden spoon in hand. "It's very therapeutic. Helps me relax."

Moving over to the stove, he stood behind her, watched her rub a handful of herbs between her palms, then drop them into a simmering pot of sauce.

"What's that?" He leaned over her shoulder to get a better look.

"Thyme. Oregano. Rosemary." As she turned her head, her cheek almost grazed his. She held her palms up to his face. "Smells good, huh?"

"Great." He caught her wrist, watched her face. Eyes even more green than usual tonight. A tiny mole at the edge of her jawline. Wisps of hair worked loose from her braid. The kids had sidled off to other parts of the house. He had a great urge to kiss her.

"Okay then." She bit her lip, looked flustered, called for

the kids. They burst into the kitchen moments later, jostling, fighting, a flurry of noise and movement.

"I get to make the salad." Julie beamed at him. "You have to wash the lettuce really good because some of it has caterpillar poo, then…" She disappeared in a cabinet and emerged with a plastic bowl. "You put it in this and dry it. If you don't get all the water off the salad, dressing doesn't stick to it."

"Is that right?" Martin walked over to the cabinet, squatted beside her. Through the open cabinet door, he could see neat stacks of colored plastic containers with matching lids. "How many of those do you think your mother has? Ten? Five hundred? Six million and ninety-two?"

Julie, kneeling on the floor, thought for a minute. "A whole big bunch." She got up, ran to the refrigerator, flung open the door. Similar containers lined the shelves. "See. She's got all these. This one is…" She pried off a lid, peered inside and wrinkled her nose. "Eew-yuk. Broccoli."

Martin grinned. "What else is there?"

"Mmm." She pointed to the containers. "This one is peaches. That one is rice. And what's this one? Uh…gravy. Mommy doesn't eat gravy, she says it makes her fat. And this one is—"

"Julie." Catherine pulled her daughter away from the refrigerator. "That's enough. Martin doesn't need a list of the contents." She gave him a bemused look. "I can't quite figure out what it is about this sort of thing that fascinates you—"

"It's the contrast. If I have leftovers, which doesn't happen often, I stand at the sink and eat them out of a saucepan. My one saucepan. That and a kettle constitutes my kitchenware."

"So you never cook?"

"Only things that can be done in one pot and only for

myself. You, on the other hand, probably entertain constantly.''

''All the time. The kids, my mother. My neighbor Darcy.'' She looked at him from under her lashes. ''Tonight, you.''

He caught the end of her braid, pulled it slightly. And found he couldn't keep the smile off his face.

WHEN THE CHILDREN were finally in bed, Catherine poured two glasses of wine, brought them into the living room and handed one to Martin. He sat on the floor, his head resting against the couch, eyes closed. He wore khakis, a navy sweater, a blue oxford shirt, open at the neck. Firelight flickered, threw shadows around him. Regardless of what she'd told her mother, the minute she'd opened the door and seen him standing there with the tulips and books for the kids she knew she was in trouble.

She would come to her senses, of course. It was early yet, something would go wrong. As they'd eaten dinner, she'd half hoped he would chew with his mouth open, anything to give her an excuse not to like him so much, but his manners were fine. He'd even helped with the dishes. And the clincher, he seemed to really enjoy the kids.

''Julie's quite the little charmer.'' He stretched his legs out in front of him, smiled as she slid down beside him. ''I don't think I scored any points with Peter though.''

''Don't take it personally.'' She swirled her glass, stared at the wine inside. Firelight caught the edge of the glass, made golden fingers of flame. ''Peter had a hard time with the divorce. He's the man of the house now.''

''Is he close to his dad then?''

''I'm not sure close really describes the relationship. Peter's always sort of hero-worshiped Gary, but...well, Gary loves scuba diving and rock climbing, physical things like that, and Peter just can't keep up. He tries, but he almost always ends up with an asthma attack. I think he feels that Gary's disappointed in him. Sometimes I think he blames himself for Gary leaving.''

"Has he told you that?"

"Not exactly, he's not very expansive. I've just picked it up. Mostly he's fine unless he thinks his territory is threatened. Fortunately that doesn't happen very often.''

"You don't date then?"

She shook her head. "I've pretty much ruled out getting involved. At least until the kids are grown.''

"They're still very young.''

"I know." She shrugged. "But they're my first priority. The divorce wasn't their fault, they shouldn't have to suffer. I grew up with parents who didn't put their children first. I know what that feels like.''

"I know a bit about it myself.'' Martin folded his hands behind his head, stared into the fire. "Different circumstances, but I ended up feeling there was no one who cared very much. My mother died when I was twelve, and my dad was so devastated that for years he just shut everyone else out of his life. Half the time it was as though my sister and I didn't exist, the rest of the time he was just angry with me.''

"How old was your sister?"

"Fifteen at the time and boy crazy, so she was never around, which I suppose made it easier for her but harder on me.''

"So what did you do to make him angry?"

He gave a wry laugh. "Being around was usually enough to set him off. My hair was too long, my music too loud, I'd amount to naught, he was always saying. Either that or a rock-and-roll singer, which in his mind was the same thing.''

She looked at him, his expression distant as though he was still remembering. It wasn't difficult to picture the lonely boy in Belfast, grieving for his mother, estranged from his father. Other—more recent—images came into her mind. That first day in the lobby in his hospital scrubs; up in the unit, his tall frame bent over a bassinet; the expression on his face as he'd looked at her across the dinner table tonight. *The way it somehow seemed so right to have him there.*

"Want some more wine?" she asked, suddenly scared of what she was feeling. "Coffee. More lasagna."

He caught her hand as she started to get up, pulled her back down next to him. "I'm fine. I was thinking of what you said about Peter blaming himself for the divorce," he said after a moment. "I felt that way after my mother's death. My dad was so devastated and so angry with me, there were times I'd almost believe it was my fault she'd died. I'd lie on the bed at night and imagine myself as a doctor, curing my mother and winning back my dad's approval."

"Was that why you went into medicine?"

"It might have had something to do with it, although Sharon was very keen on my becoming a doctor."

"Sharon?"

"My wife."

His words seemed to hang in the air for a moment.

"You're divorced?" she asked finally.

"My wife was murdered."

HE HAD BEEN in his last year of medical school at Queen's in Belfast. They'd lived in a flat, just off the Malone Road. On the morning of their first wedding anniversary, Martin stood in the kitchen doorway watching Sharon cook breakfast. She had long curly brown hair and blue eyes heavily fringed with dark lashes. She was twenty-two and, in her fourth month of pregnancy, just beginning to show.

He liked to just watch her sometimes. Marvel at the fact that she was his wife. Their marriage and all it entailed was still new to him. Having another person in his life. Waking beside her. Worrying about her. Surrendering a part of himself to her. They had very little money or material possessions. He cycled to the university, she took the bus to her job at the chemist's. Entertainment was the cinema now and then. A pint or two and a game of darts. He'd never been happier in his life.

"A year ago today, can you believe it?" Sharon smiled over her shoulder at him. Pale morning light lit her face. "Would you do it again then?"

"In a minute." He came up behind her, kissed the back of her neck. "I'm mad for you."

"Just mad is what you mean." She let her body relax against his. "And what grand plans have you to celebrate?"

"Whatever this'll buy." He pulled a few pound notes from his pocket. In fact, he'd stashed some money aside to surprise her with a dinner out. He ran his hands over the smooth, warm bulge of her belly. "A slap-up feast of fish and chips."

"Ah, well." She unwrapped three rashers of bacon from a wax-paper package, dropped them into the frying pan. "One of these days, we'll be rolling in the money. Sure, I can't make up my mind whether I'll have a Jaguar or a Rolls."

"You'd better decide soon then," He nuzzled his mouth against her warm skin. "Mmm, you're beautiful, Sharon. Let's forget the breakfast, shall we—"

"Ah go on, you daft thing." She grinned and pulled away. "Beautiful, indeed. Look at this." Lifting her red jumper, she stuck out her belly. "Fat as a cow I am. Can't even get my skirt done up now."

"Take a load off your feet then." He nudged her away from the stove. "I'll finish this."

"You're a good man, so you are." Sharon kissed him and sat down at the table. She picked up a blue airmail letter. "Have you read this letter from my sister?"

"I haven't." He broke a couple of eggs next to the bacon. In truth, he hadn't wanted to. Sharon's sister and her husband had emigrated to America the year before and quickly embarked on a vigorous campaign for Sharon and Martin to follow. Almost weekly came glowing reports of their new lifestyle. Dishwashers, a new car, new house. It was the one cloud on his horizon: Sharon wanted to go, he didn't.

Sharon, a convent girl, schooled by the nuns of the Sacred Heart, had become disenchanted with Belfast. There'd been an increase in terrorist activity in the past months: machine-gun attacks, sectarian murders, a bomb blast in the town center the week before. Security Forces had established checkpoints on all main roads and certain areas were considered dangerous. In Sharon's view, the city was no longer livable.

His father was a lapsed Catholic, his mother a Protestant. He'd grown up in the predominantly Protestant Castlereagh area, but had no particular political or religious leanings. For him, Belfast, with all its ugliness and contradictions, was home, the sectarianism part of the fabric of everyday life in Northern Ireland. It was inescapable, the clues all around. Along the Shankhill Road, graffiti said Fuck the Pope and God Save the Queen. On the Falls Road, in Catholic territory, it said Victory to the IRA. You said Londonderry if you were a British Protestant, Derry if you were a Catholic Nationalist. Even the landscape seemed sectarian.

Protestant geography was low hills, rolling farmlands and good soil. Catholics had the mountain slopes, rugged terrain and small farms of stony fields.

Evenings, the TV news would show the IRA events, the funeral processions and car-bomb attacks, but it all seemed remote and distant to him. At the end of their street, they could see the Antrim hills. The Botanic Gardens were a walk away. In their small flat, or going around the corner for a loaf of bread, he felt they were safe, untouched by the bombs and guns and violence in other parts of the city.

As he carried the plates of eggs and bacon to the table, Sharon gasped.

"God, will you look at that, Martin?" She had the newspaper spread out over the table. "See there. That's the place we were last night, isn't it?"

He read over her shoulder. A Catholic deliveryman had been shot to death at the wheel of his car, a few yards away from the Chinese takeaway restaurant where he worked. Two masked men had jumped out of a doorway, fired half a dozen shots at him and driven away.

"What time did it happen?" She leaned closer to read. "Six. I can't believe it. We weren't out of the place five minutes. Five more minutes. We could have been dead ourselves. God, it's terrible, so it is."

"There's been trouble in that area for a while now, Sharon. We should have known better ourselves than to be there." Martin sat at the table, filled now with a vague sense of foreboding. The mood of the morning had been shattered. Outside, he heard a lorry rumble down the road. The distant sound of a helicopter coming from the north. He knew where the conversation was headed.

"If there was a vote tomorrow in Northern Ireland, the IRA wouldn't get five percent of the Catholic vote, do you know that?" Spots of color appeared on Sharon's face. She speared bacon on her fork. "What have they done for anyone, I ask you? Nothing but kill more people."

He said nothing.

"And would you look at this?" She held up the paper for him to see. "There's traffic queues at security checkpoints, so they've got tips now about what to do if your motor overheats."

"Ah well, look on the bright side." He tried to jolly her. "At least we don't have to worry about my bike overheating—"

"I don't know why we stay and put up with it, I really don't." Her eyes were bright blue, angry. "At least Loren and Patrick had sense enough to get out—"

"Sharon." Martin ran his hand across his face. "Don't be starting that again."

She put the newspaper down, fixed her eyes on his face. "Loren says you could finish up at Boston University—"

"We've already talked about this." He picked up the newspaper. "I don't want to go—"

"*You* don't." She grabbed the paper out of his hands. "What about me? What about the baby? You're living in a fool's paradise, Martin. You think you can just carry on your life as though nothing is happening, don't you? We're surrounded by thugs. Thugs who know nothing except killing people."

"They're thugs, I'll grant you that." Martin finished his tea. "But going to America isn't the answer. I'm not letting them run my life and they're not going to drive me away from my own country. This is our home, Sharon."

"Ah God." She shook her head. "Will you listen to yourself? You'd stay here and be a martyr to the cause? You think it's worth dying for? Getting yourself killed to make a political point? What's the good of that? We're not safe here and that's the truth of it. *A man was shot to death, Martin, right outside the restaurant we were at.*''

"And you think nothing like that can happen in America?" He carried their dishes to the sink, ran water over them. "They're shooting each other on the streets there all the time. I don't suppose Loren writes to you about that though, does she?"

"Loren has her own car, Martin." Sharon grabbed his arm. "She didn't even drive when she was here. They've a four-bedroom house, three bathrooms and a big garden for the kiddies. What do we have? A wee flat—"

"And now we get to the real issue." He turned from the sink to look at her. "Belfast isn't the problem, is it? Sure you can ramble on about the violence, but every reason you have for wanting to go to America has to do with money—"

Her face turned red and she burst into tears. "We're still lugging clothes to the launderette. What when the baby comes?"

"Sharon." He folded her into his arms and pressed her close. "Haven't we talked about it? I'll put in a washing machine. Come on." He stroked her hair. "It's difficult right now, with money being tight, but it won't always be like that. Once I finish—"

"I'm just fed up with this bloody place." She sobbed against his shoulder.

"Come on, love." He couldn't bear to see her cry. "Let me finish school, all right? I don't have that much longer, and then we'll look into it. That's a promise."

She nodded and smiled at him through her tears. "I love you, Martin."

"I love you, too." He held her against him for a minute. "Now get a move on or we'll both be late."

HE WHEELED HIS BIKE alongside her down to the bus stop. Their breath rose in clouds of vapor in the morning air. Sharon was quiet and withdrawn, huddled inside her anorak, a red beret pulled down over her curls. The fight, even though they'd made up, hovered like an uneasy presence between them. He looked up at the sky, pale as milk, the leafless trees in black silhouette. At a pedestrian crossing, a beacon flashed, gaudy orange in the monochrome light. He sought words to break the mood.

"See there." He pointed to a woman pushing a pram. "That'll be you in five months or so."

She nodded, shivering, and gave him a wan smile. "So. Here's my bus now."

"Be careful, do you hear?" He caught her face in his hands, looked into her eyes. Blue like forget-me-nots, coal-dark lashes. "I've a surprise for you for later."

She stood on tiptoe to kiss him, fluttered her fingers and darted for the bus.

He caught a fleeting glimpse of her red beret, watched until the bus rolled out of sight and rode his bike to the university.

That night he stopped at a sweetshop and bought her a box of chocolates. Black Magic, her favorite. She wasn't there when he got back to the flat. He put the kettle on for tea, walked to the window and looked outside. It had rained and the street was dark and shining, everything turned bluish-gray by the moon. He washed for dinner, looked at the clock, made the tea. Returned to the window. At half past five, he rang the chemist's, then her parents. There was no answer at either place. At six he walked around to the bus stop, thinking she'd probably missed her bus and he'd meet her walking home. The later bus arrived, but she wasn't on it.

As he walked back to the flat, he saw, from down the

street, the Royal Ulster Constabulary car pulled up to the curb. He watched the car door open. Watched two uniformed RUC men get out, one short, the other tall. The short one turned and saw him approaching. Martin looked up at the bare branches of the trees. A drop of rain fell on his face. Then another one. The tall policemen asked his name. He told them. The policemen looked at each other for a moment, then the tall one opened his mouth to speak.

"Sorry to have to give you the bad news, son," he said. "But, there's been a tragic accident. It's to do with your wife."

CHAPTER ELEVEN

"A MASKED GUNMAN came into the chemist shop while she was working and shot her. Three times," Martin added after a moment. "In the face. By the time they told me, she'd been dead two hours."

Catherine heard her own quick intake of breath. Words whirled in her brain, but she couldn't speak. The enormity of the tragedy seemed unimaginable to her, the pain and anger too much to bear. Tears burned in her throat and she shook her head and squeezed his hand. For a few minutes they just sat there, bound together by his story, the noises around them distant and unconnected.

"I remember this sensation of cold as though something had frozen inside," he said after a while. "But I couldn't seem to grasp what had happened. I had them tell me again because I thought I might have heard wrong. It turned out to be a case of mistaken identity. The Ulster Freedom Fighters thought her brother was in the Sinn Fein, but they'd got the wrong person. She didn't have a brother."

Catherine shook her head. *A mistake.* She looked at him, seeing him as the young husband in love with his wife. Happy, anticipating the birth of their baby. And then in an instant his world was literally shattered. Blown apart by a mistake.

"I left Ireland the following year," he said. "Right after it happened, I thought I would just stay in the flat, I wanted to hold on to her somehow, all her things were still there.

At first they were a sort of comfort, then they became painful reminders. I just kept thinking that if only I'd listened to her, if we'd left as she wanted..."

"So you blamed yourself," Catherine said softly. "Just what you needed, guilt on top of everything else."

He shrugged. "Logically I knew better. But it seemed that a part of me had died with Sharon. For a long time I couldn't imagine how I would go on with my own life." He paused for a moment. "What I'm beginning to realize is that I *can* have a life again. I *can* be happy again."

She sat with her knees up to her chin and stared into the fire. After a moment, she got up, went over to the stereo and selected a Segovia recording. Then she sat on the floor beside him again, her back to the couch. He hadn't moved. Notes of a classical guitar drifted in the air. The fire crackled. Traffic rolled by on Second Street in a low roar of sound. Martin reached for her hand.

"It's funny, I was torn when I came here tonight," he said. "I wanted to see you, but my head was so full of what was going on at Western that I almost called you to cancel. Now none of that seems to matter quite so much. Eating dinner with you and the children, I feel as though I've come in from a cold place."

A moment passed and then they both spoke at once, grinning at each other as one waited for the other to start. And then they weren't smiling and the air became very charged between them, and Catherine realized she was holding her breath because he was about to kiss her. And then he did. Tentatively at first as though to test her reaction. Then again, slow and sweet. Very sweet. Very slow. And they kept kissing, long, slow, sweet kisses. Somewhere in her brain a warning shrieked. It grew louder when he hauled her up on his lap. *Stop. Red light. Stop now.* But she couldn't stop. Lost in sensation, she opened her mouth to his tongue, clutched at his hair. Felt the stir of his erection beneath her. Heard her own involuntary moan. He kissed her neck, her throat, held her so tight she felt her breasts flatten against his chest until she pulled away, out of her mind with wanting him.

Afterward, his expression was as dazed as she knew hers must be. Unless she did something, they would start kissing again, so she got up and went into the kitchen. Martin followed. As she ran water into a glass, she saw her hand shaking.

"Uh...listen." Avoiding his eyes, she walked to the refrigerator and pulled open the door. "I'm not going to sleep with you, okay? I mean, you probably thought that was implied when I invited you over and I'm sorry if I gave you the wrong idea. It's just that it wouldn't be a good thing." She opened the cheese drawer, closed it. Aligned two quart containers of milk. "Not that I'm not attracted to you, but it doesn't feel right."

"I completely agree," he said.

"I mean we've only just met." She lifted the lid off a carton of potato salad, sniffed at the contents. "I'm sure I seem hopelessly old-fashioned, but the thing is, I don't sleep around. Actually, I've never had sex with anyone besides Gary and with him I just wanted it to be over, so naturally I'm cautious."

"Quite rightly so."

"It's not as though either of us is looking to get involved, so I think it would be better if we don't get into situations that could lead to—"

"Sleeping together." He reached over her shoulder and removed the pan of leftover lasagna. "Does this go in the microwave?"

"Huh?" She turned to see him struggling not to laugh. "Okay, what's so funny?"

"You." He took her face in his hands. "Were you expecting an argument? Did you think I was going to throw you down and ravish you with your kids in the next bedroom?"

"Well, I just thought…things seemed to be moving too quickly."

"Maybe we should establish a timetable," he said, amusement still on his face. "No horizontal kissing until the second date, no clothes removed until the third."

I can't wait for the fourth one, she wanted to say, but it didn't seem like a good idea. With the way he was looking at her and the zings that kept charging through her body, she wasn't sure she could hold out until the fourth date. She took the pan of lasagna from him and stuck it in the microwave.

"Here or to go?" She glanced at the clock on the wall. It was ten, thirty minutes past the time she usually went to bed, but sleep was the furthest thing from her mind.

"Here."

BY THE TIME he'd polished off the rest of the lasagna, drank another glass of wine and they'd swapped life stories, Martin was filled with a pleasant sort of lassitude that gave him no incentive to get up and drive back to the marina. Sprawled in front of the fireplace, Catherine curled up at his side, listening to the music on the stereo, to the crackle of the fire, he felt truly happy. At that moment, he thought, as he heard her breathing grow steady and then felt himself drifting off, he wanted nothing else in the world but to be exactly where he was.

Hours later, he awoke to Catherine shaking his shoulder. He sat up, stiff and bleary-eyed. The room was cold and the music had stopped. In the dim light, he squinted at his watch and saw it was after two. With some effort, he pulled himself to his feet, then stood for a moment, dazed and still half-asleep.

Without a word, she took his hand and led him into the bedroom where he flopped down on the bed fully clothed and immediately went back to sleep.

In his dream Sharon had given birth and somehow he hadn't heard about it until days later. When he finally saw the baby, he realized that it was Kenesha Washington and she was screaming. As he tried to quiet her, Eddie Hodges suddenly appeared brandishing a hacksaw. Wildly waving it, Hodges tried to grab the baby. Martin resisted and a battle ensued. As he fought with Hodges, he heard the baby's cries grow louder and more desperate until they eventually awoke him.

For a moment he lay in bed, disoriented. Then in the blue dawn light that filled the small bedroom he saw Catherine sleeping beside him, an arm flung out across the bed. Kenesha's cries, he realized, were his beeper going off. He reached to silence it, then quietly went into the living room and called the unit. Holly had coded again, but the immediate danger was past, the resident informed him. The call was just a heads-up.

Still groggy, he hung up, then stood for a minute looking out onto Second Street and the neon lights of Morrey's Liquor Store across the road. As he watched, a street sweeper rolled by flashing yellow lights. A Long Beach Transit bus pulled up just outside the window in a belch of engine noise and hydraulic doors, and he thought about Peter's asthma and Catherine's concerns that divorce had compromised her children's living standards. And, as illogical as it was, he wanted to make everything right for her.

He bent down to pick up the empty wineglasses they'd used and carried them into the kitchen. The day Sharon had told him she was pregnant, he'd felt a sense of awe, a recognition of the way in which his life was about to change. A feeling of sheer, bursting happiness.

He reached under the sink, found a bottle of detergent and squirted emerald-green liquid over the glasses, then carefully rinsed them and set them in the wooden dish drainer. A pale beam of morning light struck a soap bubble he'd missed on one of the glasses and he watched it tremble for a moment then burst. Standing here in Catherine's tiny kitchen, he recognized that feeling again.

"Did you sleep here all night?" a small voice behind him demanded.

He turned around to see Julie, blond curls and red flannel nightgown, looking up at him, wide-eyed. As he considered what to say, Catherine appeared behind her daughter. She wore an old yellow robe and her eyes were heavy with sleep.

"Martin was very tired last night." She scooped Julie up in her arms. "It wouldn't have been safe for him to drive, so he stayed here."

"Did he sleep in your room?"

Catherine met his eyes over the top of Julie's head.

"Yes he did, sweetie." She set Julie down on the floor. "See how tall Martin is?" The child looked up and nodded. "It wouldn't be very comfortable for him to sleep on the couch, would it?"

"No." Julie giggled. "His feet would hang over the edge." She hopped around on one foot. "Oooh, I've got to go to the bathroom, Mommy. *Bad.*"

"So go then." Catherine grinned.

Filled with admiration and a little envy, Martin watched her move around the kitchen, taking mugs from the cupboard, bread from a blue enamel bin. "You handled that well, I had no idea how to answer her."

"It's something you learn." Catherine measured coffee

into a pot. "What's going on? I thought I heard your beeper go off."

"Holly coded again. She's okay for now, or as okay as she'll ever be, but I need to get over there."

"Want some coffee first?"

He shook his head. Beneath her robe, he could see the frilled neck of a pink flannel nightgown. He took her in his arms and held her and they stood for a moment, arms around each other. The smell of brewing coffee filled the air, steam misted the kitchen windows. He ran a hand slowly down her back, let it linger on the curve of her bottom. Her thigh pressed against his leg and he felt its warmth and then the shiver that ran through her body. With a smile, he pulled away to look at her.

"Are we both thinking the same thing?"

"We are." She pressed closer, and kissed him, light at first and then harder. "Unfortunately," she said after a moment, "I've got two children to get off to school."

"Tonight?" He went into the living room, grabbed his jacket from the chair, pulled it on and dug in his pocket for the car keys. "We could take the children out for pizza... Damn, that won't work, I'm on duty. I probably won't even be able to get away for lunch. What's tomorrow?"

"Wednesday." Catherine grinned, clearly amused. "Listen, Martin—"

"No, I want to see you. I think I've got a late meeting though. The Committee for the Protection and Preservation of Hospital Bureaucracy or some bloody thing like that. I'm trying to get kicked off it. What about Thursday?"

"Holly's surgery." Catherine bit her lip. "It might be kind of frantic."

"Right." A moment passed. He'd almost succeeded in blocking Holly's surgery from his mind and the thought of it now was a dark reminder of the world outside Catherine's cozy home. "Friday then?"

"There's a recital at Julie's school," she said. "A whole bunch of little six-year-old monsters, suddenly transformed into angels." One hand on the doorknob, she hesitated. "I'd invite you, but I'm supposed to meet Gary." She rolled her eyes. "For a little chat."

"All right then." He felt as though he'd been excluded from a warm room, shoved out into the cold again. He stood there, not knowing what to say.

"Hey." Catherine caught the collar of his jacket in both hands, kissed him on the mouth. "Don't look so stricken. Listen, I'm taking the children to the mountains this weekend. Want to join us?"

The sun came out again. He felt his entire face light up, an ear-to-ear grin that he couldn't stop. When he pulled her close again, he could smell her skin, faintly fragrant and still warm from sleep. "Late Saturday night all right?" he asked, his mouth against her neck. "I have to work during the day."

"Late Saturday night's fine, Sunday morning, too, if you like. I'll draw you a map for how to get there." She kissed him again. "You'll have to bring a sleeping bag, or sleep on the couch."

"This will be our second date though," he said, low enough that the children couldn't hear. "So we're allowed some horizontal kissing, right? Or, if you count lunch on the pier, it's the third one, which means we could take off our clothes."

"You are incorrigible." Her palms flat on his chest, she smiled into his eyes. "We'll see."

"God, what an incentive." For a moment, he just looked at her, struck again by how much he wanted her. About to speak, he saw Julie peep around the corner, flutter her fin-

gers and disappear. Then the grin broke out again and
wouldn't go away.

"What's so funny?"

"I feel a bit like a family man going off to work," he
said. "And I like the feeling."

"Ah, but you forgot something." She put her hands on
either side of his face. "A family man can't go off without
a goodbye kiss."

"Mommy." Julie called from inside the house.
"Daddy's on the phone."

"Tell him I'll be right there," she called over her shoulder, then turned to Martin again. "I've really got to go,"
she whispered against his mouth.

From inside the house, Julie's end of the conversation
wafted out to where they stood.

"...his name is Martin," she was saying. "And he was
too tall for the couch so he slept in Mommy's room last
night. "

"GARY THINKS he could do a better job raising the kids,"
she told Martin that evening as they sat in one of Mulligan's wooden booths. He'd found someone to cover his
shift and they'd strolled over to the tavern. "Hearing that
you'd spent the night was all the ammunition he needed.
He went on and on about what a corrupting influence having a man stay over—"

"Did you tell him I was fully dressed?" He regarded
her over a tankard of Guinness. Beer signs blinked red and
green over the long wooden bar. "Did you tell him what
you were wearing?"

"My flannel nightgown and robe?" She grinned.
"You're saying it wasn't seductive?"

"I'd find you seductive if you were wearing full body

armor,'' he said, ''but it wouldn't be my first choice. Are you concerned though?''

''About Gary?'' She frowned for a moment. ''I'm always concerned about what he's going to pull next. He likes to issue threats.''

''Want me to beat him up for you?'' He raised her hand to his mouth, kissed it. ''I'd be more than happy to take him on.''

''I can take care of myself, thanks. Anyway,'' she added, only partly in jest, ''I think you're in enough trouble as it is.'' Rumors were flying around Western that Grossman was considering legal action for the assault on his son in the parking lot. ''But I appreciate the offer.''

He smiled, leaning across the table to touch her face. On a jukebox in the corner, an Irish group was singing something unintelligible. She strained to catch the words, caught him watching her and felt something dissolve inside her.

It was as if they'd invented romance. She'd floated through the day, her thoughts full of him. His voice, his smile, the tragedy of his wife's murder. Waking up to his face next to hers this morning. Twice he'd stopped by her office, once they'd run into each other in the lobby and then, as she was leaving for the day, he'd called to invite her to Mulligan's. With only a slight twinge of guilt, she'd arranged with Darcy to pick up the children; the need to be with him so powerful that she'd turned a blind eye to the little voice in her head that warned things were moving too fast.

Arms entwined, they'd walked to Mulligan's from Western and when they'd stopped to kiss at the edge of the parking lot everything else had fled her mind. When she pulled away, her insides were churning. Please let this be the right thing to do, she prayed, because somehow I've lost control.

"That trip to the mountains this weekend?" Martin lifted his glass to drink some beer. "Does Peter know how to ski?"

"He's never tried."

"I'd like to teach him." He put the glass down, his expression animated. "Physical exercise doesn't have to aggravate his asthma, I'll keep a close eye on him. I want to win him over, Catherine. I want him to see me as a friend not a threat and...damn." The beeper on his belt sounded and he glanced at it. "It's Grossman's office," he said. "I forgot I was supposed to meet with him at six. I'd better go call him." He stood. "Be right back."

"GROSSMAN'S a little irritated that Rita had the nerve to actually express her doubts about surgery for Holly," Martin told her as they walked back to the medical center from Mulligan's. "He's particularly irked that she did it in front of the TV cameras. He'll prevail of course. I suppose you know about the press conference he's holding tomorrow to announce his plan."

She nodded. "I didn't want to spoil the evening."

"Essentially he's rationalized pushing ahead by saying that the whole issue is too complex for Rita to really understand and that I'm just adding to her confusion."

Catherine said nothing. Although her immediate impulse had been to rush to Martin's defense, she wondered whether that might not be the case.

"All I've done is explain the options," he said as though reading her thoughts. "Rita understands that surgery is one of those options. Another option is to allow nature to take its course."

"But you're biased against the surgery, Martin, and I'm sure you didn't try to hide that." He had his arm around her, and as she leaned into it, she felt him tense. "With

Peter, I was overwhelmed by all the decisions I had to make, but at least everyone agreed with what should be done. Rita's got her husband and Grossman giving their opinions and you giving yours, it's got to be torture for her.''

''*If* I thought there was any hope at all,'' he said slowly, ''I would tell Rita to go for the surgery. I'd do it if I had even the faintest hope that this whole thing wasn't a PR stunt so that Grossman can stand in front of the TV cameras and play the hero surgeon.''

''But…'' She thought of something he'd said the night before. ''You know how you said you sometimes felt guilty after your mother died? As though it were your fault?''

He nodded.

''Maybe Rita feels that way, kind of guilty that it was something she did—''

''That makes no sense. ''

''Did it make any sense that you felt guilty about your mother?'' She stopped to look at him. ''Of course it didn't, it was just the way you felt. Surgery might just make her feel that she's doing all she can. And it *is* your opinion against Grossman's. He's a respected surgeon and—''

''Dammit, Catherine.'' He dropped his arm from her shoulders. ''You work in the public relations department, so maybe it's to be expected that you'd let yourself be conned into believing Grossman can perform some sort of medical miracle. It's great press, isn't it? A nice little fairy story.''

''Thanks,'' she said, hurt now. ''You've just given me a great idea. I think I'll quit Western and go and do PR for a tobacco company, or maybe the National Rifle Association. Why not, since I obviously have no moral principles?'' They reached the van and she leaned her back against it, felt a chill that had nothing to do with the night air. "From now on, maybe we should avoid this topic."

"I'm sorry."

"So am I."

"No, I truly am." He put his hands on her shoulders, looked into her eyes. "I shouldn't have said that, I didn't mean to suggest...the thing is, Grossman essentially bribed me. He hinted that the physicians have a discretionary fund that could be used to fund WISH. If I play ball and persuade Rita Hodges to change her mind, he'd recommend using it for ongoing funding."

"Oh God." Catherine shook her head. "I wish I hadn't heard that."

"He told me to consider...how did he put it? The greater good. A single child for whom surgery may or may not be of value, depending upon one's point of view, versus a program that could prevent who knows how many premature births."

"What did you tell him?"

"I laughed."

The rain had intensified while they were talking, and she felt a drop trickle down her face. With his finger, Martin touched her cheek. Behind him, Western glowed an eerie white in the dark night. She caught his hand, brought it to her mouth. Another drop hit her face, then another.

"You're getting soaked," he said.

"You, too." His hair was plastered dark against his head. Water ran down his face.

A moment passed and then she unlocked the side door and, without a word, they both climbed in. He slid the door shut and they sat on the floor, holding each other, her face buried in his collar. She wanted not to think. Of the children at home with a sitter; of tomorrow's press conference and Holly's surgery; of what she was doing with this man. She didn't want to think about any of those things, so when he guided her shoulders down onto the carpet and kissed her, she sank into the sensation as though she were easing into a feather bed.

"I don't want Western to come between us, Catherine," he whispered against her neck. "Let's not allow that to happen."

She agreed and then they were kissing again, rolling around on the floor in a fierce heat of passion that melted guilt and resistance and time. Melted every fiber of her being. Eyes closed, head thrown back, she wrapped her legs around his body, clung to him like a drowning creature. Her hair came loose, spread out across the carpet, damp strands fell across her throat and mouth.

A car's engine started nearby. Headlights momentarily flooded the inside of the van. Startled, she sat up. Martin reached for her hand, pulled her back down beside him.

"Third date," he said

"Hmm?"

"Too many clothes."

In the dim light, she watched as he shrugged off his jacket, sat up as he helped her off with her coat. The rain had seeped through their outer clothes, and as he pulled her on top of him, she felt the damp warmth of his body against her own. They kissed some more and he held her close, murmuring endearments, stroking her face. Her breathing deepened and between kisses he began to slowly undo the buttons of her cardigan.

Her heart and thoughts raced. If she was going to stop him, it should be now, but his fingers were touching her skin and his mouth was driving her crazy and she was like the girl in *Oklahoma!* who couldn't say no and then it was too late because all the buttons were undone and he was looking at her breasts bulging out of their white cotton cups.

An image of the high-school kid who had dated her on a dare filled her brain for an instant, but Martin lowered his head to the tops of her breasts and kissed them and the old painful memory faded. He smiled up at her, the sweetly tender smile of a boy who has just unwrapped a treasured gift and, she decided, it was a gift she wanted him to have. She sat up, unclasped her bra and let her breasts tumble free. He smiled again, cupped them in his hands, brought them to his mouth and kissed one, then the other. A shudder of desire made her moan aloud.

"Hold on." He suddenly moved away from her. "I'm being attacked."

With a grin, he removed one of Peter's toy soldiers that had lodged under his hip and held it out for her to see. She looked from her son's toy in the palm of his hand, to her opened sweater and unfastened bra. Maternal and sexual urges briefly collided. Sheltered Catherine, the PTA mom, the cookie baker, baring her breasts to a blue-eyed Irish doctor. In the back of her Dodge van no less. She felt completely unlike herself, wanton and sensual, a little guilty, but more turned on than she'd ever been in her life. When he pulled her close and kissed her again, any remnant of resistance melted.

"Fourth date," she breathed after she could no longer stand the clothes that separated them. "Make love to me."

Eyes heavy lidded, he raised himself to look at her. "You're sure?" His voice was thick. "You're really sure?"

"Please." Her hips moved under him in a growing frenzy, as wild and out of control as if a demon had possessed her. "Do it. Please." The cardigan had come off her shoulders, and the bra was a tangled mess that had worked its way behind her. He stripped the garments both off and flung them aside, pushed her skirt up and, in one movement, slid her tights and panties over her hips and down below her knees all the while kissing her neck and breasts until she thought she would explode.

Breath coming in quick gasps, she fumbled at his belt, unzipped his fly. As she took him in her hand, she heard her own intake of breath and then a loud rap on the side of the van. A moment later, headlights filled the interior again.

"What the hell?" Martin sat up to peer through the window, then pushed open the door and climbed out of the van, zipping his pants as he left. The air from the open door hit her overheated body like a shower of ice water. For a moment, she lay sprawled on the floor, pulse racing. Then she looked down at herself: naked breasts, the skirt around her waist. Her face burned. She was someone she didn't even recognize. In her entire thirty-four years, nothing like it had ever happened to her. Even the knowledge that no one could have seen through the van's closed mini-blinds didn't help. By the time he returned, she had put the bra and cardigan back on, and was on her knees, pulling up her tights.

"I didn't see anyone, it was probably some kids." He climbed back inside, sat with his back against the van's wall, knees to his chin. "Whoever it was had a great sense of timing though."

"Well, it's late." She buttoned the cardigan, straightened her skirt and found she couldn't look at him. She sat against the opposite wall and braided her hair. "I should probably go."

"Catherine." He touched her shoe with his foot. "What is it?"

"Nothing."

"Come on." He watched her face. "What was it you said yesterday about trust? Obviously something is wrong. Don't you trust me enough to tell me?"

"I'm just...I feel like a slut, Martin. What we were doing. I mean, I felt like an animal in heat." Her gaze fell on Julie's plastic pail, Peter's rubber waders, and she burst into tears. "I'm a mother, for God's sake. The kids' toys are all over the van and all I wanted was to get laid."

"Come here." With one hand, he reached for her, pulled her beside him and put his arm around her shoulder. "So being a mother means you shouldn't have sexual needs? That's quite an interesting theory."

"Stop." She pushed his arm. "I guess I wasn't quite ready for the fourth-date stuff." Embarrassed now at her outburst, she blew her nose. "I told you yesterday that I didn't sleep around, and I don't. And here we are in the parking lot, for God's sake."

"Listen—" he took her face in his hands "—I never thought of this as a date, or of us even dating in that sense. It's much more than that for me, and I hope it is for you too, right?"

She nodded.

"Good, so forget the timetables." He kissed her lips. "The next time lust overtakes us, we'll pick a more discreet place, okay?"

"I don't know," she said after a moment. "Maybe it's time I broadened my experiences. They've been kind of limited to the missionary position, in bed, in a nightgown. Flannel in the winter, cotton in the summer."

"Who wore the nightgown? You or Gary?"

"Gary. It turned him on." He laughed and she relaxed against his shoulder. Rain pattered on the roof of the van. She felt the warmth of his body next to her, heard the sound of his breathing. *Wondered whether she might be in love with him.* "You probably think I'm nuts, huh?"

"I think you've spent so long thinking of everyone else's needs, that you feel guilty when you do something that's just for you."

"Well, not just for me." She shot him a sideways glance. "You seemed to be enjoying it, too."

"I was." He kissed the tip of her nose. "I want you as desperately as I've wanted anything in my life, but I also want this to be good for us. We'll go slow, all right? Whenever you don't feel comfortable, just tell me. I can wait. I'm in this for the long haul."

"THE KIDS WERE FINE," Darcy said. "Actually, it was kind of fun baby-sitting them. Julie and I talked girl stuff. She thinks it's cool that you've got a boyfriend, but she said he talks funny." She looked at Catherine for a moment. "Nadia wasn't quite so enthusiastic."

"Nadia?" The floaty, exhilarated feeling she'd had ever since she'd kissed Martin good-night was replaced by a sickening dread. "You told Nadia I was with Martin?"

"Julie did. And I might as well give you all the bad news at once. She also told your mother."

"I need some wine." She got up and found the Cabernet left from the night before. "Want some?" Darcy nodded, and Catherine poured wine into two glasses, carried them over to the table. "I don't need to hear what my mother had to say, I can already imagine her words. What about Nadia?"

Darcy rolled her eyes. "Jeez, that voice of hers. I can't believe the two of you were ever friends. She should have been a kindergarten teacher. *'Now Catherine,'"* she mimicked Nadia's high-pitched tone. *"'It's really very naughty of you to be carrying on with that bad Dr. Connaughton.'"*

Catherine drank some wine. "What *exactly* did she say?"

"Just that she and Gary were concerned about the…" With her forefingers, she drew quotes in the air. "'Quality of the children's home life' and 'the message they were getting from your having men sleep over.'"

Elbows on the table, face cupped in her hands, Catherine stared at Darcy. "Maybe I should get a notarized statement saying we were both fully clothed." Last night, at least, that was true. Tonight, while she'd been rolling around with Martin, half-naked in the back of the van, someone else had put her children to bed.

"How was Peter?" she asked.

Darcy wiggled her hand. "His nose is a little out of joint, but he'll be okay."

"Out of joint? Because of Martin?"

"Yeah, I guess. He kept talking about how his dad did this and his dad did that. I think he's got this idea in his head that you and Gary are going to get back together."

Catherine drank some more wine and wondered whether she should rescind her invitation to have Martin join them in the mountains. She'd thought Peter would enjoy having a skiing lesson, but things were spinning frighteningly close to out of control. She would have a talk with Peter in the morning, she decided.

"Quit worrying about the kids, okay?" Darcy peered at her. "You deserve some grown-up fun once in a while. And the kids need a break from you, too." She drank some wine. "Let's get to the important things. You still like this doctor guy?"

"Oh, Darcy…" Unable to find the words, Catherine just shook her head. "'Like' doesn't describe it. I've never met anyone like him. He's just incredible. Sensitive, funny, sexy as hell."

"Sounds like you've moved on from the just-friends thing?"

"Yeah." She nodded slowly. "Guess I was a bit naive about that, huh? When I'm around him, my brain turns to mush."

Darcy grinned and shook her head.

"Okay, I concede." From the cupboard, Catherine dug out the box of Little Debbies they'd started the night she'd told Darcy that she found Martin very attractive. Two left. At this rate, by the time he actually made love to her, she'd weigh a ton. She tossed one to Darcy, unwrapped the other one. "I can't explain it, I just feel safe with him. I trust him and that's something I never felt about Gary."

"Uh-oh," Darcy said. "Red flag."

Catherine broke off a piece of cake. "What?"

"God, I love Little Debbies," Darcy said around a mouthful of Banana Twist. "They are so junk-foody and awful for you and they just taste so damn good."

"Yeah, I know. Little Debbies and wine." She grinned. "Disgusting, huh? So why the red flag?"

"Remember what you said just now about being naive? You're doing it again. You don't know this guy enough to feel safe with him, and the trust thing is just nuts. He's a guy, for God's sake."

CHAPTER TWELVE

SOME DAYS START OFF poorly and go downhill from there, Martin decided as he stood in Derek Petrelli's office. This was definitely one of them. Three new admissions, a brief verbal skirmish with Eddie Hodges and the looming prospect of the news conference at noon. Not only that, but he'd developed a definite dislike for Petrelli.

"Actually, I'm looking for Catherine," he said. "We're supposed to go over some media plans."

"Have a seat." Petrelli waved at the chair beside his desk. "She should be in any time now." He sipped some coffee. "Although punctuality is not her strong suit."

"Have her ring me, will you?" Martin decided he wasn't in the mood for this, but as he turned to leave, Catherine appeared in the doorway. She wore a long red sweater, short black skirt, black hose and flat shoes. Her hair hung loose around her shoulders. A vivid and erotic image of her breasts in his hands the night before momentarily disconcerted him. She smiled at him, he winked back at her and the day seemed much brighter. What he wanted more than anything else at that moment was to be alone with her again.

"Ah good morning, Ms. Prentice," Petrelli said. "Hope we didn't drag you out of bed at too early an hour."

"Don't give me that crap, Derek. I'm fifteen minutes early." She brushed Martin's shoulder with her hand as she passed. "Let me grab some coffee and we'll get to work."

She shifted her briefcase to the other hand and looked at Derek. "I just got beeped by Claire Ovendon. Some of the nurses are going to stage a demonstration at noon to protest staffing cutbacks. They say patient care is being compromised. Someone's already called Channel 4. Can you handle that while Martin and I work on his comments for the news conference?"

"You take care of the nurses," Petrelli said. "I'll work with Dr. Connaughton on the responses—"

"Derek, I'd really rather work with Mar...Dr. Connaughton on this." Her face colored slightly. "We've already discussed some of the issues—"

"I want you to take care of the demonstration," Petrelli repeated. "I'm well aware of Dr. Connaughton's issues."

A tense silence filled the air. Martin glanced at Catherine. As much as he wanted to intervene, he suspected that nothing he said was likely to dissuade Petrelli. And refusing to do the conference might make things more difficult for her. As he sought a way out of the impasse, Catherine's beeper sounded.

She glanced at the number on the display screen, then looked at Derek. "It's nursing administration—"

"Better get over there." He waggled his eyebrows at her. "Pronto."

"Come on, Derek—" she brushed the hair off her face "—Martin and I have already discussed this. I'd really like to work on the press conference instead—"

Petrelli sat back in his chair, raised his eyes to the ceiling, let the silence lengthen. "A certain administrative meeting comes to mind," he said slowly. "Need I remind you of Ed Jordan's comments—"

"Skip it, okay?" Her face scarlet, Catherine headed for the door. "Sorry about this," she murmured to Martin. "I'll call you later."

"I sense our Ms. Prentice is having a bit of a problem with objectivity," Petrelli said after Catherine left. "She's rather enamored of you, I think."

Martin looked at him for a moment. "Listen, Petrelli, let's get something straight. I agreed to cooperate and I'll keep my word, but the next smarmy, insinuating remark I hear from you, I'm through. You can forget about me co-operating with the press—in fact, I'll say any damn thing that comes to mind. Got it?"

"I think I understand your point of view, Dr. Connaughton." His face impassive, Petrelli rose and moved to a table by the window. "If you'd like to have a seat, we'll get to work. We need to create some sound bites. First, we'll have to come up with some sort of statement about Holly's current health status. They'll want to know if you still consider her too frail for surgery, and of course, you'll—"

"Her condition hasn't changed." He exhaled. "She can't breathe without a respirator. She hasn't digested food. She hasn't grown. We've managed to lower her oxygen requirements slightly, but that's about it."

"Hmm." Petrelli chewed the end of his pen. "Let's see. Something about encouraging progress in the past few days."

AN HOUR LATER, disgruntled and feeling tainted by the interaction with Petrelli, Martin stood in the NICU, arms folded across his chest, listening to Valerie explain why she'd used epinephrine to resuscitate a frail 26-weeker in the delivery room.

"Her lungs expanded a little," Valerie said, "so I squeezed the bag, thinking that she would either improve— or she wouldn't and we'd stop." She shrugged. "The thing is, she looked terrible, but once we got her up here, her blood gasses were fine and her skin color's okay."

"I still think epinephrine's a bit radical," Martin said. He tapped his finger against a monitor that appeared to be malfunctioning and a piercing alarm filled the air. He swore and readjusted the settings. "Damn," he muttered. "Does anything around here work the way it's supposed to?"

"Someone's a little cranky this morning." Valerie's lips curved in a slight smile. "The course of true love not running smoothly?"

"Val—"

"I'm a big girl," she said. "You've moved on, I understand." She shrugged. "These things happen. Be careful though. The gossip mill loves fresh meat."

Martin looked at her, counted slowly to ten, then moved on to Holly's bassinet in time to catch the end of a conversation between a nurse and a respiratory technologist.

"...I mean, ever since the triplets arrived, people have been sending money to the hospital," the nurse said. "I've *seen* Hodges stuffing checks in his pocket. You know damn well that money's not going into a trust fund for the kids—"

"Hell no, it's probably going to the nearest liquor store." The respiratory tech rolled his eyes. "Yesterday, he showed me a check for a hundred bucks. What really pisses me off is the way he comes across like this model father, and half the time he's here you can smell beer on his breath."

Martin walked away before he heard more. He'd suspected Hodges of pocketing donations meant for the babies. It made the idea of Western picking up the tab—and his own participation in the news conference—even more of a farce. When he was with Catherine, he could ignore the twinge of conscience. Away from her, the doubts set in. He moved to examine one of the new admissions. As he put the stethoscope to the baby's chest, he heard the child's breath, like the squeak of a rubber toy.

"Sounds like he's snorting." Graham came up beside him.

"He's got a leak around his tube. It's not one of *his* better days either." Martin took his stethoscope off, folded it and stuffed it in his pocket.

"Not to add to your burdens," Graham said, "but Rita Hodges is looking for you."

Martin found Rita drinking black coffee in the parents' lounge. For a moment, he stood in the doorway watching her. She sat on the edge of an orange vinyl couch, head bowed, shoulders hunched, knees close together as though trying to take up as little space as possible. She wore a navy parka, jeans, tennis shoes and sunglasses.

"Rita." He leaned against the jamb. "Dr. Graham said you were looking for me."

"Eddie's real mad at me." She stared at him. "We got into this big fight."

"About Holly?" He came into the room, sat on the arm of one of the chairs. "Was it about the surgery?"

"Yeah. Dr. Grossman wants to do it Thursday, and I haven't signed that consent thing yet..." She looked down at her hands, red with short, bitten nubs of nails, and started to cry.

"Rita." Struck by a sudden suspicion, he crouched on the floor beside her. "Take off your glasses."

She hesitated momentarily, then removed them. One eye was purple and swollen shut. A bruise ran across the top of one eyebrow. She met his eyes for a minute, then her face crumpled.

"Did Eddie do this?"

She nodded and dabbed her eyes. "I'm sorry, Dr. C."

"For what?"

"I don't know. I'm just...I don't know who to talk to. You know how we talked about surgery and everything? I got so confused about what to do and I got this medical book from the library and when Eddie saw it last night he went into this rage—''

Martin got up and began pacing the small room.

''He starts saying all this stuff about how I'm a bad mother and I don't love Holly, then he starts hitting me.'' She looked at him through her tears. ''It's not true, Dr. C. I love Holly. I love all my kids, I just want to do what best for them.''

He looked at Rita's bruises, thought of Eddie's posturing for the TV cameras and imagined sinking a fist into the man's face. Not trusting himself to speak, he stared up at the ceiling, counting acoustic tiles until he'd calmed down.

Rita blew her nose. ''So anyway, when I get here this morning, Dr. Grossman comes up to the NICU and says he wants to talk to me. He asks me if I've had breakfast and I said no and he takes me across the street to Hoff's Hut.'' Her eyes widened. ''I couldn't believe it, this big important doctor taking me to breakfast—''

''What did he say, Rita?''

''Well, he starts talking about this surgery that Holly needs and how she won't survive without it. He said it would be this medical milestone because she's so little, and that if I was a responsible mother I'd want her to have it.''

''And what did you tell him?''

Her face clouded. ''See, that's the bad part. I mean first there's Eddie and the way he is, then Dr. Grossman says all this stuff and then he says that if I didn't agree, the hospital could get a court order and I could lose Holly.'' She bit her lip and tears welled in her eyes. ''He said if that happened I could lose the other kids, too.''

Anger coursing like an infection through his blood, Martin was on his way to confront Grossman when he ran into

Petrelli coming out of the administrative suite. With a brief nod, Martin brushed past the public relations manager.

"Oooh, whoa there." Petrelli held out an arm to stay him. "Someone's in a tearing hurry. Are we all ready to meet the press?"

"No, we're not. As a matter of fact, we've changed our mind."

"Dr. Connaughton—" Petrelli's expression was quizzical "—please tell me you're not serious."

"I'm not doing the damn thing," Martin struggled to keep his temper under control. "I'm not even sure I still want to work for this bloody hospital anymore. I'm on my way in to see Grossman and—"

"Dr. Grossman had an emergency meeting to attend in San Francisco today. I just spoke with his secretary." Petrelli looked at the leather folder he held in his hands. "All the arrangements for the press conference have been made, Dr. Connaughton. May I ask what's happened to make you change your mind? Is there something I can help you with?"

"Is it public knowledge that we coerce parents into agreeing to surgery? Is the press aware of our policy?"

"Coerce?" Petrelli frowned. "The standard accepted care for Holly's condition is to close the lesion immediately. *That's* our policy. Dr. Grossman merely explained this to the baby's mother—"

"It's also our policy to allow parents the choice of whether they want surgery, something Grossman apparently failed to mention."

Petrelli rocked on his heels. "I'm quite sure Dr. Grossman fully explained the situation—"

"And I'm equally sure he didn't. Furthermore, I'm not participating in this bloody charade of a press conference—"

Petrelli frowned again. "I really wish you would reconsider. I know that Mr. Jordan and Dr. Grossman have tried very hard to make you understand the value of good public relations to Western—"

"They have, and I'm not a convert."

"That's really too bad." He looked at Martin for a minute, his eyes flat and expressionless. "Because your refusal could make things rather difficult for Ms. Prentice."

Martin said nothing.

"Public relations assistants are a dime a dozen, you see." He stared down at his polished loafers for a moment. "Her demeanor at the administrative meeting alone would be ample reason to dismiss her. So..." He gave Martin a level look. "Let me just say that if you don't do the press conference, I will find it necessary to terminate her employment."

AT NOON, Martin sat before a bank of microphones in the administrative conference room listening to Ed Jordan explain why Western had decided to absorb the cost of Holly's surgery. On the lectern in front of him Petrelli's sheet of approved responses lay facedown.

A pulse in his temple throbbed. He searched in vain for Catherine. Petrelli, he suspected, had her occupied elsewhere. Jordan took a few questions from the press, then attention turned to Martin.

"Dr. Connaughton. How *is* Holly doing?" a female reporter asked.

"She's a fighter," he said. "She's hanging in there."

The reporter frowned. "Has her condition improved?"

"As I said, she's a fighter. She's extremely fragile, but we're doing all we can for her. Under the circumstances, she's as well as can be expected."

"Do you expect her to be discharged any time soon?"

Martin looked at the woman. "Not before Christmas."

"Christmas is a week away, Dr. Connaughton." Her tight smile did not suggest amusement.

"Dr. Connaughton—" someone waved a notebook "—this surgery that's planned for Holly? Will it allow her to lead a normal childhood? Ride a bike, play ball, that sort of thing?"

"Nothing is certain in medicine."

"Can you be more specific?"

Martin stared down at his hands and imagined answering truthfully. With surgery, Holly's prognosis is poor. Without it, poorer. Either way, she'll have problems with respiration. She has significant hydrocephalus or water on the brain. She also has a malformation at the base of her brain that will cause her neurological problems. With or without surgery she'll probably have no bladder or bowel function. In fact, she'll probably do little more than just vegetate. His stomach tensed as he searched for something positive to say. "The surgery is palliative." He paused. "It will make Holly more comfortable."

Uncomfortable with the lie, Martin barely heard the next question. He wanted to be somewhere else. Far away. As he considered possible avenues of escape, he saw Petrelli walk up to the podium and tap at his watch, signaling to the audience that the conference was over. Eddie Hodges left the podium, trailed by Rita. Ed Jordan followed on her heels. All three were soon surrounded. Martin took the steps on the opposite side and almost collided with the first reporter who had questioned him.

"Dr. Connaughton—" she caught his arm, stood so close to his face, he felt her breath "—I have some follow-up questions. Look, this kid is in pretty bad shape, isn't she?" She glanced at a sheet of paper in her hand, and without waiting for his response, reeled off a list of Holly's medical problems. "Most experts I've talked to say she's not likely to recover."

Martin shrugged. "Nothing is ever completely certain."

"But you yourself said last week you weren't optimistic."

He studied her face. The crimson lips, the heavily mascaraed eyes. He felt her waiting, poised to capture the pronouncement that would become the twenty-second sound bite. "At the moment," he said, unable to maintain the charade any longer, "I'm not particularly optimistic about anything."

FOLLOWING THE press conference, Martin sat through an interview with the *Tribune* reporter that did nothing to restore his mood. If he showered for a week, he couldn't wash away the soil that seemed to have seeped through every pore in his body. He thought of his responses, the platitudes he'd spouted, and cringed. *Happy Christmas, Holly. I've sold you out.*

Back in the NICU, he heard Catherine call his name and turned to see her coming toward him, a green gown over her street clothes.

"Hi." She smiled at him, slightly breathless, face flushed, glossy brown hair pulled back into a ponytail. "God, what a crazy day. You took off so fast after the news conference, I didn't even see you leave."

"I'd had all I could take." He rubbed the back of his neck, found it difficult to meet her eyes.

"I could tell, just watching you. I came in just as you started taking questions." She studied his face for a moment. "Listen, Martin, I'm really sorry about what happened this morning, I had no idea Derek would pull something like that…" Her smile faded slightly. "Hey, are you okay?"

"Fine." He flipped through a chart. "Were you happy with the way things went?"

"Reasonably. We had all the major TV stations. A couple of radio stations. The *Tribune*. Derek was pleased with the way it went, Jordan, too."

"Well, that's the important thing, isn't it?" He put the chart down. "Listen, we're getting a couple of new admissions—"

"Hey." She looked at him, her eyes puzzled. "What's wrong? You seem kind of, I don't know, distant. Do you feel badly about the way the press conference went?"

"It's over," he said with a shrug. "So let's forget it, all right?"

"But it's still bothering you, and I feel responsible."

"You've no reason to," he said. "It was my decision to do the thing."

"And now you wish you hadn't, right?" She touched his arm. "Look at me, Martin. Think about it for a minute. I know your feelings about Holly's surgery, but what if you *had* said what you really thought? I mean, what if you'd said, 'Oh yeah, this is all a farce. We shouldn't be treating this kid.' The hospital's not going to back down so what difference would it have made?"

"Other than you having to explain to your boss what went wrong? I don't know. Maybe it would only matter to me."

She frowned. "What do you mean?"

"Nothing. Forget it." On the other side of the unit, the transport team wheeled in a new admission. Martin pointed to the green scrub-suited figures. "Any minute now they're going to come and get me..."

"What's happened since last night?" Her face was troubled. "I feel as though I've done something, and I don't really know what it is."

He shifted his weight, looked at her, looked across at the transport team, back at her. "Forget it."

She stared at him for a minute. "Look, I just want to understand what's going on, okay? You're acting like a stranger. What is it?"

He said nothing. His thoughts were like tangled yarn, hopelessly raveled. He knew what he wanted. Catherine. With her he'd seen beyond the black void of loneliness. Still, he couldn't escape the image of Rita Hodges's bruised face. What he wanted came with a price and he wasn't sure he could live with himself if he went on paying it. Weary suddenly, he just wanted to retreat.

Catherine stood with her arms at her sides, looking up at him. Her eyes softened. "I care about you," she said quietly. "A lot. If something is wrong, or if things have changed for you, then tell me, okay? I might not like it, but I'd rather know. Don't shut me out like this. "

Across the unit, someone called his name. He signaled he'd heard. "I don't know what to tell you, Catherine. It's everything. Nothing. I don't know."

"Maybe you need a break from Western," she said. "I'm taking the kids ice-skating tonight. Want to join us?"

"Thanks." With his foot, he hit the seat of a chair, watched it spin for a moment. "But I don't think I'd be very good company."

"Dammit." Her eyes bright with anger, she clutched at her hair. "This kind of thing makes me want to scream. Clearly something is wrong. Why can't you just tell me what it is? Have *I* done something?"

"No. It's me." He ran his hand across his face, wanted just to end the exchange. "I need to go, I'm sorry."

"Fine." She studied his face for a moment. "But the next time you tell someone you're in for the long haul, I'd suggest you think about what that really means."

CHAPTER THIRTEEN

"MOMMY." Julie rapped on the bathroom door. "Peter called me a weirdo."

"Well, she stuck her dumb Barbie in my face," Peter said.

"She was just giving you a little kiss." Julie giggled. "She said you're her boyfriend."

Catherine heard Peter's howl of indignation. "Listen you guys, just be good for a little while, okay? I'll be out in five minutes." She lay in the tub, her hair pinned in a knot on the top of her head, her body submerged in scented aqua water. All evening she'd managed to keep her emotions in check. Hand in hand with the kids, she'd skated around the rink, smiling, refusing to admit thoughts of Martin. But now, even as she willed herself not to think about him, she realized her ears were tuned to the phone.

"Mom." Peter rapped again. "I'm hungry. When are you coming out?"

"Five minutes, Peter, I just told you."

She wanted to sit in the tub and cry. Wallow in her misery. Analyze what had gone wrong. *Analyze.* She threw her sponge against the wall. Who was she fooling? He'd changed—literally overnight. Convinced her they had something special and shown up the next day acting like a distant stranger. The answer was so damn obvious. He'd gone from her to another woman. She just didn't want to see it. The way she hadn't wanted to see Gary's affair with Nadia.

She slowly soaped her breasts and arms, looked down at her body in the steaming water. Recalled the feeling of Martin's mouth on hers. The graze of his stubble against her cheek. His body hard against her own. Desire pulsed through her, tugged at her stomach. Needs, denied out of necessity after Gary's rejection, clamored now to be met. Damn him. He'd walked out on her, just as her father had, just as Gary had. What made it worse, she'd actually believed he might be different.

"Mommy," Julie called. "When are you coming out?"

"Now, sweetie." Catherine climbed out of the tub, dried herself with a rough towel, dressed and pulled on jeans and a sweater. She started to dry her hair then realized she wouldn't be able to hear the phone over the noise of the drier, so she turned it off. Then, furious with herself, she turned it on full blast. Not loud enough to drown out the phone though. When it rang she bolted into the living room. *Please, please, please,* she muttered under her breath.

The ringing stopped.

"D'you get it?" She looked at Peter, stretched out on the floor in private communion with a Nintendo game.

He nodded, his eyes fixed on the game.

"Who was it?"

"I don't know. It was a wrong number. Mom, what's for dinner?"

"Chicken." Disappointment rose like a lump in her throat. "Peter, look at me for a minute. Are you sure it was a wrong number? Was it a man or a woman?"

"A man."

"Did he ask for me by name?"

"Jeez, Mom." He shot her an exasperated look. "It was

some guy who wanted to speak to a Jose Gonzalez, okay? What's with you anyway?''

What *was* with her? She looked at her son, waiting for dinner while his mother obsessed over a man she hardly knew. Good question. She'd gotten her priorities confused. *That's* what was with her.

"MY EX OWNS a chain of gourmet markets.'' The blonde smiled at Martin across the flickering candles on the table of the Newport Beach restaurant. The light from the flames glanced off her diamond earrings. "They're in all the up-scale areas. Merchant Michael's. You may have heard of them?''

Martin shook his head, struggled to keep his mind from drifting. As he'd left the unit, Tim Graham had reminded him about a blind date arranged weeks ago that Martin had completely forgotten. The meeting he might have used as an excuse had been canceled. Too late to back out, he'd reluctantly let himself be dragged along, but his thoughts were elsewhere.

"They have a *wonderful* line in pâté. The duck with truffles is absolutely to die for. And the chanterelles with cracked black pepper...?'' She reached over and tapped his arm with a long scarlet nail. "*Omigod.* Orgasm time.''

"Do they sell tins of stew?''

"Excuse me?''

"Tinned stew. I quite like it. Corned beef's nice too, especially with a bit of HP Sauce. I like to wash it all down with a pint of Guinness.''

The woman smiled uncertainly and turned to Tim's wife. "I don't know about you, Ruthie, but I need to visit the little girls' room.'' Both women gathered their purses, rose and headed off across the restaurant.

"So what d'you think of her?" Tim grinned at Martin. "Attractive, isn't she?"

His thoughts on Catherine, Martin nodded a vague assent. The day's events lodged heavily, like an ill-digested meal. He'd sold out for Catherine and then let her down. And despite Rita's concerns, Holly's surgery would take place as planned. Grossman would be the star of the evening news. Across the table, he realized, Tim had launched into a story about his wife.

"...so she says, 'Do whatever you like.'" He imitated his wife with a mincing falsetto. "Of course, that means don't do whatever you like."

"That's the way it works, is it?"

"Right." Tim drank some wine. "That's how wives are. Do whatever you like, but don't do it. I tell you, sometimes I look back to the good old days when I only had myself to think of." He smiled nostalgically. "Ah, freedom."

"You miss it?"

"*Aagh*, I don't know. Some days, when I come home after a bitch of a day and Ruth's on a tear about one thing or another—usually what I have or haven't done, I guess I think about the single days." He took a bread stick from a wicker basket on the table, broke it in two. "There's other days though... It doesn't matter what's gone on in the unit, when I get home, Ruth and the kids put everything into perspective."

"Grossman told me that my life needs balance," Martin said. The words were out before he'd had time to consider them. "He said it improves clinical judgment."

"He's right." Tim met Martin's eyes. "Work's only part of the equation. I mean, when I'm there, I'm there one hundred percent, but don't call me in the middle of the night when I'm not on duty. I've got another life." He thought for a minute. "It's more than that though. You need someone you can be yourself with, let your guard down once in a while.'' His expression turned quizzical. "How come you mentioned Grossman's comment? Don't tell me you're actually considering his advice.''

Martin grinned. "What do you think?''

"I'm surprised it even registered.''

Martin stared across the restaurant. An image of Catherine's face floated across his consciousness. He'd seen the hurt in her eyes this afternoon, had wanted to reach out, make a conciliatory gesture, but he hadn't been able to find the words. Out of habit, he'd retreated behind the wall that now seemed higher than ever. His mind was still on Catherine, when the two women returned from the rest room, but he forced it in another direction. Grossman was a train barreling down the track to surgery, with Holly his passenger. His own task, he knew with absolute clarity, was to derail it. His action would be an atonement of sorts. The only way he could live with his conscience.

After that, he would allow himself to think about Catherine again.

"HEY, FORGET ABOUT HIM,'' Darcy said from her customary spot at the kitchen table. "Let me fix you up with someone else.''

"No thanks.'' Catherine stared at the recipe for the third time, then glanced up at Darcy. "Damn, I don't remember if I put any baking soda in—''

"That's what you get for going on a baking binge at ten o'clock at night.''

"Therapy.'' Catherine took a pinch of cookie dough, estimated the calorie count, shrugged, and washed it down with a sip of wine. In the oven, a tray of chocolate chip cookies slowly browned. Oatmeal raisin cookies cooled on the counter. She'd started to review a pecan pie recipe when she realized her therapeutic session was getting out of control. Still, at least she'd sorted things out in her mind. Bottom line: she didn't need one more man screwing up her life.

"So Gary's threatening you again?" Darcy had been there to overhear Gary's call just after the children went to bed.

"Ever since he heard about Martin. He pumps Julie for details about 'Mommy's boyfriend' and then blows everything out of proportion. He makes it sound as though we're practically living together." She shot Darcy a wry grin. "Little does he know, huh?" With one hand, she opened the oven, bent to peer inside. Hot air blasted her face. "Anyway, I'm getting sick of his damn threats, At first I took them seriously, but now I'm beginning to think he doesn't really want the kids, he just wants to intimidate me and make my life difficult."

"Speaking of making life difficult, I saw your guy on the news again talking about the triplets," Darcy said. "He didn't look too happy to be there though."

"He wasn't." Catherine took a deep breath. *Do not cry.* "And he's not my guy."

"Cath—"

"I'm fine." She grabbed a paper towel and blew her nose.

"I warned you he'd be trouble," Darcy said. "I mean, maybe he's great and everything, but so many guys are like that. One minute you're the most wonderful thing they've ever seen, and the next it's 'Who the hell are you?' Right now, he's probably out there telling his story to someone else."

Catherine mashed cookie crumbs with her index finger. The discussion felt disloyal somehow. She got up, went to the refrigerator, searching for something to fill the emptiness inside. "I just hate the way I feel right now." She closed the door. Food wasn't the answer, she'd learned that after Gary left. Ten pounds later. "I'm behaving like an idiot," she said after she'd sat down again. "I'm not a teenager, I've got two kids to support. A job to do, and all I can think about is Martin. Every time the phone rings, I think it might be him. Before all this happened, I was content—"

Darcy sniffed the air, got up and checked the oven. "Uh-oh." She pulled out a tray of cookies. "You're letting these things burn." She ran a spatula under the cookies, dumped them on a plate and brought it over to the table. "You *thought* you were content," she corrected.

"No." Catherine fished a cookie crumb out of her wine. "I *was.*"

"Listen, you might think you had everything you needed, but you didn't. I mean, you've got to have more in your life than kids and work." She shrugged. "This guy's just the wrong one for you. Maybe he got scared. He told you about his wife and maybe that made him feel closer to you than he wants to admit."

"You think?" Hating herself, she couldn't help hoping.

"Maybe." Darcy's doubtful expression belied her response.

"God, it's so embarrassing." Catherine stared at the cookie in her hand. "If someone hadn't knocked on the side of the van, we would have made love right there in the parking lot."

"So you were horny. Big deal. When was the last time you had sex?"

She tried to do a quick mental calculation, then gave up. "Probably the consolation screw Gary gave me before he told me he was in love with Nadia. First sex we'd had for six months."

"There you go then. You've got the hots."

"I have, but only for Martin." The wine had loosened her tongue, caused her to ignore her resolution. "I think I might be in love with him." She held up her thumb and index finger. "Just a teeny bit."

"Nah—" Darcy flapped her hand "—you're not in love. You're in lust. Big difference."

Catherine shrugged. Maybe Darcy had a point. Nothing had prepared her for the explosion of feeling she'd had with Martin. Even now, thinking about it made her stomach lurch. Darcy, she realized, had launched into a story about losing her virginity.

"...and I was fifteen." She poured more wine into their glasses. "Back in Saint Louis. This Italian guy, Antonio Bongiavanni. He lived in a boardinghouse and he had these really great eyes. Long lashes. He'd always look so sad when I stopped him. One night, I'd had three or four beers and he'd managed to get most of my clothes off." She shook her head at the memory. "I'm lying nearly naked in the back seat of his car and I thought, What the hell? Mostly, I was so damn cold, I just wanted to get it over with so I could get dressed. Eight weeks later, when I told him I thought I was pregnant, he dumped me."

"Men are bad news." Catherine put her elbows on the table, gazed across at Darcy. "I don't want to talk about them anymore. The thing with Martin is over, kaput. I mean it."

"Good." Darcy went to the refrigerator and removed a bowl of risotto. "He's trouble, I already told you that. One, you like him way too much and, two, he's probably still got this thing for his wife." She set the bowl down on the table. "No one will ever live up to her memory. I mean she's *dead,* for God's sake. How the hell can you ever hope to match up? And three—"

"No—" Catherine dug her a fork into the risotto "—that's enough."

"Tough. I'm going to tell you. Three..." Darcy scrunched up her face. "Shit, I've forgotten. Wait, let me think. Oh, I know. Three. He's obviously one of those guys you never know where you are with." She took a helping of risotto. "Look, I'm just saying you need to meet other people—"

"Dammit." Catherine put her fork down. "I can't believe I'm eating this stuff. Cold, too. I'm going to gain back all the weight I lost."

Darcy gave her a critical look. "I don't think you've gained any. But we've got to keep up the jogging. The other thing is I'm going to fix you up. It's the only way you're going to get over this guy."

Catherine shook her head. Another man wasn't the answer. And maybe Martin wasn't either. Gary had knocked her around emotionally. Today, she had allowed Martin to do the same thing. But it wouldn't happen again. It didn't matter how she felt about him. From now on she'd be on her guard around Dr. Martin Connaughton.

Just one more encounter with him when Holly had her surgery, and then it would be over. If Holly pulled through the procedure, Grossman would have his moment in the sun; Western would reap the publicity rewards; the TV cameras and swarming reporters would move on to the next news story, and Catherine would forget the last few days ever happened.

But when the phone rang at ten, she grabbed it on the first ring. When she heard her mother's voice, she burst into tears.

THURSDAY MORNING, the day of Holly's surgery, Martin sat in one of the burgundy leather armchairs that stood on either side of Grossman's desk and tried once again to reason with the neurosurgeon.

"I just want to ask you one more time not to do this." He looked at Grossman. "Clearly the mother doesn't want the operation for the child. Obviously it's futile—"

"In your opinion, Connaughton. Not everyone feels the same way. Many of these children lead happy, normal lives—"

"How many with the life-threatening problems Holly has? The whole thing is inhumane, Nate."

Grossman's lips twitched. "Perhaps we should just get a pillow and hold it over the child's head."

"That might be kinder."

Grossman studied him for a moment. "You're looking at this patient with your heart and not your mind, Connaughton. It happens to physicians sometimes. For one reason or another, they become emotionally overinvolved and fail to use sound clinical judgment. Your position is not rational."

"Right, well, there's a lot of things going on around here that aren't very rational." He knew he'd lost the battle and suddenly felt reckless. He rose from the leather armchair and began pacing the office. Adrenaline made his heart pound. "I don't find it particularly rational that we've got crack-addicted babies up in the NICU while your son is out in the parking lot actively drumming up business."

"My son has entered a recovery program." Grossman's voice grew very quiet. "Which has nothing to do with the question of surgery for this child. You will spare yourself a lot of emotional turmoil by understanding that with or without the mother's consent, the child *will* have the surgery. It's the appropriate course of action. Medically, ethically—and legally. Were we to abide by the mother's wishes and not operate, the father would almost certainly sue us. I would advise you to accept the inevitable and move on.'' He leaned back in his chair, studied Martin for a moment. ''What you need to realize is that around here only one of us gets to play God, and I've already got the job.''

''Is that so?'' Rage building until he could contain it no longer, Martin walked across the expanse of pale gray carpeting and placed one hand on either side of the antique desk. He saw the flicker of fear in Grossman's brown eyes, a pulse beating in his neck. Then he caught the edges of the desk and tipped it. As he left the room, he glanced over his shoulder and saw the surgeon's face visible through the spindly wooden legs. ''Looks as though I just toppled you off your throne, doesn't it.''

He closed the door behind him as he left. Five minutes later, he sat across the desk from Dan Hanrahan, Western Memorial's in-house attorney.

''Let me ask you something Dan. What's the precedent for a doctor going to court and arguing for a baby on the grounds of wrongful life?''

''Wrongful life?'' Hanrahan ran his index finger along the bone of his nose and pushed his glasses up. ''Keeping the kid alive technologically even though it's not viable? Is that what you mean?''

''Right.'' Martin nodded. ''Severe disabilities that she's never going to outgrow. Unjustified pain and suffering.'' He looked at Hanrahan and tried to keep his tone casual. ''Anyone ever won a case like that?''

Hanrahan gave him a quizzical look. ''You'd make a terrible poker player. I know damn well where this is going. It's the Hodges kid, right?''

Martin nodded.

''Grossman's going to prevail. He's going to do this surgery, and even if the kid dies, he'll be forging new ground.

You're fighting a losing battle, pal, and if you're not careful you're going to lose a hell of a lot more than that."

LOSE A HELL OF A LOT more than that. An hour later, he stood at the window in the corridor looking out over the skyline of downtown Long Beach. When he stepped away, his own reflection stared back at him, hollow-eyed and weary. He felt defeated and drained and lonelier than he'd ever been in his life. He'd lost the battle to protect Holly. Had he lost even more than that? There was only one way to find out.

CHAPTER FOURTEEN

PHONE LODGED between her head and shoulder, Catherine scraped out the last of the nonfat strawberry yogurt and explained to yet another reporter that while he couldn't bring his camera crew into the OR, there would be pool footage of Holly's surgery available. She tossed the empty carton in the trash bin under her desk, looked at the to-do list and tried to think of anything she might have forgotten.

Derek had assigned her all the arrangements for press coverage of the surgery and she'd spent most of the morning pulling everything together. Things were a little strained between Derek and her, but she intended to demonstrate beyond a shadow of a doubt that her slight lapse in judgment over Martin hadn't compromised her ability to get the job done.

Convincing Gary that she wasn't compromising her moral standards with overnight guests wouldn't be so easy, but she couldn't think about that now. Compartmentalizing was the trick to successfully juggling responsibilities, she decided. Not thinking about Western when she was at home with the kids and keeping thoughts of home…she looked up to see Martin standing in the doorway.

He leaned against the door frame watching her. Green scrubs, stethoscope dangling from the pocket of his white lab coat. He looked exhausted, beaten. Eyes dark, a shadow of beard at his jaw, an uncertain smile that flickered like a candle caught in a draft. The smile tugged at her heart.

Steeling herself against it, she folded her arms across her chest, gave him a level stare that belied the churning in her stomach.

"I should be getting good at this apology thing," he said. "I'm definitely getting enough practice at it."

She kept looking at him, forced herself not to speak.

"I'm truly sorry," he said. "I did some stupid things, I thought I could block Holly's surgery, but I was wrong. I thought I could compromise a bit and go along with it all, but..." He ran his hand around the back of his neck, as though not sure what to say next. "Anyway, after that press conference, I realized that I'd sold out. I knew that unless I did all I could to try and stop the surgery, I couldn't live with myself."

"And you couldn't have just told me this when I came up to the unit?"

"I didn't handle it well, Catherine, I know that. That's what I'm trying to tell you. Nothing has changed about the way I feel...the things we talked about the other night. I want us—"

"No." She shook her head. "I don't want to hear that. You could have told me what was wrong. I asked you enough times, but you shut me out. If you choose to hide behind some kind of emotional wall whenever things go wrong, that's your problem."

He walked around to her side of the desk, sat on the edge. "Want to help me tear it down?"

"I can't." She folded her hands on the desk, looked down at them for a moment. A phone rang in Derek's office, a door slammed. "I've got my own walls. The reason I've avoided relationships is that I'm scared to death of getting hurt all over again. I tell myself it's because of the children, but I know the real reason. With you, I sort of peeked over the top, but now..."

"You've retreated again."

She looked up at him, and neither of them spoke. A moment passed, and then she saw the flicker of a smile around his eyes, felt a reluctant smile on her own face. She couldn't help it. The image struck her as funny, both of them hunkered down behind their own walls, both wanting to come out but not knowing how to do it. The problem was she didn't want to go back to her side—now that she'd glimpsed life beyond the wall.

"When we were talking about Holly the other day," he said finally, "I told you there are times when you just have to recognize there's nothing else that can be done. That it's time to give up and accept the way things are. Maybe that happens in some relationships, too. There isn't much to fight for. But I don't feel that way about us."

"So what happens when the walls come up?"

"We knock 'em down."

"Which might be easier said than done. You weren't exactly willing to let me try after the press conference."

"It won't be easy." His face turned solemn. "For either of us, but I'd like to try. How about you?"

She didn't answer, but her brain and heart were both battling for dominance. *You don't need the complications,* her brain said. *You love him,* her heart said. *You'll get hurt,* her brain said. *It's worth the risk,* her heart said. Martin was watching her, waiting for her response. On her desk was a ceremonial hammer that had been used in a celebrity auction. She reached for it.

"Okay, I'll try a little demolition, but if you break my heart…"

"I won't break your heart, Catherine. I promise," he said softly. "Things may not always go smoothly, but if you're willing to take the risk, I'll do my best to make you happy. I want you to promise me something though."

Before she could respond, Martin's beeper sounded. He used the phone on her desk and she went into the outer office to get coffee. When she returned, he was smiling.

"Holly's spiked a fever," he said. "Her surgery's off."

Catherine smiled back at him. It seemed like an omen. A good one.

Martin took her face in his hands. "Let the demolition begin."

TONIGHT THEY would celebrate their new pact, Martin decided as he left Catherine's office and started back to the unit. Whistling "Deck the Halls," he stopped by his office to check on his mail. It seemed a lifetime ago since he'd sat in the parking lot thinking about Kenesha Washington and wondering whether there was any point to his own life. And then a woman with long brown hair and blue-green eyes had transformed it. Just turned it around.

Holly's surgery had been postponed. Catherine had agreed to give him another chance. Maybe even WISH could be rescued, although his altercation with Grossman might have scuttled the program. Still, life seemed filled with promise.

"OF COURSE you didn't hear me, you were too busy exchanging sweet nothings with your boyfriend." Derek took a handful of jelly beans from the jar on Catherine's desk. "About our latest failure-to-fly kid—"

"Derek." Catherine winced at the flip term he'd used to describe the child who had fallen out of an upper-story window. "He's got multiple broken bones, head—"

"Let's turn it into a positive," Derek said. "Find one of the E.R. docs to talk about what safety precautions parents should take to avoid these accidents, then find the mommy, see what she has to say."

"I already tried, she's pretty hysterical right now." Catherine fought a surge of irritation. She'd been on the run since Martin had left. Nonstop calls to and from reporters about the cancellation of Holly Hodges's surgery and, in the last hour, media inquiries about the child who had fallen through the window. "The boy's got serious head injuries." She looked Derek straight in the eye. "I can't start bugging his mother about talking to reporters—"

"Did you try?"

"No, not yet."

"So how do you know?"

"If it were my son, the last thing I'd care about would be talking to the media."

"I'm losing tolerance for your attitude." He frowned down at his tie—red-patterned with mistletoe—and flicked away a piece of lint. "Did you finish the publicity package for the imaging center? I need it by the end of the day."

"Derek." She stared at him, dumbfounded. "I asked you if you wanted me to work on that and you quite clearly said you would take care of it."

He regarded her for a moment. "Perhaps I expected you to take some initiative—"

Anger suddenly boiled over. "Listen, I've been knocking myself out all morning and not one damn thing I've done has been right for you." She rose and walked around the desk to stand next to him. There was a psychological advantage to being four inches taller than her boss, she decided as she glared down at his face. "Why don't you just tell me what the real problem is?"

"Frankly, I'm extremely disappointed that your *boyfriend*—" he paused for emphasis "—has managed to sabotage the whole press effort with the Hodges kid. We had a news conference planned. Grossman was all set to go—"

"For God's sake, Derek, you've got to be kidding." It

was ludicrous, but the man actually saw the cancellation as a personal affront. "Martin didn't sabotage anything. The baby got an infection. Preemies get them all the time. What do you think he did, deliberately infect her?"

"It's not beyond the realm of possibility. And don't think I'm the only one to entertain the idea," he added, apparently reading the incredulity on her face.

She wanted to laugh. On days like this she could see why she had never wanted a career. When she'd stayed home with her children, she'd dealt with real problems, real issues, not ridiculous flights of fancy motivated by political posturing and professional jealousies.

"Maybe you're not aware of the fact that he struck Dr. Grossman." Derek took the bowl of jelly beans off her desk, spent a minute or so picking out the black ones, then looked up at her. "Not satisfied with that, he tried to remove Holly's name from the schedule. Obviously there's very little he won't do to get his own way."

Catherine folded her arms across her chest, stared down at her shoes and considered what Derek had just told her. Was this what Martin had meant when he said he'd done some stupid things to stop the surgery? A small tug of fear knotted her stomach. His conviction that surgery would prolong Holly's suffering was unshakable. Surely he wouldn't have... She pushed the thought away and sat down behind her desk again.

"The fact is, Connaughton never wanted to cooperate with the publicity effort in the first place," Derek said. "I really don't understand why he said he would." He dropped into the chair opposite her, slouched down, head back, face to the ceiling. "Are you aware that he did the press conference under duress?"

"Duress?" Catherine frowned. "No, he agreed to do it. You know that, Derek. We were all there in your office."

"Ah, but later in the day he changed his mind, with some notion or other that Grossman was coercing Rita Hodges into signing. I ran into him when he stormed in to confront Nate." He met her eyes for a moment. "I convinced him that if he didn't participate, I'd fire you."

All the air seemed to go out of her lungs. Catherine stared at Derek openmouthed.

"I told him you were expendable." He drummed his fingers on the armrests of his chair for a moment, then he sat up straight. "Which is true. You're approaching your three-month probationary period, and I've been giving some thought as to whether you're really working out for us."

Hardly able to breathe, let alone speak, she sat there, heart beating so hard it almost hurt. She watched Derek get up and close the door. This was it then. She folded her hands in her lap to stop them shaking. He was about to fire her. Her thoughts raced. Maybe she should preempt him by resigning first. And then what? Gary would snatch the kids from her before she could get to her first interview for a new job. A wave of nausea hit her. Derek sat down again, folded his arms across his chest and looked at some spot over her shoulder.

"A lot of changes will be taking place in the next month or so," he started. "Ed Jordan wants to expand this department and create an assistant director position. Which is what I wanted to talk to you about." His eyes finally met hers. "Would you be interested?"

Catherine took a couple of deep breaths. It was as if she'd stood before the firing squad, heard the click of the rifles and then, instead of bullets, they'd fired rose petals at her. Relief overwhelmed her, but quickly gave way to anger. Derek must have known how his remark about the probationary period would affect her. Once again he'd manipulated her by creating fear and uncertainty.

In that way, he and Gary were alike. Both of them used the tactic as a way to bolster their own egos. The awareness did little to change the fact that both of them could, if they wished, do more than threaten. Both had the power to wreak actual havoc on her life. Derek, she realized, was waiting for an answer.

"Obviously I'd be interested in the job." She looked at him and voiced a sudden suspicion. "But something tells me there's more to this than just the offer of a promotion."

"You're right. While I'm generally satisfied with the quality and quantity of your work, I think your involvement with Connaughton compromises your efforts. You've resisted me every step of the way with the Hodges publicity—"

"Derek, that's—"

"I'm not interested in hearing justifications. Obviously your involvement with him has priority over professional responsibilities."

Catherine looked at him. Face flushed, all the usual coy mannerisms gone, he was furious. She'd never seen him so angry.

"We deal with a lot of sensitive and highly charged issues in this department. What you don't seem to appreciate is that Connaughton is a loose cannon with an uncanny knack for getting into the spotlight. I doubt very much whether we've heard the last of the Holly Hodges matter. I've no doubt he has some tricks up his sleeve ready for when Grossman returns from Greece and—"

"Derek, why don't you just tell me what it is you're trying to say."

"I realize that your personal life is your own concern, but I think in this case my position is justified. Unless I'm

confident that you've ended this…fling with Connaughton,
I'll have difficulty recommending you for a promotion, or
for that matter, continuing your employment at all.'' He
glanced at the calendar on her wall. "Today is Thursday,
I'll be at an off-site meeting all day tomorrow. Think about
it over the weekend and get back to me Monday.''

"I can give you an answer right now, Derek.'' She
looked directly at him. "I'm not having a casual fling with
Martin. I could come in next week and tell you we've
ended it and then we could try and keep it secret, but I
don't want to do that. I don't want to sneak around and
hide. And—'' she paused ''—I *won't* be threatened.''

"So you're willing to give up your job for him?''

"I don't want to. I'm supporting two children.'' She bit
her lip again and took a deep breath. "But you've put me
in a position where I don't have any choice.''

"And how do you think Connaughton will take this?''

"I don't know. That's not really the point though, is it?
It's my job, my decision to make.''

"So do I consider this your two weeks' notice?''

"If that's the way it has to be.''

"Very well.'' He stood and walked to the door. "I'll
inform personnel.''

She barely made it to the rest room after Derek left before she threw up.

STILL NUMB with shock, she met Martin in Mulligan's that
night, not quite ready to tell him what had happened. While
he got their drinks, she opened an emerald-green door
marked Colleens and tried to repair the ravages to her face.
The cold water and an application of makeup didn't help
much though. Every time she thought of what she'd done,
tears filled her eyes again. Her hands on either side of the
washbasin, she stood there shaking and crying, mascara

running down her cheeks. Laughter and conversation from
the bar filtered in.

She blew her nose, checked her reflection in the mirror
and reminded herself of why she'd done what she did; what
she was going to do about it now and why there was no
reason—well, maybe just a little—to panic. It helped. As
best she could, she fixed her face again and then, still
shaky, but with the tears in check, she made her way back
through the crowd and found him near the end of the long
line at the bar.

"Are you all right?" Concern in his eyes, he looked at
her for a moment, then put his arm around her shoulder
and squeezed her against him. "You look done in. Go and
sit down, I'll be there in just a bit. It's the same booth we
had last time." He grinned and glanced around the packed
room. "Don't ask how I managed it, but a bit of blarney
helps."

"I'm sure it does." She tweaked his chin and smiled up
at him. He looked terrific. Tall and good-looking with his
cream cable-neck sweater and dark red hair brushed back
off his forehead. An excitement in his eyes that she'd never
seen before. He seemed almost buzzing with it, charged
with an energy that lit up his face. She pushed through the
throng around the bar to the booth he had reserved, pulled
off her jacket and sat down. The crowd included a smattering of people she recognized from the medical center.
Two women from the marketing department, a few nurses
she knew. It served to remind her that in two weeks she
would no longer be part of Western's workforce. The
thought made her eyes fill and she held her breath until she
got her emotions under control.

Over at the bar, through the haze of blue cigarette smoke,
she could see the back of Martin's head. On the jukebox,
a group sang "Whiskey in the Jar." A few weeks ago, she

wouldn't have recognized the piece, but after he'd asked if she'd like to hear some Irish music, she'd gone out and bought some tapes of traditional songs.

Her thoughts returned, inevitably, to the exchange with Derek. In a sense, he had called her bluff. Until he'd actually walked out of her office, she'd been sure he would back down. It had even crossed her mind that he might tell her he admired her honesty. Even as he closed the door behind him, she'd half thought he would turn and make one of his snide comments and the whole exchange would be forgotten. In fact, he hadn't said another word to her for the rest of the day. Once the reality set in, she had started into his office to tell him she'd reconsidered. Twice she'd made it to his door and twice she'd changed her mind.

And not just because of how she felt about Martin. What stopped her was the thought of allowing Derek to control her life the way Gary had. No one would have that power again. If anyone was going to wreck her life again, she would have no one to blame but herself.

But that wouldn't happen. As terrified as she felt by what she'd done that afternoon, she also felt a new surge of confidence. While she was up in the mountains with the children, she would update her résumé. Sunday she would check the classifieds. If Derek thought she could be an assistant director, obviously she had the capability to get another job.

She watched Martin work his way through the crowd, a bottle in one hand, a couple of glasses in the other. What she would say to him about it, she hadn't decided. No telling what he might do if he knew she had quit because of him. An image of him decking Derek made her grin despite herself. He'd stood up for what he'd believed and had refused to compromise his principles.

"I think the entire population of Long Beach must be in

here ordering drinks." He set the bottle and glasses on the table and sat down opposite her. "All right, are you? I was afraid that I'd find you dead of thirst. And to be sure," he said in an exaggerated brogue, "that would be the end of me."

Her heart turned over, and she had to bite her lip very hard not to cry. Until this afternoon, she'd never understood what it was about some men that would make a woman give up absolutely everything. Now she did. With a need that edged on desperation, she wanted nothing more at that moment than for him to make love to her. To lie naked under him, to feel the weight of his body on hers, to open her body to his. Terrified by the intensity of the feeling, she shivered. Beneath the long sleeves of her silk blouse, goose bumps had formed on her arms.

"Where are you?" Martin flicked her hand with his fingers.

Overcome by a complex rush of feeling, she shook her head and glanced down at the table. After a moment it registered that instead of the Guinness he usually drank and the white wine she'd expected for herself, he had brought a bottle of champagne. Through her lashes, she glanced up at him.

"WISH is being fully funded for two years," he replied to her unspoken question. With a grin, he popped the cork, poured champagne into both glasses. "But I'm no longer involved with it. Jordan gave me the sack."

"MARTIN." At the first part of his sentence, Catherine had started to lift her glass in a toast. Now she froze, open-mouthed. "What happened?"

"My various transgressions." He shrugged. "I'd be long gone already if we weren't short of neonatalogists."

"God, I don't know what to say." Catherine watched his face. "How do you feel? What are you going to do?"

"Well, I'm very glad that WISH is still going to go on, I really am, but I want to be a part of the effort. If I'm not, there's no reason for me to stay at Western any longer."

She felt her mouth go dry. The music and conversation around her faded until it seemed she could only hear her heart beating. Her hands folded on the table, she sat very still and watched his face.

"I've been thinking about what else I can do. I contacted a few people I know in this area, but no one was really interested in anything like WISH. But I rang the hospital in Boston where I used to work." He paused and then a smile broke across his face. "They want me to start a program there, in fact they've offered me carte blanche to go back and direct it. I can have it all, Catherine. The staff, the budget, administration's full commitment. Everything that I've been knocking myself out to accomplish here at Western."

The words had come out in an unstoppable rush. His face was rapt, his eyes bright with excitement. Jubilation was there in the set of his shoulders, the musical cadence of his voice. It was a side of him she had never seen before.

"God, there's so much I want to do." He picked at the edge of the label on the champagne bottle. "It's funny…for the last few days, I've been trying to do for Holly what I couldn't do for Kenesha. Even though they're quite different clinically, I think they've come to represent the same thing in my mind. Pain and suffering that, one way or another, might have been avoided." His forehead knit in a frown and for a moment he seemed lost in his thoughts. "But if I take the Boston offer, I'll be able to help all the Keneshas…" Suddenly he threw his head back and laughed. The sound seemed to linger in the air for a minute, then he looked at her, a huge grin on his face. "I suppose you can't tell I'm just a bit pleased about it, right?"

Catherine smiled across the table at him. How could she not be happy for him? Still, she didn't trust herself to speak. The bar seemed suddenly cold. An image of herself as a child playing on the beach ran through her head. The damp sand at the water's edge was the best kind for molding into shapes, so she always built her castles there, but just as she'd get the perfect castle built, a wave would inevitably roll in and demolish it and she'd have to start again. Deep down she tried to convince herself she'd really known that one day Martin would leave. First Ethiopia, now Boston.

"You gave them an answer?" she finally managed to say.

"All but..." He hesitated then reached into his pants pocket and withdrew a small brown paper bag. "I wanted to talk to you before I signed the deal."

She watched as he withdrew a black velvet-covered square. Attached to it was a brass ring with a green glass stone, the kind of toy jewelry Julie liked to wear to play dress-up. With one hand, he pulled the ring off the cardboard.

"It's just a symbol," he said with a little smile. "It was all they had in the gift shop, but I promise we'll go and get a real one tomorrow." He reached across the table for her left hand and slipped the ring on her fourth finger. "I want you to go with me, Catherine. You and the children. Marry me and let's start a new life together in Boston."

CHAPTER FIFTEEN

FOR THE SECOND TIME that day, she felt as though a gun had gone off at close range. All sound and movement stopped. Words tumbled around in her brain, but she couldn't impose any order on them. She looked down at the ring on her finger. The glass stone glinted in the smoky air. Still the words wouldn't come. Tears in her eyes, she looked up and saw the confusion in Martin's eyes. Then she slowly took the ring off her finger and put it on the table between them.

"I can't do it, Martin." Now she couldn't bring herself to look at him, couldn't bear the stricken expression she knew she would see. "I just can't do it," she repeated. "I can't."

"You've said that. Three times. Now tell me why."

She dug her nail into a groove on the table and tried to sort through her thoughts. "First of all," she said slowly, "I can't just uproot the children to follow you across the country. If Gary didn't fight it, which I know he would, there's the whole issue of uprooting them again. They're still adjusting to the changes from the divorce."

"Children adapt, Catherine." He picked up the ring, held it in the palm of his hand. "As for Gary, I'm sure if he decided to move for some reason, he'd do it and you'd be left figuring out what to do about it. You can't let him dictate your life. What else?"

"I don't know. I..." A panicky feeling hit her, and she

looked around as though for an escape route. *Because I love you too much? Because I'm scared to death that I'll lose myself in you? Because I can't let myself be rescued again?* "It's hard to explain." She shredded the edge of the cocktail mat. "I guess it has something to do with proving myself. Figuring out who I am and making it on my own. I mean, I've just started to do that, I can't risk everything I've gained."

"Your job you mean? Is that it?"

Her heart racing, Catherine just looked at him.

"Because if that's the reason…" He hesitated. "When I told them about you, they offered to find a position in the public relations department. Not that I don't think you could get a job on your own," he added with a wry grin. "So don't start down that road. Look…" He reached for her hand across the table. "You don't even have to work if you don't want to. You always worry that you're compromising the children by working. Stay home with them. I'd love to come home to the smell of cakes baking. Maybe we could even have a baby," he said softly. "What do you think?"

Catherine swallowed. If the devil had dreamed up a way to tempt her, he couldn't have found anything more compelling than what Martin had just offered. Damn him. She wanted to scream that it wasn't fair. Hardening herself to the look in his eyes, she pulled her hands away.

"What?" He shook his head. "Tell me."

"Don't you see what you're doing? I've tried to explain and you sweep it all away. What you're saying is that my work isn't important enough to really matter. Sure, just give it up, stay home and make cakes and babies, that's what you do best anyway."

"No, that's not what I'm bloody well saying." His eyes were dark with anger. "God, Gary certainly did a number on you. What I'm saying is that I think raising children in the way you want them raised is the most important thing you can do. *You're* the one who undervalues staying home, Catherine. Whenever you talk about it, you get this note of apology in your voice. What is it you call it, your Becky-Home-ecky role? Somehow you've convinced yourself that churning out damn press releases has more intrinsic value than being there full-time for your children. I don't happen to feel that way myself, but it's *your* choice. I'll support you either way.''

''Oh God, Martin.'' She put her elbows on the table, held her head in her hands. *''You'll support me.* That's the whole problem. Someone's been supporting me my entire life. Until now, I've never done it alone. You've had the freedom, the autonomy. You've been independent for a long time. It's different for you.''

He looked at her silently for a while. Then he said, ''Let me tell you about my experience with independence. Sure, I had the freedom to go wherever I wanted. Plenty of autonomy. No one to answer to, no one to consider. No one to give a bloody damn what I did. They were the loneliest, bleakest, most desolate years of my life. Less than a month ago, I sat in the parking lot and thought about my independence and wasn't sure I even wanted to go on with my life. I never want to know that kind of independence again.''

Undone by the crack of emotion in his voice, by the light that had gone out of his face, she looked at him through a shimmer of tears. *God, it would be so easy to bring that light back.* Tears clogged her throat and her nose, trickled down her face and dropped onto the wooden table. A thick silence filled the air between them. She wouldn't let herself say the words she knew he wanted to hear, the words she wanted to say.

"Is it Boston?" Martin finally asked. "Is that the problem?"

Miserable, she shook her head. She knew that as much as he wanted to accept the Boston offer, he would turn it down if she refused to go with him. Just as she had given up the Columbia scholarship for Gary. Willingly, she'd thought at the time, but it had changed her life, and the deep undercurrent of resentment never entirely went away. WISH meant too much to him and he meant too much to her to risk it.

"Martin." Catherine addressed her hands on the table, then risked a brief glance at him; all the eye contact she could manage without breaking down. "This is difficult advice for me to give you, but...I think you should take the Boston offer."

"Go without you?" he asked, his voice flat and expressionless. "Is that what you're saying?"

"I know how important the project is to you. Think about what you were willing to do to get WISH funded at Western. Talking to a bunch of yammering reporters, going along with all that puffery rubbish. Remember?" She'd hoped to make him smile, but when she risked another glance, she saw a wariness in his eyes. Quickly, before she could give in to the urge to walk around the table and fling her arms around him, she looked away. "You already know that there aren't many hospitals willing to make the kind of commitment you want." Now she addressed the shoulder of his sweater. "It's an opportunity I don't think you should turn down."

"I thought we were in this together, Catherine." His eyes lowered to the ring in his hand. "Isn't that what we've talked about?"

"I know..." She swallowed, unable to finish the sentence. "But I'm not ready for the kind of commitment you're talking about. I haven't even been divorced a year yet, this is my first relationship. I think what I need to do is take some time, maybe see other people and figure out my own life.''

For a moment, he sat very still. His face did not change expression. He did not move. He did not speak. He just looked at her, his gaze steady on hers.

"I'm sorry." She bit her lip hard, but it didn't stop the tears, so she got up from the table and pulled on her jacket. As she did, she saw, like a still life, the two untouched glasses of champagne, the ring and the braided pattern on the sleeve of his cream sweater.

FOR AN HOUR after Catherine left Mulligan's, Martin just stayed in the booth watching the bubbles go out of the champagne. Then he made his way over to the bar, ordered a pint of Guinness and watched that go flat. Leaning on his elbows, he stared into the glass and reflected that it was a pity that when Catherine made him promise not to break her heart, he hadn't extracted a similar promise from her.

Oblivious to the noisy cheer all around, he wallowed in morose contemplation. As a small boy, whenever he'd suffered some minor bump or scrape, his mother would preempt his tears by telling him it didn't really hurt. It always confused him, her denial of his pain, but he never contradicted her, and after a while it really didn't hurt anymore. After an hour or so he grew weary of the music and smoke and noise, threw some money on the bar and walked back to the medical center.

In the lobby, carolers dressed in Dickensian costumes clustered around the Christmas tree. Martin punched the button for the elevator and when it didn't come immediately, ran up the five flights of stairs to the unit, the notes of ''Joy to the World'' drifting in the air like mockery. In the locker room he changed clothes, scrubbed up, then started across the unit to look at Holly. On the way down the line of isolettes, he found Valerie Webb drawing blood from a baby girl. She glanced up at him as he approached, smiled, then turned her attention back to the baby.

He watched as she lifted the tiny arm and swabbed it with antiseptic. When the first attempt was unsuccessful, she tried again and the baby's stomach rose and fell spasmodically. Like most of the babies in the NICU, she had a tube between her vocal cords that prevented her from crying out. As he looked at the baby in her clear-walled isolette, he heard in his head her screams of silent anguish. As he walked away, he felt a wave of the old desolation. The black void seemed very real once more.

THE RECITAL had already started by the time Catherine slipped into the auditorium on Friday evening. In the back row, she found an empty metal chair, sat down and located Julie's blond head in the crowd of first-graders lined up on the stage. Gary had left a message on her machine at home to say he wouldn't make the recital but he would pick up the kids afterward and take them out for pizza. He and Catherine could talk later after he'd dropped them off. The prospect had all the appeal of a root canal.

As the final notes of "Frosty the Snowman" faded, and the kids launched into "Silver Bells," Catherine dabbed at her eyes. Children singing always made her cry. The lisping, high-pitched voices. The toothy smiles. Whatever they'd been up to before—fighting, screaming, shouting, driving adults to distraction—once they opened their mouths to sing, they became little angels. Tonight, though, it wasn't just the children making her cry.

As cameras clicked and video recorders whirred all around her, two images kept appearing over and over. The happiness on Martin's face last night when he'd told her about Boston and his face as she'd left. God, it would have been so easy to say yes. Determined not to start second-guessing herself, Catherine blew her nose into a tissue. She couldn't marry him. Beneath the veneer of the new Catherine, the woman he loved, too much of the old needy Catherine remained. A self-sacrificing martyr of a woman who would slowly, inexorably, return. She couldn't do it to him, couldn't do it to herself. The decision she'd made had been the right one. Ultimately it would prove best for both of them. Like a mantra, she repeated that thought to herself throughout the recital, every time she felt her eyes fill.

When she got home from the recital just after seven, she found a letter from Gary's attorney. A custody matter, the note said. She needed to call his office. The mail also included a note from her landlord that her rent was to be increased by fifty dollars a month, and one from the bank informing her that her checking account was overdrawn by ninety-five dollars.

Hoping for better news, she checked the message machine. It occurred to her that there might be a message from Martin, although why he would call after what had happened, she didn't know. No message. Chilled, she wrapped her arms around herself. Action, that's what she needed. In the bedroom, she changed into jeans and a sweater, tied her hair up in a ponytail, then took out the trash, washed and put away the dishes and vacuumed the living room. As she mopped the kitchen floor, she repeated the mantra. It didn't help for long.

She felt split in two. Part inconsolable child crying, unable to understand why she couldn't have something she wanted, part stern parent doing what was best for everyone. The child wouldn't be consoled though. Martin's voice filled her head. Desperate for a distraction, she called Darcy. No one home. In the kitchen, she opened the fridge, closed it, made a batch of oatmeal cookies and wept into the mixture. While they baked, she turned on the Christmas-tree lights and sat in the twinkling house, her head back against the couch, tears rolling down her face. By the time Gary arrived with the kids, she was exhausted, cried out, but determined to stick by her decision.

After the kids were in bed, she handed Gary the letter she'd received from his attorney. Aware of his eyes on her, she folded her arms across her chest. Her black sweater felt uncomfortably tight. Twice, he'd complimented her on her appearance, told her she looked good, that she'd changed over the past few months. As he sat on the couch, his jacket and tie off, he might have been a date relaxing after an evening out. "I take it you've seen this," she said with a nod at the letter.

A shadow passed over his face. Earlier, while she'd been supervising the children's baths, he had built a small fire and poured two glasses of wine. When she returned to the living room, she'd found him sprawled comfortably on the couch, feet up on the coffee table. Since most of their contacts after the divorce had been conducted in public places, this cozy domesticity was something new. A little disconcerted, she decided to establish control by taking the offensive.

"I can't believe you really want to do this, Gary." She perched on the edge of the couch. "I mean, the whole time we were married you hardly spent any time with the kids. How can you really think they would be better off with you?"

He sighed deeply, leaned forward to put the letter on the coffee table and turned to look at her. "To be perfectly honest with you, Cath, I don't think they would be. I guess

I've always been more oriented toward business than family, but...well, I'll level with you. It was Nadia's idea. She likes the idea of a family and she keeps hoping we'll have one together, but it's not happening."

"Oh really?" White-hot anger burning away all traces of fatigue, she stared at him for a moment. "So she's willing to settle for my kids. Breaking up my marriage wasn't enough, huh? And you, of course, were willing to go along with it. Whatever Nadia wants, is that it? To hell with everyone else."

"Cath, stop. Look, can we take off the boxing gloves for a minute? I did go along with the idea at first, but now that I've had some time to think about it, I can see it wouldn't be the best thing for the kids. You're a good mother, I know that."

Catherine met his eyes for a moment, then he gestured at the letter.

"I'll call it off tomorrow first thing, okay? I'm sorry, really. I've made a lot of mistakes, not just with this custody thing but all through our marriage. You were always so wrapped up in running the house, taking care of the kids. When Nadia came along I was just lonely and—"

"Stop, okay? I don't want to go into that. It's all in the past. History." Unwilling to look him in the eye, she picked at the frayed denim on the knees of her jeans. "All I care about now is that we come to an agreement on what's best for the kids. And I don't want to live under constant threats from you."

"I said I'm sorry, Cath." He picked up the letter from the table and tore it in two. "Okay? No more threats."

She shot him a sideways glance, long enough to see the look on his face. The I've-been-a-bad-boy-but-how-can-you-resist-me grin that he'd used, usually with success, throughout their marriage.

"Sometimes I miss us all being together, you know?" He put his arm along the back of the couch. "All the things we used to laugh about. Remember that time when my mother was visiting? All of us ready to go out, and then Julie got in the tub with her clothes on and she splashed all over your dress?"

Catherine nodded. The event was memorable for more than the ruined silk dress. After removing Julie from the tub, she'd left his mother watching the kids and had dashed into the bedroom, stripped off the wet dress and underwear. As she stood there, nude, Gary came into the room and embraced her from behind. Then he carried her to the bed and made love to her. It had been one of the few moments of spontaneity in their marriage. Out of all the childhood anecdotes, she wondered why Gary had chosen this one.

"To be honest, Nadj and I, well we've had a few problems lately." He paused for a moment. "Not that I'm blaming her or anything, but she can be pretty strong-willed. Once she got this idea into her head that the kids would be better off with us, I couldn't shake it."

Catherine felt the embers of anger reignite, but as she opened her mouth to speak, Gary reached over and caught her hand.

"It's okay, Cath, I told you. The issue's closed. I'm just trying to explain how Nadia... Well, the thing is, I'm not happy with her." He blurted out the words. "It's not working. We fight about everything. It's like she's trying to rule my life. She doesn't want a husband, she wants someone she can order around, 'do this, do that.'" The words came faster, his face colored slightly. "I mean, we go somewhere and it's like she's the star and I'm this underling, running around doing whatever she wants me to do."

Fighting the urge to say, *Now you know how it feels,* Catherine edged her hand out of his grip.

"I can't live my life like that." He got up from the couch, walked over to the Christmas tree and stood for a moment, watching the colored lights blink on and off. With one finger, he gently touched a clay gingerbread boy, painted in red-and-blue stripes. "Peter made this, didn't he?"

"In kindergarten." She glanced at her watch. It was late and she wanted to go to bed. Gary's problems with Nadia were of no concern to her. The events of the day felt like fragile objects precariously stacked up around her. One false move would send them crashing down around her. Thoughts of Martin constantly crept into her head. A sick feeling percolated up from her stomach. The certainty that she'd done the right thing had given way to sheer need. If she could see his face, hear his voice, feel his arms around her again, nothing else would matter.

Gary walked back to the couch and sat down beside her again. "We had a pretty good life, you know? Twelve years—obviously something about it had to work." He turned to her, reached out as though to take her hand again, then drew back. "I guess what I'm leading up to is, I thought maybe we could give it another try."

Jarred from her reverie, unable to believe what she'd heard, Catherine just stared at him.

"I'm doing well financially, the law firm's growing. Money's coming in. We could get a house down in Newport or Laguna. Something decent." He glanced around the small living room. "Not to knock what you're trying to do, Cath, I know you've got this thing about making it on your own, but this is a pretty tacky little place."

"Thanks."

"I didn't mean it like that."

"Bull. You know exactly what you said. This *tacky little place* happens to be my home."

"Come on—"

"No, you come on. You're doing exactly what you've always done. Criticize whatever I try to do. Make fun of it. Belittle it. It just kills you to think I might be able to make it on my own, doesn't it?"

He said nothing for a while, just sat with his eyes downcast. Finally, he looked up at her. "We've gotten off to a bad start, Cath, and that wasn't what I meant to happen. All I'm trying to say is that I want us to put all this crap…all the stuff that's happened the past year, behind us and start again. I think—"

"Gary, stop." She looked at him, took a deep breath. "I shouldn't get angry, because you obviously have no idea. You sit there and describe your life with Nadia, tell me how unhappy you are, and it doesn't even occur to you that it's exactly the same way I lived when we were married—"

"That's ridiculous." His face darkened. "You had everything. A big house, all the money you needed. You were raising our kids, taking care of a home, being my wife. It's totally different."

"The only difference is you've realized the problem sooner than I did. I had nothing, Gary. No independence—"

"You've got nothing now. I mean it's pretty damn obvious you can't make it. Peter's sneakers look like they came from a goddamn discount store. And Julie's jacket—"

"I guess if they were name brands—"

"Look, I don't want to turn this into a fight. I've made mistakes, I know that. I'm just asking for another chance. Let's try and make a go of it, okay? It would be better for the kids, better for you. You could give up that damn job, go back to school maybe. We'd all be better off."

Before she could reply, the cell phone in Gary's shirt

pocket rang. He frowned then clicked it open. From the conversation, she deduced that Nadia was on the line. Catherine got up, went into the kitchen and filled a glass at the sink. Gary's voice carried over the running water. Nadia was apparently telling him something that surprised him. Catherine waited until she heard him say goodbye before she walked back into the living room. Gary looked up from the sofa, a frown on his face.

"Nadj was at this big marketing shindig tonight, and I guess your boss was there." He paused. "She said Petrelli told her you quit. I said she had to have it wrong."

Catherine felt her heart speed up. No point in denying it, she decided. "It's true," she said.

"God." He shook his head. "That was a damn good job. You were lucky to get it. Why the hell would you do something like that?"

"Petrelli gave me an ultimatum that I couldn't accept."

"What kind of ultimatum?"

"It's personal. I don't want to talk about it."

"Personal?" Gary's eyes narrowed. "Well Petrelli's gay, so for damn sure he didn't proposition you." He watched her face for a moment as though the answer might reveal itself on her forehead. "Julie said some guy's been sleeping here."

Catherine opened her mouth to speak, closed it. She didn't owe him an explanation.

"Who is it? Someone you work with?"

"You know what, Gary? This is none of your business."

"Sure it's my business. They're my kids. If you're involved with some guy, I have a right to know he's not some... Damn." He shook his head. "I just figured it out. It's that Irish doctor who was on TV...the one who delivered those kids on the freeway. Nadj said she's heard some gossip about the two of you—"

"I said this is none of your business. I'm entitled to a personal life."

"And I have a right to know my kids are okay." He gripped her upper arm. "It's him, isn't it? He's been sleeping here."

"Just let me go, okay?" She tried to pull away but he tightened his grip. "I mean it. Let go of my arm."

"You got horny, is that it?" He pinned her arms to the wall. "So you crawl into bed with the first guy who looks twice at you, the hell with the kids. And then you go and quit your goddamn job." Enraged now, his face dark with anger, he shoved his knee between her legs. "Sounds pretty responsible, doesn't it?"

She stayed completely still, her eyes on his. He had never physically abused her during their marriage, but she had never incited jealousy in him before. For what seemed like eternity, he silently held her against the wall while the colored tree lights threw patterns onto his face and his eyes bored into hers.

"You think you've got it all figured out, don't you?" When she didn't answer, he shook her shoulders. "Don't you? Miss Independent. Do you think you're just going to waltz straight into another job? Or are you going to have your boyfriend support you?"

She bit the inside of her lip, willed herself not to respond. Whatever she said would only incite him. And what would she say anyway? No, I don't have it figured out. I'm scared to death.

Then he kissed her, hard enough that she tasted blood as his teeth ground into her lips.

"Bitch," he said when she wrenched her head away. "I'm pouring my heart out to you, trying to make things right between us again and you don't give a shit, do you? You're just the same cold bitch you've always been.

Twelve years we were married and I worked my ass off and what thanks do I get?'' He flung her arms away, grabbed his jacket and opened the front door. ''When you're out there with no job and no roof over your head and you've lost custody of the kids, just don't come crying to me, okay?'' The door slammed behind him, then opened again. ''Oh yeah, forget about having the kids for Christmas.''

CHAPTER SIXTEEN

As SHE DROVE UP to Big Bear on Saturday evening, Catherine tried to blot out the thoughts of last night's fight with Gary. Because of it, she'd stayed up half the night, finally fallen asleep around three, overslept and, as a result, ended up getting off to a very late start. Now it was getting dark and she hated driving the mountain roads in anything but perfect conditions. She glanced at the sign for Big Bear Village. Only another five miles down the road. She could do it. And they were going to have a good time. She kept repeating the words like a mantra. She wouldn't think about her soon-to-be-unemployed status; wouldn't think about Gary. And Martin? Snowflakes swarmed against the van's windshield, flurried like moths around the car's headlights. She would try not to think about Martin.

They were going to have a good time. Snow blanketed the roofs of the cabins that dotted the road leading into the village, piled up in pillowy banks along the sides of the roads. Perfect conditions for Peter to try out his sled. She'd lashed it to the roof of the van, packed toys, games and books and enough brownies and cookies to bring on insulin shock. It would be a fun, relaxing weekend. Just the three of them.

"Looking forward to getting out in the snow?" She reached over and squeezed Peter's knee. "It's been a long time, huh?"

"The last time was with Dad." Peter stared gloomily out

of the window. "It's getting thicker. Dad said we should take chains."

"I called the highway patrol and they said we wouldn't need them." She turned on the wipers. Crusted clumps of soft white crystals fell from the blades. "It's only another fifteen minutes or so, we'll be fine," she said as much to reassure herself as Peter.

Last night, after Gary left, she'd found Peter lying wide awake on his bed with the door ajar. Apparently he'd overheard the whole thing. He hadn't wanted to talk to her and had barely suffered her good-night kiss. Now, despite her resolve not to think about her ex-husband, she couldn't help wondering whether he might have talked to Peter about the possibility of a reconciliation even before he'd mentioned it to her. Gary probably looked like the good guy to Peter, wanting only to get the family back together again. She decided she would try again to get Peter to talk. Perhaps tonight, after Julie went to bed.

With the palm of her hand, she rubbed a clear spot on the steamed-up windshield, turned the defrost to high. Despite her resolve, she couldn't stop the worry creeping in. Last night, she'd succumbed to a raging panic attack that had her pacing the floor for hours. Gary would take the kids, she would never find another job, Martin would fall in love with someone in Boston and she would be out on the streets. Childless, jobless, homeless. Loveless.

The snow was getting heavier, thick and disorienting. Twice she felt the tires start to slip. Her hands tightened on the steering wheel. Out of the corner of her eye, she could see Peter, distant and glum. Daylight had diminished some of her fears, but now in the warm confines of the van she began to feel claustrophobic and panicky again. No telling what revenge Gary might exact. Peter had said he didn't want to live with his father, but if Gary really pushed, who knew? Unless she got another job right away, she had played right into his hands.

And Martin. She swallowed hard, trying to wrest control of her feelings. Despite everything, a tiny flicker of hope that he might turn up at the cabin anyway refused to be extinguished. Longing filled her. In the back seat, Julie stirred and whimpered in her sleep. Without taking her eyes from the road, Catherine reached across the back of the seat and patted her daughter's leg.

A sudden thought made her smile. Julie's all-time favorite bedtime story was "The Three Little Pigs." Julie would insist, over and over, that Catherine demonstrate just how hard the wolf tried to blow the house down. Finally satisfied that the wolf couldn't make it, no matter how hard he tried, she would smile sleepily and close her eyes.

She cranked up the heater a little and imagined the cabin with its beamed ceilings and cozy loft where the children liked to sleep. She would light the fire, put something together for dinner. After that, maybe they'd play a couple of games. Cozy and snug in their own little world, safe against the swirling, blowing snow outside. She started to feel a little better. Things would be all right. Gary could huff and puff, but she wouldn't let him blow their world apart again.

It was a little harder to inject the same note of optimism into her thoughts about Martin. In time maybe she'd actually believe that she'd made the right decision.

They passed through the village, ablaze with twinkling Christmas lights, the colors blurred by the blowing snow. As she glanced at the speedometer, she tried to remember whether the road to the cabin was five or ten miles outside the village. In the past, they'd always made the trip during daylight hours, and because Gary had driven, she had never really paid attention, an omission that now made her retrospectively angry at the sheltered woman she had once been.

At the five-mile marker she slowed the van, but the blowing snow made it difficult to see the unlit and unmarked side streets they passed. Driving at a crawl, she leaned forward in the seat, peered into the milky air. Just as she decided they had another five miles to go, she remembered something familiar about the clump of trees at the road they'd passed and glanced back over her shoulder.

"You missed it." Peter snapped out of his silence long enough to inform her. "It was that one back there."

"Jeez, Peter, you might have said something sooner." She braked and glanced into the side-view mirror. The road behind them was empty, lit only by the van's red taillights. As she backed up, the tires slipped in the soft snow then slid toward a ditch. Her heart thudding, she righted the wheels and started slowly up the hill. Fifteen years ago when her mother had bought the cabin, it had been the only one for several miles around. Now the road was paved, and a few A-frames had been added, but the area was still sparsely populated. As she glanced up the hill, she couldn't see a single tire track on the pristine stretch of freshly fallen snow.

"Mommy." Julie's sleepy voice came from the back seat. "I have to go to the bathroom."

"Can you hold on a minute?" She gritted her teeth as the van spun out again. "One more bend in the road and we're there."

"I'm hungry too," Julie said.

"I know you are, sweetie, and you're being a very good girl...damn." The van skidded halfway across the road, spun a couple of times then slid into a snowbank.

She turned to look at Julie, wide eyed in the back seat. "You okay?" Julie nodded and Catherine looked at Peter.

"How about you?" She shot him a shaky grin. "It's getting pretty slick out there, huh?"

Peter gave her a faintly disdainful look and returned to his silent contemplation.

"I'm scared." Julie whimpered. "I don't like it here."

"Just be patient a little longer, okay, sweetie?" Catherine started up the van again and heard the rear wheels whine as they spun treadlessly in the snow. After a moment, she tried again with the same result. "Dammit." Her hand pounded the steering wheel. "I can't believe this."

"Want me to put a blanket under the back wheels?" Peter's face seemed to suddenly come alive. "I know how to do it, Dad showed me."

"Might as well give it a try." Catherine pulled on her parka, tied a woolen scarf around her neck and started to open the door. "Put on your jacket and do it all the way up," she called over her shoulder to Peter. "Julie, throw me that old gray blanket on the back seat."

Minutes later, she watched as Peter, vapor pouring from his mouth, spread the blanket out behind the van's rear tires. Panting, he surveyed his handiwork then began issuing instructions on what she should do. His sullen mood had totally evaporated. Recalling his man-of-the-house remark of a week or so ago, she smiled behind the woolen scarf that covered her mouth. His nose and the tips of his ears were pink with cold and she fought a sudden urge to hug him.

"You go start up the car, Mom." He stomped his feet against the chill. "And I'll push."

Ten minutes later, they'd pushed and pushed, rocked the van back and forth all to no avail.

"It's no good, Peter." She stuck her head out the driver's window to look at him. "The cabin's just at the top of the hill. I think we're going to have to go up and call for help."

She looked at him, his face pinched now, his breathing raspy. "Are you okay? Your asthma bothering you?"

"It's fine, Mom, quit fussing over me like I'm a little kid."

"Sorry." Her heart turned over. He looked *exactly* like a little kid trying hard to play a man's role.

He hunched his shoulders, jammed his hands into the pockets of his parka. "If we had some buckets of sand, I could do it."

"I know you could, sweetie." Her mind already on what they would need to carry up the hill with them, she climbed into the back seat and began piling food and clothes into bags. "But it's really really cold and I think it would be better if we called someone."

Peter slammed the van's door shut as he got back in and she glanced over her shoulder to say something, but the look on his face chased the words out of her head. He sat in three quarter profile, shoulders slumped, his face shadowed in the dim interior light. All the animation had vanished. A chill ran through her that had nothing to do with the cold. He looked defeated.

THIRTY MINUTES LATER, they stood shivering in the middle of the unheated cabin. Peter hadn't said a word during their trudge up the hall. He'd shrugged away her arm when she'd tried to put it around his shoulder, snapped at Julie and walked on ahead, a small solitary figure locked in his own world.

Catherine dragged her eyes away from him, forced herself to concentrate on what needed to be done. Heat was the first priority, she decided as she stamped her feet to restore circulation. Both children stood huddled and shivering, Peter's face buried deep in his parka. With relief, she noted the wood and kindling left from a previous visit still stacked beside a huge wood-burning stove, the cabin's sole source of heat.

"Tell you what, Peter." She started to take off then changed her mind. "While I call someone about the van, why don't you see if you can get a fire started?"

He shrugged, but moved over to the stove and began crumpling newspaper.

She watched him for a moment and tried not to worry. He'd snap out of it, she told herself as she dragged a phone book from a shelf in the kitchen. Maybe what she needed to do was assign him more responsibility. Build up his confidence. Make him feel manly. Manly, but not arrogantly male like his father. Her head started to throb as she thumbed through the Yellow Pages to garages. Nothing about being a parent was easy.

Ten minutes later, the smell of smoke drew her back into the living room. Through billowing black clouds, she peered at Peter still squatting in front of the stove. Julie, at his side, looked up as Catherine approached and shivered dramatically.

"Peter used a whole box of matches, Mommy, and it's still not lit. *Brrr,* I'm freezing to death."

"Shut up, Julie." Peter poked at the paper. "The wood's wet. We need some fire lighter."

Catherine sneezed and surveyed the ashy gray newspapers in the grate, felt the sting of acrid smoke in her nose and eyes. Her teeth chattering in the frigid cabin, she wrapped her arms around herself and considered bundling the kids up and finding the nearest motel. Then she remembered the immobilized van. Not one of the garages she'd called had been open, so they were stuck until morning, by which time they could all freeze to death. Eyes smarting, she looked at Peter still valiantly balling up newspapers. Torn between the need for warmth and fear of wounding his pride, she knelt on the floor beside him.

"Sweetie, it isn't good for you to be breathing this stuff. Let me help, okay?" She picked up a couple of sticks of kindling. "I'm not sure I could do any better, but I'd be glad to give it a try."

"I can do it." He ignored the wood she held out, struck another match, touched it to the newspaper.

A brief blaze warmed her face as the newspaper caught fire, then it faded and dissolved into gray ash. Black clouds billowed all around them. She sneezed again. "Pete, I know you're trying to help, but this is going to make you wheeze." As she tugged on his arm to pull him away from the smoke, she heard the front door open and slam. A sudden blast of even colder air filled the room. Peter's arm stiffened in her grasp, and Julie's eyes widened.

Still on her knees, her heart thudding, Catherine reached for a piece of wood. The weapon clutched tight in her right fist, she looked through the smoky haze to see a tall angular figure dressed in jeans, boots and a heavy parka.

"You must be Cinderella." Martin took a step toward her, his face solemn. "Could you tell me where I might find Catherine Prentice?"

She rubbed her eyes, felt the grit of ash, and sat back on her heels. Fear gave way to a surge of more complex emotions that made her heart pound and robbed her of words. As though she were watching the scene from a distance, she saw Julie dart across the room and hurtle into Martin, heard her squeals of excitement as he, pretending that Julie had knocked him off balance, swooped her up into his arms.

"We've been trying to unstick the van." Julie grinned at him. "But it's still stuck, and Peter can't make the fire go, he started coughing when the smoke got in his face and now we're all really, really cold."

"Shut up, Julie." Peter shot his sister a dark look. "The wood was wet."

Martin set Julie down, and she scampered back to the stove. Blood beating in her ears, Catherine sat rooted, one arm around her daughter, the other around her son.

Shoulders slightly hunched, his expression uncertain now, Martin stood in the middle of the room. Unshaven, his face flushed from the cold, he wore a heavy navy parka, opened to reveal a red flannel shirt. Crystals of melted snow clung to his hair, his sleeves, the legs of his faded jeans. Catherine's hands ached to brush them away. An electric jolt swept through her. If she made one move toward him, everything would change. He would put his arms around her and all her resolve would fade, and if he asked her to go to Boston or the moon, she would.

Her heart leaped at the thought even as her brain commanded her to stay put. Moments passed. Martin's eyes dark, almost navy, didn't move from her face. The silence between them lengthened, broken only by the sound of Peter crumpling newspaper.

"I saw your van down the hill," he finally said. "Couldn't get it out, eh?"

"Peter and I both tried." Catherine glanced down at her son. "But I drove it in there pretty good. None of the garages in town are open."

"I'll go and take a look at it," he said in the neutral voice of a stranger. "Living in Boston, I got quite a bit of practice at dealing with that sort of thing." He moved past her and over to the stove, where he squatted beside Peter. "What's going on here, son?" One hand ruffled the boy's hair. "The wood's a bit damp, is it?"

"I guess," Peter replied, his voice sullen.

Martin peered into the ashy mess. "A long, long time ago, I was a Boy Scout. Maybe between the two of us, we can get a fire going. What d'you think?"

"Fine, I don't care." Peter jumped up and started across the room, but Catherine shot out her hand and caught him

as he tried to pass. With a cry, he squirmed out of her grasp
and ran up the wooden ladder to the loft. "I'm not his son,"
he called, his voice defiant. "I've already got a dad and I
wish I was with him instead of here."

IGNORING HER IMMEDIATE impulse to rush after Peter,
Catherine glanced over at Martin. In the dim light of the
cabin, his face was shadowed. Fatigue showed in his eyes,
the set of his shoulders. Tears burned in her throat. It was
as though something life-affirming was ebbing out of him.
What clutched at her heart was the knowledge that she had
the power to stanch the flow.

"Martin, I'm sorry." She focused her eyes on the stitch-
ing around the neck of the black T-shirt he wore under the
flannel shirt. "About what Peter said, I mean. He's a little
touchy about someone taking Gary's place, I guess, and—"

"Right. Well…" He looked at her for a moment and a
muscle twitched in his cheek. "I'll get this lit for you and
then take a look at your van."

Ten minutes later, the fire blazing, she watched him
trudge down the snow-covered driveway. A solitary figure
surrounded by empty whiteness. Her eyes filled and she
started for the door to call out to him. Behind her, she heard
Peter's asthmatic cough. For a moment, she stood para-
lyzed. Pulled in two directions. Then Peter coughed again
and she made her choice.

THERE WAS NO REASON to stay, Martin kept telling himself
as he stood in the kitchen watching Catherine put dinner
dishes away. He had completed his good deeds. Lit the fire,
freed the van with the help of a couple of passing motorists
and driven it back up to the cabin. The kids had gone to
bed. Julie had planted a kiss on his cheek, but Peter maintained a sullen silence.

What did it matter anyway? He had no reason to be here.

Still he couldn't bring himself to leave. He'd come because he needed to know whether Catherine really meant what she'd said at Mulligan's. On the way up, he had convinced himself that she hadn't. In his mind, she'd flung her arms around him, tearfully admitting that she'd been wrong, that she wanted to go to Boston with him.

Reality was another story. From the moment he'd walked in, he felt like an intruder. Now Catherine was peppering him with questions about Western, about the drive up, about the snow. About anything except what was happening between them. Her tone was that of a distant acquaintance. Worse, he found himself responding in kind, unable to break through either her reserve or his own barriers. Catherine looked over at him and he realized she'd asked a question.

"Sorry?"

"What happens with Holly's surgery once your rotation's over?" She put a carton of milk in the refrigerator. "Who will be the attending physician?"

"John Nillson." The thought of the portly physician he'd tangled with a few days earlier made his spirits drop further. One of Grossman's cronies, Nillson had made it pretty clear he agreed with the neurosurgeon on the prospect of surgery for Holly. "Once I'm gone, there'll be nothing standing in his way."

"So I guess Holly's infection was just a temporary reprieve, huh?"

"That's one way to look at it."

"Is that how it works with the rotations?" She wiped her palms down the sides of her jeans. "Nillson might not agree with you, but he doesn't get involved until he's the attending?"

"There's a sort of unwritten protocol that we step out of each other's way when it's not our month. It's about the only way we can all work together.'' *Why the hell were they talking about this?*

She looked up, caught him watching her and their eyes locked for a moment. Unresolved tension filled the air between them. It was as if they'd entered a silent pact to avoid the one thing he knew they were both thinking.

''Well…'' He grabbed his parka and started for the door. Catherine followed him and they walked in silence to where he'd parked the Fiat. A huge pine tree hid the house from view. Unable to hold back any longer, he turned to her, caught her arm and pushed her roughly against the trunk.

''Dammit, Catherine.'' He stared into her eyes. ''Why are you doing this?''

''You know why.'' Her teeth were chattering. ''I've told you.''

''Tell me again.'' He moved closer until he felt her body against his. ''I can't remember. You don't give a damn about us, is that it?''

''I didn't say that.''

''Tell me.'' He caught her shoulders, pinned her against the trunk and kissed her until her mouth opened under his. Kissed her throat, her neck, leaned hard against her. She murmured his name and shuddered against him. He looked up at her. ''Tell me why it won't work between us, I forget what you said.''

''Martin, please.'' She tore free from his grasp, caught his head in her hands and kissed him, her tongue in his mouth, body pressed tight to his. ''God, I love you,'' she breathed, her voice almost a sob.

''Wait.'' His mouth still on hers, he maneuvered them until his back pressed against the tree. Her body trembled against his. ''Say that again.''

''I love you.'' Shaking now, she buried her face in his collar. ''Don't make a big deal about it, okay? I shouldn't have said it.''

"Catherine." He pulled away from her, took his parka off, slipped it around her shoulders. In the dim light from the porch, he could see the tears running down her face. "What's all this about?"

"I'm sorry." She sniffed and wiped the back of her hand under her nose. "I need a tissue."

"Here." He pulled the rag he'd used on the van from the pocket of his jacket. "Watch for the oil."

"I quit my job yesterday." She blew her nose, gave him a wan grin. "So I'm a little emotional."

For a moment, her words didn't register. Then they did and his spirits soared. *She had decided to go with him.* From somewhere down in the valley, he heard a car's engine. Catherine stared at him, her eyes huge in the dark night.

"You quit? So you mean—"

"No, it's not what you're thinking." She'd evidently read his expression. "Derek was angry about all that's happened with the Hodges case and…" She hesitated. "Well, he gave me the choice of continuing my relationship with you," she said, looking away, "or keeping my job. So I quit."

He stared at her, openmouthed. "Are you serious?"

"Yep." She met his eyes. "Pretty amazing, huh? I'm having trouble believing it myself."

"When did this happen?" he asked, struck by a suspicion. "Before I told you about Boston?"

"A few hours earlier." Tears glittered as she shook her head. "It's so damn ironic. Telling Derek had to be the scariest thing I've ever done. I felt like I was walking this high wire and suddenly you were holding out a safety net. You have no idea how hard it was to say no to you."

"But you did." He couldn't keep the bitterness from his voice. "Unemployment being preferable to marriage, I suppose."

"Thanks." Her tone matched his. "That's just about the most helpful comment you could have made."

"I'm sorry." He took her in his arms again, his thoughts in turmoil. "Why the hell couldn't you have just told me before you did it? You've got children to support. For you to just quit your job because of me, I don't know, it seems—"

"It seems what, Martin?" She pulled away to look at him. "Go ahead and say it. Gary already has. Irresponsible? Is that what you think?"

"Don't put words in my mouth. I'm just concerned. I don't want you and the children to pay the price for my... I know how important this job is to you. Why *didn't* you just talk to me first? We could have worked something else out."

"Because it was *my* decision." She stabbed at her chest. "*Mine.* If I'd told you we had to end things because of my job, you would have resigned, wouldn't you?" Her eyes glittered in the darkness. "Solved the problem for me? Tried to save me?"

"So what? It's not as though I have some great love for Western. If it would have helped you out, what harm would it have done for me to quit? I did anyway."

"We've been through this," she said quietly. A frown creased her forehead. With her finger, she traced a pattern on his chest. "I don't want someone else solving all my problems. I don't want to be rescued. I have to know that I can make it by myself." She looked up at him. "And I can."

He looked at her, lost for words. "What I don't understand," he finally said, "is why you feel you have to shut me out in order to prove yourself. Doesn't it occur to you that I could be there to encourage you? To cheer you on?"

"But it wouldn't happen that way. You'd want to rescue

me.'' She put her hands on his shoulders, as though to soften the words. ''Just like when you agreed to do the press conference because Derek threatened to take away my job. It would happen over and over. I wouldn't be able to fall because you wouldn't let me.''

He said nothing. She was right, he knew that. He could make promises, but they would be empty. A scene ran through his mind. One that he'd never discussed although it had haunted his dreams for years. He saw himself walking into the chemist shop to see Sharon. Sun slanted through the windows, fell across her face as she looked up and saw him. Then he heard the click of the trigger behind him, saw the smile fade from Sharon's face. In an instant, he had knocked the pistol from the gunman's hand, jumped across the counter, swept Sharon up in his arms and carried her out of harm's way. Boldly and heroically he had saved her life. And then he would wake up to the mockery of reality.

Sure, he could promise Catherine that he wouldn't step in to rescue her, but the truth was, he wanted to do for this woman what he had been unable to do for his wife.

She pressed her chin into his shoulder and he put his arms around her and stroked her hair, but even as he held her, he felt the old grief rise. His need to save was as strong as Catherine's own need to prove herself. For the first time since the conversation in Mulligan's, it occurred to him that perhaps she had been right in urging him to go to Boston.

''Well, then...'' He pulled away to look at her face. ''I suppose that's it. Have a happy Christmas, Catherine.'' She nodded, tears in her eyes. There seemed to be nothing else to say, so he climbed into the Fiat and drove down the mountain.

CHAPTER SEVENTEEN

CHRISTMAS EVE MORNING Catherine sat in her office drinking coffee and feeling miserable enough to indulge in a cinnamon bun from the cafeteria. She hadn't been scheduled to work, but around eight in the morning Derek had called to ask her to cover this year's reunion of all the kids born in the NICU. The event was scheduled for that afternoon. Derek had a raging fever, he said, and couldn't be around small babies. Considering that he'd essentially forced her resignation, she'd been tempted to tell him to go to hell, but decided it might be unwise if she needed references.

Besides, as Gary was now calling to remind her—for at least the third time—he was picking up the kids from her mother's to spend Christmas Day and the rest of that week with him and Nadia. Since Christmas kind of lost its magic without the kids around, she figured she might just as well be at work.

"Four days," Gary said again. "You got any problems with that?"

As if it would make any difference anyway. Her fingers tightened around the receiver. "Please make sure Peter uses his inhaler, okay? And it might help if you kept the dog out of the house. You are aware he's allergic to it, right?"

Gary mumbled something about her attitude, but she cut him off by carefully replacing the receiver. Then she ate a jelly bean from the jar on her desk, chewed it well, and shoved a handful in her mouth. Okay, this had to stop. She couldn't afford the luxury of self-pity. For the next two weeks, at least, she had a job to keep her busy. Beyond that, things were more uncertain.

There were no suitable jobs in the Sunday classifieds, a fact on which she didn't care to dwell. It had occurred to her that since Martin was leaving Western, perhaps it wouldn't be necessary for her to quit, but the thought made her uneasy. If she stayed, it would be because, even without realizing it, he had made it possible for her to stay.

Even as she'd watched Martin's taillights disappear down the hill, she'd imagined herself getting into the van to go after him. Why the hell was she so determined to prove she could make it alone, anyway?

Restless, she got up, paced around her small office, taking in the homey touches—pictures of the children, trailing plants, knickknacks—all intended to make her feel as though she belonged. But it was an illusion. Derek could take it all from her, just as Gary had. All of it was so damn transitory. Jobs, possessions. Relationships.

Martin's wife, gone in the blink of an eye, her life along with that of her unborn child snuffed out. The whole direction of his life changed in a way he could have never foreseen. Looking into the future was like looking at an incompletely developed Polaroid film. Blurry, barely recognizable images. And yet for this uncertain tomorrow she had banished any chance of happiness today.

Tears burning in her throat, she gathered her folder and camera from the desk and headed for the elevators. *Dammit, she loved him.* Loved him with every part of her being. To hell with tomorrow, she wanted to fall into his arms today, sink into the feeling as if it were a featherbed. It was like being on a diet and craving chocolate-chip-cookie-dough ice cream. Once in a while, the urge proves irresistible. Enough! She punched the button for the fifth floor. The food thoughts had to stop.

She got off the elevator and headed down the corridor to the NICU conference room where the holiday reunion was going on. The noise from inside filtered into the corridor. More than one hundred children and their parents were expected at the annual event which, Derek had pointedly remarked to her, also drew heavy media coverage.

As she pushed open the double doors, Catherine scanned the room, transformed with balloons and streamers and packed end to end with parents, staff and exuberant children. At the far end she caught a glimpse of a TV crew partially surrounding a tall figure in green scrubs. For a moment she froze and then the figure turned and she saw it was one of the other neonatologists. Relief left her weak in the knees. And desolate with disappointment. She took a deep breath and worked her way through the crowd. It will get easier, she promised herself, once he leaves. Once he's on the other side of the country.

Eager to turn her mind to something else, she waved at the reporter from the local NBC affiliate. Three TV crews and a radio reporter had called to say they were attending. Earlier that morning she'd set up photo sessions for the print media. More coverage than Derek had managed to draw the previous year, she realized with grim satisfaction. If she had to leave Western, she would go in a blaze of glory. It was one of the few thoughts from which she could draw much consolation.

"THIS PLACE LOOKS LIKE a tornado struck." Tim Graham stood in the door of Martin's office and surveyed the half-filled packing boxes stacked around the room, the desk littered with disposable coffee cups and orange peel. "You look kind of rough yourself. What d'you do, camp out all night in here?''

"Just about." Martin ran his hand across his chin. He'd already packed up most of his books and papers. News of his imminent departure had spread through the unit like an epidemic. People had dropped in all morning to say good-bye. Once the decision had been made, he'd really wanted to leave immediately, but had reluctantly agreed to stay until the end of the month when one of the other neonatologists returned from a family emergency.

Graham cleared off a packing box from a chair and sat down. "Got much more to do?"

"This is about it." The few possession he had on the boat, already listed with a broker, were packed. He would drive the Fiat to Boston.

"You're lucky you don't have a wife and kids," Graham said. "When Ruth and I moved here from Phoenix..." He rolled his eyes. "A garage full of bikes and roller skates and God knows what else. I never want to go through that again."

Martin glanced at the Christmas gift one of the receptionists had left on his desk. A glass globe with a tiny figure inside it, surfing on a plastic ocean. Miniature palm trees fringed the shore. A reminder of California, she had told him. He lifted the globe, turned it upside down, then set it back on the desk. It struck him that at one time he would have related to the figure locked inside. Isolated, contained in his own world, closed off from the life going on all around.

He tried to find that same detachment now, but something protective had been torn away, and the raw, aching emptiness hurt more than he would have believed possible. Twice that morning, he'd started up to the public relations office, then turned back, reminding himself that this was what Catherine wanted. The intercom buzzed on his desk, and the unit secretary reminded him that his presence was expected at the NICU reunion.

Minutes later, across the packed conference room, he spotted Catherine. Watched her until a woman carrying a smiling red-haired toddler in a blue velvet dress approached him and blocked his view.

"Dr. Connaughton." The woman smiled. "I heard you're leaving Western and I wanted to be sure you got to see Debra." She held out the child for his inspection. "Two pounds at birth. Amazing, isn't it?" Her smile broadened. "But I'm sure with all these kids around here, there's no way you can remember."

He glanced at the woman's name tag, moved his head to avoid the cookie the toddler was trying to force into his mouth, and apologized for his bad memory. Across the room, he saw Catherine talking to a female reporter he recognized from the first press conference he'd done. Both women glanced over in his direction. He forced his eyes away from Catherine, smiled at the mother and child and tried to remember what she had asked him. She patted his arm.

"I'm not going to take up any more of your time." She began to move away. "Good luck. Where is it you're going?"

"Boston." He watched as Catherine, a camera crew in tow, worked her way through the crowd to where he stood. She wore a dark green wool dress that hugged the lines of her body, and her hair was piled up in a knot on the top of her head the way it had been that night in the van. The night she had begged him to make love to her. She moved closer, her eyes studiously avoiding his, her bottom lip caught in her teeth.

And then she was there in front of him, addressing his

left shoulder as she explained that the reporter at her side wanted an interview with him. Wisps of hair brushed her cheek. She'd chewed off her lipstick. He didn't respond to her request, just kept his eyes on her face until she slowly looked up at him. Seconds passed, neither of them looked away. For a moment it seemed they were alone in the room, oblivious to the noisy, squealing children all around.

"I'll do it on one condition," he finally said. "Which I'll explain later."

Selena Bliss laughed. "How can she agree to something if she doesn't know the terms?"

"It's okay." Catherine held his gaze. "I accept."

SHE STOOD OUTSIDE the conference room, her back against the wall, arms wrapped around her leather folder. A few feet away, Selena Bliss interviewed Martin about the reunion. She heard him talk about improved outcomes for premature babies, the miracles of modern medicine. Once, he glanced over at her, held her eyes for a moment. The charge had shot through her body. She felt suspended somehow, on a different plane from all of those bustling around her. Everything in soft focus, but the tall man talking to Selena Bliss.

The crowd from the conference room began to trickle out. Finally, Selena finished the interview and left with her crew. A moment later, Martin walked over to where Catherine stood. Without a word, he glanced over his shoulder at the exit door, pulled it open with one hand and, with the other, pulled her into the deserted stairwell. Then he backed her against the wall, put his hands on either side of her shoulders and kissed her hard. His tongue in her mouth, body pressed up against hers, he kissed her until she thought her knees would give way.

When they finally parted, he kept his hands on the wall,

stared into her eyes. "I think we should finish what we started the other night. I want to make love to you, Catherine."

"If that was the condition—" her voice was ragged "—I've already accepted it."

"I don't know what's going to happen." His eyes searched her face. "Saturday night, I decided you were probably right about Boston and maybe you are. Maybe we're all wrong for each other, but…I'm so bloody miserable without you. It's like an unbearable pain and there's only one thing that will help it." His lips brushed her throat and she arched her neck back. "What are you doing tonight?" he asked softly.

"Nothing. Gary's picking up the kids later today. He's got them for Christmas."

"*Christmas.*" He shook his head as though suddenly aware of the date. "So you'll be alone?"

She nodded. "You, too?"

"No. I'll be with you. Let's just forget about everything else. Can we do that? No talk about tomorrow, or next week. Just us in the moment?"

Shaking with desire, she stared into his eyes, drank in the details of his face. Then he kissed her again and her brain ceased to function. "Tonight," she managed to say a moment later.

"Tonight then," he said, and kissed her again. "Merry Christmas."

FULL FUNCTION DIDN'T RETURN to her brain for hours. Even when Jordan dropped into her office to congratulate her on the press coverage for the NICU reunion. Even when Derek called to say that he'd heard Martin was leaving Western and would she reconsider her resignation and stay on. Even when she'd shocked herself by agreeing to do so, but only as assistant manager. She'd briefly snapped out of her trance when he'd agreed to her terms, but before long her mind was counting down the hours to the moment she would see Martin again.

On the way home from Western, she joined the last-minute throng of holiday shoppers at the mall. For a moment she lingered at the door of a brightly lit store, then impulsively, her face warm, she stepped inside. Lingerie surrounded her, billowing in creamy drifts of lace and silk from shelves and displays, pouring out of gift-wrapped boxes, clinging sinuously to mannequin bodies. Along one wall, stylized silver torsos wore shimmering panties in rainbow colors. On another, they sported jungle motifs—zebra stripes, leopard spots, monkey paws.

Like a tourist in an exotic and foreign country, Catherine stared at the women all around her. Watched as they touched, discarded, selected. Were they all anticipating a Christmas Eve seduction? From a drawer overflowing with frothy garments, she withdrew a confection of peach silk. Panties, constructed entirely of satin ribbon, designed only to be untied. Suddenly overwhelmed by it all, she hastily selected an armful of lingerie, found a cubicle and stripped off her clothes.

Clad in only her own white cotton panties, she looked critically at herself in the full-length mirror. Turned sideways. Peered over her shoulder at her rear. Definitely no reed-thin mannequin. In a charitable mood, she could see her body as womanly. Large breasts, rounded hips. Gary had called them childbearing hips. Less charitably, they were broad. Would Martin be disappointed? She tried on a lacy cream camisole, discarded it. A peach bra, from which her breasts burst like overripe fruit. A diaphanous slip that clung like a casing to her belly and hips.

The pile of discarded items grew. With her fingers, she

combed her hair about her shoulders, licked her lips. In truth, she no longer had any idea how her body looked. Its image had been wildly distorted, first by Gary's disinterest, then by his abandonment. Now, in the dressing room's artificial light, her skin looked sallow, her body fleshy and soft. Gripped by panic, she quickly dressed, suddenly seeing herself as a mediocre gift, made attractive by its paper and ribbons, but, unwrapped, a disappointment.

She hastily separated a black lace bra and panties from the jumble of lingerie and started for the cash register. Still not too late to call and cancel, a voice in her head reminded her, even as she fished for the credit card in her wallet. Better to leave him with an illusion. She handed her card to the sales assistant in a Santa hat.

THE CASE OF NERVES lingered even as she sat across from Martin in the Spanish restaurant he'd chosen. Sprigs of mistletoe adorned pictures of bullfighters, festively dressed diners toasted each other with sangria, and she was yakking on, endlessly, about paella. "They use this special pan to make it." She touched her fork to the round shallow pan on the table between them. "In some parts of Spain, they put the pan right on the fire and just eat directly from it."

"Not a bad idea." Martin stuck a fork in the mixture of seafood and rice and grinned at her.

She watched as he extracted a shrimp and ate it in one bite. Martin wasn't the only reason she was rushing to fill the silences. A fight with Gary when he'd come to pick up the children hadn't exactly been a tension reducer. When Peter heard she was spending Christmas Eve with Martin, he'd decided, suddenly, that he didn't want to go with his father. Gary had accused her of trying to alienate the boy's affections. She suspected that Peter was jealous and the thought tore at her.

She drank some wine. A candle in an earthenware bottle flickered, dripped ribbons of wax. "Paella's a regional sort of thing," she rattled on. "Every area uses ingredients that grow locally. In an inland area you might get sausages and pork, for example. On the coast, you'd have fish." *God, this was ridiculous. Someone make her shut up.* A waiter in a short red jacket and black trousers moved between the tables. Catherine looked at Martin.

He winked.

She stared at the pile of shrimp tails, the empty mussel and clam shells and racked her brain for something to say. All the fantasizing about making love to this man had come down to this. *She was scared to death.* A busboy removed the dishes. On his heels a waiter arrived to ask about dessert. He reeled off a list of offerings that included a dense, chocolatey and highly caloric confection she'd first tasted in Valencia.

"I usually cover my ears at this point," she said, although on her own, she would have ordered three of everything. Buried her face in chocolate goo. "Anyway, I'm stuffed."

"Ah, come on. This is Christmas Eve. I think you should indulge." Martin glanced at the waiter. "One of the chocolate things and a couple of cognacs."

"You're wicked." Catherine shook her head at him, tried to relax. "Dissolute."

"One of my better qualities actually." He put his elbows on the table, leaned forward, eyes on her face. "Are you all right? You seem a bit tense."

She grinned, relieved to have it out between them. "You could say that."

"What is it? The kids? Us?"

"All of it." She looked at him. "But especially the us part. All I've been able to think of is being with you tonight, and now I'm suddenly panicking…I don't know, it's not like I'm twenty and flawless. There are bags and sags." She stopped. "Jeez, even with the wine I'm getting embarrassed."

"Catherine." He caught her hands. "I'm not twenty and flawless either. I wouldn't even want twenty and flawless—"

"I know…neither would I." She laughed. "It sounds so stupid now, but I went shopping earlier today." She told him about the lingerie shop experience. "And I just sort of freaked."

He grinned, shook his head and stared at her for a moment. "You don't have a very accurate perception of yourself, do you? You're a good-looking woman. Desirable, sensuous…"

She looked at him, bit her lip. "Thank you."

"I mean it. It's difficult for me to even imagine why you'd worry."

"Maybe it's a woman thing, I don't know."

He moved his glass on the table, looked at her. "Listen, if you'd rather not—"

"No, I want to. God, this is ridiculous. I'm coming off like some blushing teenage virgin—"

"Well, you're blushing—"

"I know, my face feels as though it's on fire." She sat back in her chair as the waiter brought the cognac and dessert, drank some water, let the ice melt in her mouth.

Martin raised his glass. "What shall we drink to?"

"Christmas." She touched her glass to his, watched his face for a moment. Imagined spending other Christmas Eves with him. *No. Not allowed.* "Tell me what you're thinking right now," she said, mostly just to block out her thoughts.

"Given your concerns—" he met her eyes "—it might not be wise."

"Tell me." She held her glass in both hands, stared at him over the rim. "Come on."

"Of ripping off your clothes, throwing you onto the bed and making love to you for most of the night." His knees touched hers. "And then waking up in the morning with you next to me and doing it all over again."

She swallowed. Desire fought nerves and won hands down. *God, she wanted him.* "You know what I'm thinking?"

"Tell me."

She slowly licked chocolate mousse off her spoon, stared into his eyes.

"Really?"

"Mmm." The tip of her tongue circled the bowl of the spoon. "I wasn't sure you spoke that language." She smiled slowly. "But I'm glad you do."

He slipped one shoe off and, his eyes on her face, ran his foot up the inside of her thigh. She spread her legs slightly, wriggled against his toe.

"If you keep doing that," he said, "I might have to take you right here."

She glanced around the crowded restaurant, then her eyes went back to him. "Right on the table?"

He swallowed. "Uh-huh."

Her face went hot. "No clothes on?"

"Completely naked."

"Spread out across the table?"

He nodded, watching her eyes.

"Do you think anyone would mind?"

He grinned. "Who cares?"

She glanced down at the front of her dress. Her nipples were erect against the fabric. "Look at me."

"You should see me."

They both spoke at once. "Let's get out of here."

CHAPTER EIGHTEEN

"CHEZ CONNAUGHTON." Tie undone, jacket opened, Martin put his arm around Catherine's shoulders, and they walked down the wooden gangway to the boat. At the bottom, they stopped and kissed. Her hands in his hair, tongue in his mouth. He tasted chocolate, wine. Heat.

"I just want you to know…" She smiled into his eyes. "That at this very moment, I couldn't think of a better way to spend Christmas Eve than being here with you."

He hugged her close, knew exactly what she meant. For now, he was exactly where he wanted to be. Despite their pact, he felt like a love-struck adolescent out with his girl. Sex later on was a given, an erotic subtext to the evening. But for the moment there was a magic to standing in the cool air, arms entwined.

She turned to look across the darkened water at the lighted Christmas trees in Alamitos Bay. He stood behind her, his arms around her waist. Above them, a patch of fog hung like a shawl over a slender crescent moon. The plaintive wail of a saxophone from a party across the bay drifted in the air.

"It's beautiful," she said. "It must be nice living here on the water. Very romantic."

"Gardening's a bit tricky though," he said. "Very difficult to put down roots." The thought of the marina as romantic hadn't occurred to him but, through her eyes, he experienced it as though for the first time. The fugue of waterfront sounds, the damp salt tang to the air.

She leaned back against him, and he ran his hands across her belly, up and down her thighs, the soft velvet of her short dress sensuous under his palms, inching up between his fingers.

"Do you think…" She covered his hands with her own, guiding them along the lines of her body. "That those people in the houses across the water are sitting there with binoculars watching us?"

"No." He nuzzled her neck, inched the dress higher. Except for the distant lights, they were cocooned in the concealing blackness. "They're all old and blind and go to bed at six. We could take off all our clothes and dance a jig and none of them would know."

"Might be a little cold though." She leaned into his body, her bottom pressed against his groin. "What exactly is it you're doing with your hand?"

"Checking to see if your new underwear includes panty hose."

"And?"

He felt smooth, warm skin above the top of her stockings.

She smiled.

He edged a finger between her thighs, felt her slight tremor. A breeze blew strands of her hair across his face. Out in the bay, a lighted pleasure boat rocked the dark water, left a churning wake. Sounds of laughter, revelry, floated out to them. With his mouth, he parted her hair, kissed the back of her neck. The prospecting finger explored, she squirmed against it, gave a low moan.

"I think," she said softly, "that you've just struck gold."

He slid his finger higher, stroked her until she slumped

against him, her breath coming in short gasps. A few moments later, he turned her around, kissed her and led her to the boat. With one fluid movement, he jumped aboard then held out his hand for her.

HER BODY STILL HOT and swollen from his hand, her legs shaking with desire, she watched Martin pull off his jacket and tie. Then he lit a candle, put a jazz CD on the stereo and drew her into his arms.

"Let's see," he said. "Where were we?"

"You were doing something wicked to me." Her arms around his neck, she swayed against him to the soft beat of the music. Smiling into his eyes, she ran her fingertips inside the collar of his shirt, massaged the muscles at the base of his neck. The saxophone throbbed and wailed and they kissed and swayed some more in the candlelight.

"I think..." He located the zipper at the back of her velvet dress. "That you're wearing far too many clothes." With the palms of his hands, he pushed the dress off her shoulders and down her body. It slid to the floor and she stood there, clad only in black lace bra and panties and the sheer stockings that clung to the tops of her thighs. Torn between wanting to get naked on the bed with him and the sensual thrill of the slow striptease, she watched him kiss the tops of her breasts. Through the portholes, the marina lights blinked golden in the dark night; beneath their feet, the boat gently rocked. With one hand he unclasped the front of her bra, tossed it off and took her breast in his mouth.

She shuddered at the touch of his teeth on her nipple, at his hands on her body, at the sheer eroticism of the evening. They kissed again and, without taking her mouth from his, she removed his shirt and they swayed together, her breasts against his chest, skin against skin. No matter what they'd

told each other, no matter what happened after tonight, she
knew without a doubt that she loved him. Loved him and
wanted him with an intensity that stunned her. Slowly, sa-
voring the moment, she unbuckled his pants, lowered them
over his hips, then hooked her fingers in the waist of his
shorts and pulled them down. For a moment she just looked
at him: Martin, naked in front of her. Tall, lean and fully
erect in the flickering candlelight.

"Where's your bedroom?" she whispered.

"I'll show you in a minute. First though, we still need
to get rid of some more clothes."

With one hand, he pushed her onto the padded bench
that ran down one side of the cabin, stripped off the sheer
black stockings and touched his lips to the black lace at her
crotch. The kiss sent a tremor through her body that left
her trembling and weak. Head thrown back, knees spread
wide, she gave herself up to sensation. Nothing existed but
this hot center of her and Martin's mouth against it. His
teeth tugged at the lace, pushed it aside. His tongue lapped
and probed, darted up inside her, hotter and higher, faster,
chasing the heat. Some part of her brain registered the silver
ribbons of moonlight on his hair, the lap of water against
the sides of the boat, but the heat kept building inside her,
building and growing until the tension finally broke and
she cried out.

ON CHRISTMAS MORNING, she woke to the creak of the boat
against the dock, the raucous cawing of a couple of gulls
and Martin beside her. She lay on her back, eyes still
closed, lulled by the sway of the boat on the water. In the
distance, she heard the rumble of traffic across the Alamitos
Bay Bridge, the same sounds she heard from her own bedroom every morning. Less than a mile away, but it seemed
a different world.

He lay with one hand loose on her breast, a leg sprawled across hers. Early-morning sunlight shimmered over their bodies, fell in patches on his chest and stomach, her thighs.

Disentangling herself, she turned onto her side to face him, her head raised on one elbow. In sleep, his head thrown back against the pillow, the intensity of expression gone, he seemed younger, vulnerable. She gazed at him, absorbing details. Unruly hair that, depending on the light, seemed either red or brown. A small scar by his mouth. His body long and spare, chest and arms faintly tanned.

Memories of the night before filtered in, and she imagined seeing him at the hospital now. The way she had first seen him. *Dr.* Connaughton tearing down the corridors, white coat flapping behind him. In the NICU, examining an infant, his face serious and intent. It would be different now. And then she remembered she would never see him at Western again. The thought brought a lump to her throat.

He stirred, opened his eyes and smiled lazily at her. "Hi."

"Hi." She leaned across to kiss him, felt his beard graze her breast. "Merry Christmas."

"You, too." He rolled over to face her. "By the way, that was a fantastic gift you gave me last night."

She smiled. "As good as the one this morning?"

"Almost." With his thumb, he traced the outline of her jaw. "Are there more where that one came from?"

"Lots." Still smiling, she rolled over on her back. "God, this is fantastic. Just being here with you like this. It's all a new experience. Not hearing cartoons on somewhere. I feel as though I should jump up and start pouring the milk and Cheerios. Go look for schoolbooks or something."

"I'm glad you're here instead."

"Me, too." She smiled into his eyes, thinking how terrific he looked. *I am so nuts about you, I can't see straight.*

She held his face in her hands, looked into his eyes. Reminded herself that they'd made a pact. No thought beyond the moment. But she would never feel quite this way again. She knew that. Martin filled her body, her heart, her brain. Her soul. Even now, after they'd made love half the night, she felt weak with desire for him.

"Hey you…" She brought his hand to her mouth. "What was that you said last night about waking up in the morning and doing it all over again?"

"We did."

"That was hours ago." She climbed astride him. "It doesn't count."

"SO WAS SHOWERING *à deux* one of the new experiences you were seeking?" Martin asked some time later that morning. His hair still damp, he was barefoot, in jeans and a white T-shirt.

"It was and I liked it." She grinned. "That and everything else."

She stood in the small galley scrambling eggs for breakfast. The day was sunny and unseasonably warm for Christmas and she wore an old pair of Martin's denim cutoffs and a loose red cotton shirt that she'd packed in an overnight bag. No bra. The straps had slid down her shoulders, so she'd abandoned it in keeping with the unfettered spirit of their day together. Eventually, she would have to return to the real world, but for now she was living out her fantasy.

"So the plan is…" Martin peeled an orange, broke it off into sections and put one in her mouth. "No plan. We just lounge around here all day like a couple of indolent sloths."

"Sounds good to me," she said through a mouthful of orange. "Too bad you have to go in tonight."

"Right, but you'll be here waiting for me and it's the last day of on-call." A shadow passed across his face and he frowned at the piece of orange peel in his hand. "I wasn't going to say anything, but there was a message on the machine. The phone must have rung while we were— busy." His mouth twitched. "Anyway, it was Tim Graham wanting to let me know that Grossman is back from Europe."

"Which means?"

"That he'll undoubtedly want to do the surgery. Probably in the next day or so. After today, I'm gone. There'll be nothing standing in Grossman's way."

Catherine wrapped her arms around his waist, leaned her face against his back. Whatever objectivity he might have gained, the emotional torment he felt over Holly was clearly still close to the surface. She felt an enormous surge of tenderness and an almost equal feeling of helplessness.

He ran his hands across his face. "Listen, let's not talk about Western. Today is our time to be together." His face brightened. "I've got an idea. Let's take the boat out, okay? I don't have to be at the hospital until five, so we'll have a few hours to ourselves."

"Fine." She met his eyes. "But if you want to talk about it, I'm here."

"CALL THE HOSPITAL and tell them you have a serious malady and you won't be in." She said that later, after the boat was back in the marina. They were in the rear bunk, lying naked on rumpled sheets and drinking champagne when her cell phone rang. Catherine sat up. "Uh-oh. It's in my purse in the other cabin. I better go see what's going on."

Martin nodded, but felt a stab of resentment at the intrusion. She's got kids, he reminded himself. Responsibilities. He watched as she padded, naked, into the main cabin, then he closed his eyes. From her end of the conversation, he realized something had happened to Peter. Immediately, he reached for his clothes on the floor.

"Gary," she said a few minutes later. She sat down on the edge of the bed. "Peter's in the emergency room at Western. He fell off his bike. It's nothing serious, no broken bones, but…" She bit her lip hard. "Gary says he's kind of upset."

"Did you talk to him?"

"No, Gary wouldn't let me. He just started laying this guilt trip on me."

"Guilt trip? What do you have to feel guilty about?"

"That I'm out screwing around, as he put it, while my son is in the hospital." She pulled on her shirt, buttoned it up. Bent to retrieve her shorts and underpants. "He said I'm always going on about how important the kids are, but when one of them needs me, I'm more interested in getting laid." Her eyes filled and brimmed over. "God, Martin, I feel terrible. I'm going to have to go. Gary's furious."

"Catherine." He looked at her. "What right exactly does Gary have to be furious? He's their father. The agreement was that they stay with him for a few days. He's perfectly capable of looking after them."

"I know." She wiped her knuckle across her eyes. "I just think I should be with them."

He sat up, swung his legs off the bed to sit beside her. Shoulders hunched, she held the jeans and underwear bunched up in her lap. With one finger, he brushed back a lock of long brown hair from her shoulder. "I know you want to be with Peter right now, Catherine. But don't let Gary bully you into feeling guilty. It's pretty obvious he's jealous of the idea of you being with me."

"That's not it. If Peter hadn't had an accident—"

"Peter's fine now. You heard that yourself. Kids fall off

their bikes all the time. Gary just needed an excuse. What you're doing is letting him come between us. You need to stand up to him—''

"Don't tell me what I *need* to do, Martin, okay? I'm sorry if you can't understand that my first priority is to my kids, but that's the way it is."

He studied her face for a minute. "I'm trying to understand what's going on here. I feel as though the rules have suddenly been changed, but no one's told me what they are. Is there something else I'm not picking up on?"

"I don't know." She wouldn't look at him. "Maybe I just got a dose of reality. Being here with you was great, but now it's time to go back to the real world."

"The perfect excuse to leave. Is that it?"

"Martin, stop, okay?" She finished dressing. "We both agreed that this was just an in-the-moment thing and…well, the moment's passed. Gary's threatened before to take custody of them. I'm not giving him any ammunition—''

"So you'll let him blackmail you."

"Look, I'm not going to get into this with you." She picked her way across the clutter of his discarded clothes and the empty champagne glasses. "Can you just take me home?"

He followed her into the main cabin. "Remember what we said about hiding behind walls?"

She shook her head. "This is different. Let's just drop the subject, okay? We both got what we wanted—''

"No." He grabbed her arms, forced her to look at him. "Dammit, Catherine, you know it's more than that. I don't care what we agreed on. I love you. Can't you see that?"

"I don't know. I don't know what to think. Right now, I just want to go home."

The phone rang again. His phone. Grossman had scheduled Holly's surgery for tomorrow. He looked at Catherine. "Do you have your things together?"

She nodded, her expression uncertain. "What are you going to do?"

"I'm going back to the hospital. I think I have a better grasp of the parameters there than I do here." He picked his keys up off the table. "Ready?"

They drove back to her house in silence. He pulled up outside, stunned at how quickly the euphoria of the day had dissolved into this. Catherine, clearly fighting back tears, rubbed her sleeve across her eyes.

"I'm sorry about the way things turned out," she said.

"So am I." He left the engine running. He drove away before she'd even reached the front door.

CHAPTER NINETEEN

As SHE STOOD at the refrigerator eating a Christmas dinner of cold spaghetti from a Tupperware container, Catherine decided that this would probably go down as one of the loneliest, most depressing Christmas Days she'd ever had.

After effectively ruining her time with Martin, Gary had decided the kids would stay with him after all. When she'd finally managed to talk to Peter, he'd seemed fine. More interested in the video game he was playing than talking on the phone to her. Julie, busy helping Nadia bake sugar cookies, had been only slightly more conversational. After Catherine hung up, she'd felt almost miserable enough to consider driving over to her mother's house for the low-fat, low-cholesterol, low-calorie dinner her mother was preparing for a few friends in her wellness support group.

Almost. Instead, she finished the spaghetti and opened the freezer. Caramel pecan ice cream wouldn't make her feel any better about Martin, but it couldn't make her feel much worse. Twice she'd started to call him at the hospital then hung up. What was the point? Seeing him would only weaken her resolve. And nothing he could say would rid her of the fear of what could happen if she allowed herself to really need him.

By the time the phone rang at 4:45 a.m., she'd drifted off into a fitful doze. She picked it up on the first ring, sank back against the pillow.

"Martin. Hi."

There was a pause. "No. It's Derek." Another pause.
"Listen, sorry to wake you at this hour, but we've got a
major crisis. A baby in the NICU was found dead just before midnight. It's unofficial at this point, details are still
coming in, but they're calling it an apparent homicide."

"Oh my God." Catherine reached for the pen and notebook she kept on her nightstand. She sat up. "Who is it?
Do we have a name?"

"Yeah. Holly Hodges."

"*Holly.*" Catherine's hand shot to her mouth. "What
happened? Does Martin know?"

"He's the main suspect, kiddo."

THE DETECTIVE HAD a wide, florid face, thinning gray hair,
gold-rimmed glasses and a paunch that strained the fabric
of his white shirt. Martin glanced at the clock on his desk.
Not quite noon. The man had been questioning him for
more than an hour. The phone on the desk rang, and Martin
ignored it, not wanting to conduct a conversation in front
of the detective. The previous call had been from Gary
Prentice who'd made a thinly veiled threat about Catherine
losing custody of the kids if she continued the relationship.
Martin turned his attention to the detective.

"According to a number of people in the medical center,
Dr. Connaughton, you have an explosive temper." The detective's voice was casual, conversational. "Would you
agree with that assessment?"

"It's what I've been told."

"But do *you* agree?"

"I suppose so."

The detective looked at him. "What does that mean exactly?"

Tempted to give him a demonstration, Martin thought

better of it. He stared at the desktop, looked up at the detective. "It means yes, I lose my temper easily."

The detective made a note. "Now, Dr. Connaughton, you were opposed to surgery for this child, right?"

"I was."

"To the point that you actually erased Grossman's name from the surgery schedule."

"I did."

"And your professional relationship with Dr. Grossman? How would you describe it?"

"You've already asked that. Twice."

"I'm asking again."

"We're not exactly a mutual admiration society."

"You dislike him?"

"You could say that."

"According to Dr. Grossman, you became so irate about the prospect of surgery for this patient that you knocked him out of his chair. Do you recall that incident?"

"I do."

"You told a TV reporter, in relation to this case, that you believe death is preferable to questionable treatment. Do you recall saying something like that?"

"I may have. I don't know that it necessarily related to this case."

The phone on the desk rang again. The detective motioned to it. "Why don't you go ahead and answer it, Doctor? Maybe it's important." Martin shrugged and picked up the phone. Hanrahan, the hospital's lawyer. Martin hung up, stood and walked around to where the detective sat. "We're going to have to wrap this up. I've been advised not to say anything more to you without an attorney present."

The detective put away his notebook. "Well, thanks for

your trouble, Dr. Connaughton." He got to his feet. "What's your accent?"

"Irish."

"Are you an American citizen?"

"No." Martin sipped some lukewarm coffee from a disposable cup. "I'm here on a permanent visa. I have a green card."

"Not thinking about taking any trips back to the old country in the foreseeable future, are you?"

Martin shrugged.

The detective gave him an assessing look. "Well, I wouldn't plan any if I were you. I'd strongly advise you to stick around for a while."

After the detective left, Martin slumped down behind his desk and tried to bring some order to his thoughts, which, like events of the past twenty-four hours, spun wildly out of control. The phone rang, he picked it up immediately, hoping it might be Catherine. Instead it was Hanrahan's secretary calling to change the time of their appointment later that day.

AFTER THE MEETING with Hanrahan, Martin headed for the NICU. Glancing around the lobby to make sure there were no camera crews lurking nearby, he punched the elevator button for the sixth floor. In the same instant, he realized that he had no reason to be in the NICU. His rotation was over. *Holly was dead.*

The reality hit him as though for the first time, leaving him feeling newly bereft. He let the elevator go and stood in the brightly lit lobby, stared unseeing into the gift shop's plate-glass windows. He leaned against the wall of the telephone enclosure, questions hurtling around in his brain.

On a whim, he dialed directory assistance and got the number and address of an Edward Hodges in North Long

Beach. His hand hovered over the receiver, then he changed his mind.

Twenty minutes later, he pulled up outside a small stucco house in a side street off Atlantic Boulevard. A chain-link fence surrounded the small weed-choked front yard. More weeds sprouted in the concrete walkway and along cracks in the three concrete steps leading to the front door. After turning off the ignition, he sat staring through the rain-spattered windshield. A couple of teenagers in black clothes walked by, heads shaven, smoking, shoulders hunched against the cool night air. A dog barked somewhere. In the gutters, trash made sodden by the rain, glimmered under the streetlights.

When the windshield began to fog, Martin got out and knocked at the front door. While he waited, he took a step backward, peering at a window to his right. Light from a TV screen glowed through the drapes. From inside, he heard movement, then the door opened slightly against a chain.

A face peered through the opening. Eyes widened. Then the door was closed for a moment and flung open.

Rita's face was gaunt and pallid. Her eyes had an empty, distant look. Her shapeless gray sweatshirt and faded jeans hung like rags on her thin frame. She started to speak, and then her face seemed to collapse.

He put his arms around her. There weren't any words, he thought. Nothing meaningful to say. He held her, felt her tears against his skin. Comforting her and feeling somehow comforted himself. Rita's grief seemed close to his own. Grief for Holly, for the child who might have been. They stood together until her sobbing subsided and she pulled away.

"D'you want some coffee?" She dabbed at her eyes with wadded tissues. "A soda or something?"

He shook his head and sat down at one end of a battered orange couch, which, with a matching recliner, a TV and an aluminum Christmas tree winking blue lights in one corner, constituted the living-room furnishings. The air in the room was heavy with stale cigarette smoke and lingering cooking odors. A tortoiseshell cat snaked against Martin's legs.

Rita sat down on the opposite end of the couch. "The other kids are with my folks," she said. "Eddie's out." She twisted the tissue in her hands. "He's taking this real badly."

Martin refrained from comment. The TV was showing a Christmas special. Actors in biblical costumes warbled "Away in a Manger." He stared at it, suddenly, inexplicably, at a loss for words. He'd counseled enough bereaved parents through the grieving process. He knew the stages. Knew how the anger often surprised them. "It's like you've prepared a big celebration," he'd sometimes tell them, "and the guest of honor just turns around and leaves. Naturally, you'd feel hurt and rejected. You'd probably be angry, too." He'd never felt facile or glib, but now, struggling with his own emotions, the words he'd so easily uttered seemed empty and meaningless. Not much more than a greeting card sentiment.

"I loved her..." Rita sat on the edge of the sofa now, knees together, looking down at her hands folded in her lap. "She was so tiny, but she knew me. When I played that little music box for her... 'You Are My Sunshine.' She *was,* you know. I'll never hear that song again without..." Her voice broke, and she started to cry again.

Caught up in her emotions, Martin looked away.

"She was so brave. All she went through..." Rita got up from the couch, took a box of tissues from the top of the TV and blew her nose. "All I wanted was what was best for her. But it was so hard. One minute I'd be watching her little face, the way it kind of crumpled up like she was really hurting, and I'd think no, she shouldn't go through any more. Then the next minute I'd think well, maybe she deserves the chance—"

"I'm sorry if I made things more difficult. I wanted what was best for her, too."

"I know you did. You were just doing what you thought was right. I understand. She's better off where she is now, I know that."

He looked at her, wondered for a moment whether she thought he had murdered her baby as an act of compassion and was now offering him her forgiveness. As he struggled momentarily for words, Rita put her hand on his arm.

"I wanted to call you this morning, but, well, Eddie was here and everything. Anyway, what I was saying was, I was standing there, looking at Holly and all of a sudden, it was like she was trying to tell me something. For a minute, I didn't believe it, but I swear, Dr. C., it was like she was saying, 'No more.'"

Martin saw the far-off look in her eyes and felt a sudden chill.

She cleared her throat and for a few moments stared silently at the TV. "I leaned over and kissed her and told her I loved her and…" She stopped, held a tissue against her mouth for a moment. "There was this little soft blanket. It was folded up into a small square. I just held it over her face. She looked so peaceful after, Dr. C.…"

He heard the words a moment before they actually registered and he felt his body tense. Rita, he was dimly aware, was still talking. Words and tears flowing unquenched.

"I wanted to talk to someone, but everyone was so busy. They were short-staffed, so Holly's nurse had to go help with a delivery. Then there was all this commotion down at the other end of the nursery."

She began to cry again, and Martin moved next to her and took her hand. A pulse above his right eye began to twitch as the realization of what she'd told him sank in.

"I still think it was right, what I did," she said, more composed now. "It's just that afterward, I got kind of scared like I'd done something bad. Do you think it was bad, Dr. C.?"

"I think you did it because you loved Holly." Martin chose his words carefully. "You wanted what you thought was best for her."

"That's what I keep telling myself."

"Rita, who else knows about this?"

"No one."

"Not even Eddie?"

"No." She shook her head. "Eddie's one reason I did it. I couldn't fight him anymore. He was so dead set on Holly having the surgery, and it wasn't right for her. You always said that, Dr. C."

Martin said nothing.

"Then Dr. Grossman was calling me a bad mother and saying if I loved her I'd want her to have the operation. I just couldn't deal with them anymore."

"Why did you tell me, Rita?"

"I knew you'd understand. I mean, you felt the same way as me." She paused. "And I guess because I've always trusted you. It's like, well, you were the one there right at the beginning, you know? I just...wanted you to know. I don't know what's going to happen now though."

Elbows on his knees, his head in his hands, Martin pondered this latest reality. Outside, a car door slammed. Rita jumped up from the couch as though she'd been shot.

"It's Eddie!" Her eyes went wide with fear. "Please don't tell him, Dr. C."

As she ran to open the front door, Martin got up from the couch. Eddie Hodges wore tight blue jeans, a heavy flannel shirt over a red T-shirt and cowboy boots. From across the room, Martin smelled the alcohol on the other man's breath.

Eddie's face froze. "Want to tell me what the hell you're doing here?"

"I came to see Rita."

"Yeah?" Hodges took a step forward. "Well, you've seen her. Now get out."

"Eddie." Rita reached to touch his arm. "Dr. C. was just—"

"Stay the hell out of this, Rita, okay?" Hodges kept his eyes on Martin's face. "If she'd had the surgery in the first place, like Dr. Grossman wanted, none of this shit would have happened."

"Right then." Martin turned to Rita. "I should go. If there's anything I can do, you know how to get in touch with me." He started for the door.

"Don't you ignore me." Hodges grabbed Martin's sleeve. "You know something? I never trusted you from goddamn day one."

"The feeling's mutual." He jerked his arm free from Hodges's grasp.

"You and your goddamn negative attitude. They're goin' to get you for this, you know that? I hope you rot in jail." He balled his knuckles into a menacing fist, brought it up to Martin's face. "Baby killer, I ought to beat the crap out of you."

Adrenaline pumping, Martin felt his own fists clench. While a swift blow to Hodges's jaw would get rid of a lot of tension, Rita's frightened face behind Eddie's shoulders persuaded him that two men brawling on her front doorstep was the last thing she needed. It took every bit of willpower he could muster to walk away.

HALF AN HOUR LATER, elbows on the bar, head in his hands, Martin sat in the Long Beach Marina Jolly Roger, trying with a couple of beers to achieve what a punch in Hodges's face might have accomplished. Light glimmered off liquor bottles lined up on glass shelves along the bar. Behind them, through the plate-glass windows, he could see the masts bobbing in the black water. In the distance, amber streetlights glimmered like jewels in the night sky.

Life was a bit like navigating in unfamiliar waters, he thought. You make a mistake, don't realize it but keep going along until suddenly you realize your whole direction has changed. He'd done that, gone off course somewhere. He'd thought he was acting in Holly's best interests. He still did. But now Holly was dead. By her mother's hand. Was he partly to blame? Had he confused Rita to the point that she'd felt compelled to do what she had done?

He thought of Rita's surviving babies still in the hospital, of her older kids with the grandmother. He pulled out the detective's card, looked at it, drank some more beer. Images of Catherine in her little house. Her children. Peter and Julie with Catherine. Smiling. He'd wanted to see himself as part of the picture and for a while it almost came into focus. Almost, but not quite.

He got up from the bar stool, dropped some money on the counter and started for the door. Still holding the detective's card in his right hand, he wondered whether he should wait till the morning to call.

"YOU'RE NOT EVEN READY." Darcy, in a pale blue track-suit stood at the front door and jogged in place. "Weren't we supposed to run this morning?"

"We were." Catherine, still wearing a robe and slippers, held a coffee cup in both hands and shivered in the early-morning air. "I've been up half the night though, it was after four before I got to sleep."

Darcy followed her into the kitchen. "Martin?"

"I'm scared to death for him. Grossman and his cronies would be thrilled to see him take the rap for Holly's death, and I'm terrified they might succeed."

"You haven't spoken to him?"

"Not since he dropped me off. I don't even know where he is. There was no answer when I called him at the boat and he's not at the hospital, but his rotation is over, so that's not too surprising." She glanced at the clock on the kitchen wall. It was six-thirty. "I thought I'd wait until seven and try calling him again. If he's not there, I'll go by the boat."

"You don't think the police maybe picked him up?"

"It's possible, I guess." Her stomach tensed at the thought. "But I think Derek would have called me. He'd probably want to put out some kind of press announcement." As she raised the coffee cup to her mouth, the phone rang. Startled, she splashed coffee down her robe, but caught the phone on the second ring. It was Derek.

"Catherine, is Connaughton there with you?"

"No." Her fingers gripped the receiver. "I've been try-ing to reach him. What's going on?"

"After the police got his statement," Derek told her, "he just took off. He didn't show up at the hospital today and there's no answer at his home number. You probably haven't heard, the media only just found out... The mother did it. She broke down last night and confessed to the detectives. Called them herself. Her other kids have been placed in protective custody.''

''Rita did it?'' Engulfed by an overwhelming mixture of sadness and relief, she couldn't speak for a moment. ''What will happen to her?''

''There's a lot of sympathy out there for her. My guess is they'll plead temporary insanity. That whole postpartum-blues thing. Hanrahan thinks she'll get off with a light sentence, or even probation.''

''Does Martin know?''

''He has to. Everybody has been leaving messages for him. Jordan is falling all over himself to make amends. Listen, it's crazy time around here again. Eddie Hodges is holding a news conference at ten to announce that he's divorcing Rita. One of the nurses said she saw him this morning all dressed in black. Total sleazebag. Administration wants us to distance ourselves from him. Anyway, we need to plan some kind of press update, put a release on the wires. Every reporter in town wants to speak to Connaughton. I know you're supposed to be off for a few days, but if you could come in, I'd appreciate it.''

CHAPTER TWENTY

"I DON'T KNOW WHAT Martin said to the detective, but my guess is that after Rita told him she'd killed the baby, he got it into his head that he had to take the rap for her." Tim Graham shifted on the bar stool, glanced around Mulligan's smoky interior. They'd walked over there at six, after Catherine got off work. "He probably figured he'd rather go to jail himself than see a mother with kids put away—especially if he's convinced himself that he was somehow to blame. Like I said, it's a guess, but knowing Martin—"

"As much as anyone knows him."

"True." He looked at her. "Hell, what am I thinking? I'm sure you know him better than I do. Doesn't that seem like a likely scenario?"

"Yeah." She nodded slowly. "And then when Rita confessed to the detectives, he probably felt there was nothing else he could do. At that point the whole thing was just too painful to deal with and he..." She paused, felt Tim watching her.

"He what?"

"I don't know." She stared down at her hands on the wooden bar. "Disappeared behind the wall."

"You've lost me."

"Just a figure of speech." Around them, she heard lilting accents that tore at something inside. As she listened, hearing sounds rather than content, an idea slowly emerged, fragile and tentative as a springtime shoot. For the moment, she couldn't look at it too closely. Later, she decided.

Graham drank some beer. "You're pretty serious about him, aren't you?"

"I guess you could say that." She gave a wry laugh. "It's kind of strange. My whole life, I've thought of myself as this needy person. Always dependent on someone else." A lighted bar sign flickered its message in red then green. Behind her two men talked football. "So what do I do? Fall in love with someone who actually needs *me*."

"But can't ask for help."

Surprised, she turned to him. "That's how you see him, too? I thought maybe it was just my own interpretation."

"No, I think you're right on. Martin's a loner. He'd sooner walk away from a situation than admit he needed someone." Graham signaled for another round. "Listen, Catherine, for what it's worth, you're important to him. We could all see the change in him in the last few weeks." He hesitated. "Even Val Webb said his temper had improved."

She grinned.

"I'm serious. Not that she was too thrilled that it was you and not her who was responsible for the change."

Catherine nodded, still smiling.

"So what are you going to do now?" Graham asked.

"I don't have all the details worked out yet." In her briefcase were a couple of addresses and phone numbers she'd wangled from a sympathetic clerk in personnel. "But I'm going to try and carry out a promise I made to him."

"WILL YOU BE JOINING us for a wee drink tonight, Martin?" Joan asked. "Sure, you can't see the new year in without a bit of a celebration."

Martin didn't answer. He stood in the parlor of his father's house in Belfast and leaned a shoulder against the casing. Through lace curtains, he could see out to the front garden, and the street beyond. Misty rain dripped off bare, black tree branches, fell like tears onto the drenched ground below. Behind him, his father and sister drank tea, huddled around the electric fire. Despite the heavy cable-knit sweater and flannel shirt he wore, he felt colder than he'd ever felt in his life. A chill that seemed to wrap around his bones, seep into his blood.

"Oh, come on Martin, it'll do you good to get out for a bit. You're walking around with the weight of the world on your shoulders."

Martin wiped condensation from the window, watched an elderly woman in a long dark coat trundle a shopping cart on wheels, her head bowed against the driving rain. The landscape seemed insubstantial, everything wrapped in a filmy shroud, the passersby shadowy figures who drifted through the gloom.

He moved from the window, stared at the red coils of the electric fire. Away from the window's drafts and cool panes, the room felt stifling and overheated, the air redolent of the eggs and black sausage they'd eaten an hour earlier. His father and sister watched him, faces expectant.

"So what about this girl of yours, Martin?" Joan reached into a cavernous cloth bag at her feet, pulled out a piece of knitting. "The one with the children?"

"Catherine." He returned to the window to stare out at the street again. Touched his hand to the condensation. Drops of water trickled down the pane. "Catherine is better off without me," he said after a moment. "I've already complicated her life enough. She doesn't need more problems."

"Did she decide that?" Joan's knitting needles clicked. "Or did you?"

"It makes no difference."

"Of course it makes a difference. And what you're *not* telling me answers my question." She stopped to count stitches on the needle. "So you ran away again, did you? Ah well, always easier than staying to work things out, isn't it?"

Anger igniting like a flame, Martin turned from the window to face her. "What the hell is that supposed to mean?"

"What it sounds like." Joan's eyes, blue like his own, darkened. She dropped the knitting in her lap. "You've done exactly as you did after Sharon died. Run away from everything—"

He glared at her. "I didn't bloody well run away—"

"Sure you did. You left Ireland in the first place because it was easier than living with what had happened. Not that you ever wanted to leave, mind you. It was a way to punish yourself, wasn't it? Just as you've gone on doing all these years and just as you're still doing."

"Balls." He stalked into the kitchen, grabbed his jacket from a hook on the back of the door. His sister on his heels snatched it from his hands.

"You're going to listen to me, Martin Connaughton." She held his arm in a fierce grip. "You blamed yourself for Sharon, now you're blaming yourself for this baby—"

"I didn't say that."

"Do you take me for a fool, then? You don't have to say it, it's written all over your face. Look at yourself. You've barely said half a dozen words since you got here. And you look like death warmed over."

"I'm tired, for God's sake, Joan. I don't feel like listening to this rubbish." He took his jacket from her, pulled it on and opened the back door.

She caught the knob, held it for a moment. "Go on then. Off with you. Have your way and go. But mind what I've said. You've atoned enough. Don't start the whole thing over again. Even prisoners get their sentences commuted.''

HE WALKED FOR HOURS. Through the streets of Belfast. Down Dublin Road, along Royal Avenue, past the shops, among the pedestrians. Water worked through the soles of his thin California shoes, soaked through his jacket. Rain turned to hail, bounced off the streets like popcorn, turned to slush under his feet. Red taillights of passing cars jeweled the gray wintry light. He walked until he lost track of time. Through the maze of narrow streets, past small houses dominated by mill chimneys and chapel spires.

In the cemetery, he stood in the rain by Sharon's grave. Stood for a long time. Once, he'd imagined tracking down the killer, exacting a measure of revenge. Now he probed for the pain and anger but felt only a faint dull ache. He left the cemetery, kept walking. The chemist shop she'd worked in was now a video store. The flat they'd lived in, leveled to a parking lot. Shoulders hunched against the damp chill, he walked on, seeking something he couldn't name.

Streets that had once seemed a part of him were familiar but strange, as though he were seeing them in a dream. Joan was right, he hadn't wanted to leave Belfast, but now he longer belonged. He looked up at the Antrim hills, their outlines blurred by mist, and imagined not returning to California. Imagined moving on as he had always done and felt a raw emptiness. He walked on.

On a street off Falls Road, he stood and watched a couple of workers chip away at what was left of a wall. ''Peace walls,'' they were called, put up to keep neighbors from becoming angry enough to kill each other. What you don't hear or see isn't happening.

"Need something?" One of the workmen looked over at him.

"No," Martin said. "Just watching."

The workman nodded. "Bloody things should have been torn down years ago."

Martin watched the pieces fall away, finally saw through to the other side. Two little girls stood there, giggling under a red umbrella, splashing their feet in the puddles. One of them, blue eyes and blond hair, flashed him a shy smile. He winked at her and headed on down the street. As he turned the corner, he looked back to the place where the wall had been. The girls' red umbrella bobbed and glistened like a tropical flower in the gray watery light.

Almost running, he reached his father's house, already working out in his head the time distance between where he was now and where he wanted to be. Breathing hard, he let himself in through the front door, walked down the narrow hallway and into the kitchen.

The warmth of the room hit him first, then the smell of a roast cooking. And then he saw the conspiratorial smiles on the faces of Joan and his father who sat at the table drinking tea. Finally, he noticed the third person at the table with them. For a moment he stood in the doorway, transfixed.

Catherine smiled at him.

HE STARED, speechless. She wore a long, blue cotton skirt and a loose sweater in the same color. California clothes. Her braid hung over one shoulder. As she raised a hand to her face, the silver charm bracelet lodged against the cuff of her sweater. In the next instant, he was across the room, his arms around her, his face buried in her neck.

"I promised I'd come and find you," she said. "Drag

you out from behind the wall. I'm just keeping that promise. Of course, if it's not what you want—''

He held her in his arms. "I'm sorry—"

"You're sorry?" Clearly fighting a grin, Catherine pulled away to look at him. "You take off without a goodbye, force me to chase halfway across the world to find you and all you can say is you're sorry."

"You're looking for abject groveling, is that it?"

"Something along those lines."

"I've already told you, that's not something I'm very good at."

"Which doesn't say you can't learn," she said.

"THE KIDS BOTH said to tell you hi," Catherine said later that night. They'd eaten dinner at his father's house and then around eleven had walked down to the pub on the corner to see in the new year. To her amusement, this pub didn't look nearly as Irish as Mulligan's, although Martin had insisted the Guinness was far superior. As they waited for the countdown to midnight, she sipped the glass he'd bought for her and tried to not grimace at the bitterness. Martin watched her across the table, his expression amused.

"It's an acquired taste," he said. "So the children are fine?"

"Terrific. Julie said she wants to marry you when she grows up, and Peter wants you to teach him how to light a fire the way you did at the cabin. Apparently he was quite impressed."

Martin grinned. "He hid it well."

"Well, he just takes a little longer to come around. Actually, he was all in favor of my coming here." She smiled. "He even offered to contribute his allowance toward the plane ticket. My mother was also pleased."

"Your mother? She's never even met me."

"Yeah, I know, but you're a doctor."

"And what? I've loads of money, is that what she thinks? Did you set her straight?"

"It has nothing to do with money." She took another sip of Guinness and slid the glass across the table to him. "God, I can't drink this stuff. Anyway, my mom just kind of likes the idea of having a medical expert on hand. Be warned, she'll have a list of questions to ask you. Everything from St. John's Wort to Saw Palmetto."

"Saw Palmetto?" He frowned. "Why—"

"Don't ask. Just wait till you meet her."

"So the kids are staying with her?" He lifted his glass. "What about Gary? He knows you're here, does he?"

"Yeah. We had a long talk. I'm not sure it's going to make a whole lot of difference, but Nadia's pregnant. So he's kind of got other things on his mind. I'm hoping that means he'll back off a bit."

"Catherine." Martin reached for her hands across the table, looked into her eyes. "I'm not going to take the job in Boston. I don't know for sure yet, but I think I can get back on staff at Western. When Jordan told me about what had happened with Rita, we cleared the air about a few other things, and he told me to talk to him if I changed my mind about Boston."

"But what about WISH? Will they let you be involved again?"

"I feel pretty certain we can work that out, too. Plus, I know someone influential in the public relations department."

"Listen, if you think she's going to pull any strings for you…" She looked down at her hands in his, up into his eyes. "I love you, Martin. If you'd told me you were going to Boston anyway and you still wanted us to go with you,

I would have because I love you enough to take the risk. But I'm glad you decided to stay."

He smiled and squeezed her hands.

"After the divorce, I felt as though I was living under a black cloud," she said. "It was like this storm always on the horizon, I just kept waiting for something else bad to happen. On the flight over here, I started worrying that maybe it was a mistake coming to find you, even though I'd promised I would. I kept thinking that maybe your leaving was one more bad thing, and I should just accept it and move on."

"Lucky for me you didn't."

"Me, too. I guess we've both had our share of black clouds but that doesn't mean we can't expect sunshine."

"Unless of course we stayed in Ireland," he said.

"Huh?"

"A weather joke." He reached into his pocket and produced a small box. "But you're right. Maybe we're both overdue for a little sunshine." He set the box on the table between them. "What I'm trying to say is I love you very much and I think we should get married. It doesn't have to be next week, or next month, just…sometime. Preferably sooner rather than later." He opened the box.

Catherine looked at the ring, then up at him.

"I think I've seen this before," she finally said.

"You have. I'm going to keep bringing it out until I get the answer I want."

"And what happens then?"

"Then I'll get you a real one." He slid the ring onto her finger. "What do you say? When we get back to California—"

"Actually, I kind of like this one. I like this one a whole lot. Was that the answer you were looking for?"

Martin smiled and started to answer, but his words were

lost as the raucous countdown began. All around them people kissed and hugged, yelling out "Happy New Year."
The band struck up "Auld Lang Syne" and paper streamers
were released from the ceiling. They hung in ribbons from
Martin's hair, draped like a shawl around Catherine's
shoulders. Laughing, Martin tipped her chin and kissed her
and then his arms were around her and the sound of the
festivities receded. Overcome by a sudden wave of emotion, Catherine buried her face in his shoulder. The uncertainty of the past week only heightened the happiness of
the moment. It all seemed so incredible. Just to hold him
again, to brush her mouth against his skin, to actually be
here in Ireland with Martin, talking about their future together. So incredible that she couldn't even try to describe
it. Instead, she brought her lips to his. When she finally
pulled away to look into his eyes, she knew without a doubt
this was going to be a very happy new year.